SUICIDE NOTE?

Between the pages of *Final Exit*, the little book by the Hemlock Society, in the pocket of Denise's robe, was a piece of paper.

March 3

Denise,
You asked me to think about it and I've thought about it. I'm willing to go through with it if you are. In business, when an enterprise has failed, you close the doors. There is no sin in that and there is no sin in this. But the suggestion that you go alone is unbearable for me. I love you and, despite everything, you still have some feeling for me. It must be both of us or neither of us, my darling.
You say that if we are going to do this, we have to do it before things get any worse. I know I must be the one to choose the time and the method for us. I promise you, the method will be both foolproof and painless. And the time will be soon. Now and forever . . .

Also by Pat Frieder

SIGNATURE MURDER

PRIVILEGED COMMUNICATIONS

PAT FRIEDER

BANTAM BOOKS

NEW YORK TORONTO LONDON SYDNEY AUCKLAND

PRIVILEGED COMMUNICATIONS

A Bantam Crime Line Book / June 2000

CRIME LINE and the portrayal of a boxed "cl" are trademarks of
Bantam Books, a division of Random House, Inc.

ISBN 0-553-57613-5

Published simultaneously in the United States and Canada

Bantam Books are published by Bantam Books, a division of Random House, Inc. Its
trademark, consisting of the words "Bantam Books" and the portrayal of a rooster, is
Registered in U.S. Patent and Trademark Office and in other countries. Marca
Registrada. Bantam Books, 1540 Broadway, New York, New York 10036.

PRINTED IN THE UNITED STATES OF AMERICA

OPM   10   9   8   7   6   5   4   3   2   1

This book is dedicated to my husband,
Brian Frieder,
with much love and gratitude for his untiring support.

ACKNOWLEDGMENTS

I am grateful to my sister, Deborah Bianco, and to Rosalind Block and Paula Paul for their willingness to read the manuscript in its early stages and for their very helpful suggestions. I also want to thank my editor, Kate Miciak, for her wise and thoughtful edit and my agent, Maria Massie, for her consistent support and encouragement.

PRIVILEGED COMMUNICATIONS

A licensed psychologist shall not be examined without the consent of his client as to any communication made by the client to him. . . .

CHAPTER 61, ARTICLE 9, SECTION 18,
NEW MEXICO STATUTES ANNOTATED

The engine idled and the Cadillac slowly filled with exhaust. The gentle rumble-hum of the expensive Northstar fuel-injected engine blanketed the hiss of gasoline spraying from a loose fuel-line coupling onto the hot manifold. But neither Alan Prather nor his wife, Denise, seated side-by-side in their plush leather seats, would have heard the sound. Their heads lolled in tranquillity against the side windows, his to the left and hers to the right. Their money troubles and their marriage were finally near an end.

Eventually the heat of the manifold ignited the spraying gasoline and the flame raced up the fuel line. A whoosh of oxygen rushed toward the fire. Moments later, the first explosion, then . . . the second. The Cadillac erupted. Hood and radiator, steering wheel and windshield, doors and armrests and arms careened off each other from the epicenter of the blast. Denise Prather's head left her neck. Joined to the headrest in mid-flight, it sailed through the rear window and out the widening maw of what had been the garage door.

In the coming days, Alan and Denise Prather's garage would invariably be described as a "crematorium." Its reinforced concrete walls contained most of the fire and thus intensified it. The heat boiled the Prathers' blood and fused their flesh with the leather seats of the Cadillac. The flames charred metal and bone alike.

ONE

~~~

"HOW DO YOU SPELL YOUR NAME?"

Angie's kid, Sam, addresses me solemnly, as he always does when trying to teach himself something. With messy five-year-old fingers he's taping a fresh sheet of typing paper to the top of his writing box.

"Which name?" I ask Sam. "Matty or Donahue?"

"Both. But say the letters slow," he commands. "And tell me when the first name is over."

"M ... A ... T ... T ... Y ..."

While he completes each letter with grave concentration, I surreptitiously loosen my bra a notch, settle deeper into the hammock, and dangle my fingers toward the stack of weeks-old newspapers on the ground.

I skim the papers chronologically beginning with that first Sunday in April, the day after the explosion. On that day, nearly all of the *Santa Fe Sun* and four separate sections of the *New Mexican* were dedicated to the deaths of Alan and Denise Prather.

Section A has photos of the devastated garage and a list of the hard evidence of suicide that had already been released by that time: the idling engine, the metal hose-ends wired into the end of the Cadillac's exhaust pipe and the driver's side window, carbon monoxide in the only piece of soft tissue recovered from the ash.

"That's all of the first name," I say to Sam. "Tell me when you're ready for Donahue."

"Is Matty a real lady's name? Is it short for a bigger name? My name is short for Samuel. Why does it need two T's for? If I spell Matty with one T, does it sound the same?"

This is typical. Sam's questions drive Angie crazy but make her brag when he's out of earshot.

"He's so damn smart," she'll say. "How'd I get a kid so smart?"

Angie herself is part of the explanation for this brainy little kid. But it's the other part of Sam's gene pool, the Jimmy Abeyta part, that is lately contracting Angie's stomach into a knot so hard, she can't keep food down. It's for Jimmy's sake that Angie arrived this morning carrying the armload of old newspapers she dumped here beneath my hammock.

"The garage explosion? The double suicide up at Irongate?" I'd asked her. "Angie, this is old news. What's it got to do with Jimmy?"

"Nothing! That's just it," she'd said. "Absolutely nothing!"

"Then, why . . . ?"

"I swear, Jimmy didn't have anything to do with the explosion, or whatever it was, but . . . but if somebody doesn't do something . . . Please, Matty!"

That was several hours ago, and she'd sounded almost crazed. I'd lifted my head an inch or so from the hammock pillow and squinted up at her. Angie's naturally orange hair was more spiky than usual. Her freckles and red-rimmed eyes were stark against her pale skin.

"Sure," I'd said, "okay."

She gestured toward the newspapers with one fist, her other absently digging into her belly.

"Jimmy will be here in a little while . . . it would help if you'd read these before you see him. Matty, I'm pretty sure Jimmy needs a lawyer."

Angie knows I'm not much of a lawyer anymore. She sees me, day in and day out, lying out here in this hammock, contemplating my navel and the drifting white blossoms as they float down from the biggest blooming apple tree in the state of New Mexico. Six years ago, it was because of this damned tree that I forked over first and last month's rent for my ridiculous loft-apartment that clings like a baby monkey to the back of the two-story, adobe mother house next door.

A while back, after a bleak time, I had a little windfall: a one-client one-case one-shot windfall from which all blessings flowed—for a while. I paid old debts and started living large. In the grip of manic grandiosity and inspired by this frigging apple tree, I bought into the American Dream. I signed the contract and made a down payment on the whole kit and caboodle here—house and loft and apple tree too.

I concocted a fantasy wherein new clients would beat a path to my door and, unlike the herd of look-alike, think-alike suits whose days are filled with time-sheet mendacities, I would do the impossible for a practicing lawyer. I would live a life of human proportions: I would garden and sculpt and read for pleasure. I would support myself from the rent off the big house and by taking interesting, lucrative cases right here—right out of my own loft apartment. I'd need to add just a small corner—maybe the back porch under the big-house balcony could be converted into an office? How hard could it be to enclose a porch? Renovations commenced.

It was, of course, a bone-stupid idea. The mortgage payments stretch far into the future. The renovations have become a sinkhole; the licensed contractor quit after the third payment delay. The clients who do show up are pitiful scraps from the bountiful tables of real law firms.

Mickey the Mick, for instance, visits me here in my backyard about once a week. Mickey chose to open a marine equipment store here in the desert Southwest and is doing about as well at it as you would imagine. Among other things, Mickey is being sued by his current bank for failure to disclose that he owed a hundred thousand dollars to his former bank. Mickey keeps all of his business and tax records loose in

the trunk of his car, so, during appointments, we drag my two
lawn chairs out to the compound's gravel parking area. I
watch him rummage in the car's wheel well for documents
he's sure he brought this time and so must be in there somewhere. Mickey is my best client.

Angie's had plenty of opportunity to see what kind of
lawyer I am. She was what was left of the renovation crew
when the licensed contractor bailed out. At about the same
time, the contractor fired her for bringing her kid to work
with her, so Angie and I took a mutual leap of faith together.
She gave me a fair price on the rest of the construction and
has stuck to it, without complaint, and despite a jillion un-
foreseen problems. She's here every day now, usually with Sam
in tow. My apartment and house are choked with sawdust or
plaster dust or dust dust at every hour of the day. So I practice
law—and watch Sam—and observe floating blossoms—and
occasionally rest my eyes, right from this hammock. I'm
pretty sure a person can actually think more clearly from a
horizonal position.

"Just read these . . . and talk to him," Angie'd begged.
"Please."

The "crematorium garage" headline had run statewide
and the story stayed on page one, above the fold, for more
than a week. By the third week after the conflagration at the
Prather mansion, the hard news had begun to be replaced
with journalist speculation about the victims and the nature
of suicide. What would it take, one wondered, to induce two
wealthy, mature adults to commit suicide together? Would
the wife's failing health do it? Were the couple's financial
problems too crushing? The lawsuits too awful to bear?

I study the flowchart illustrating the tangle of lawsuits that
besieged the Prathers up to the moment of their death. Two
civil fraud claims had been filed against Alan Prather personally, six more against his companies. He'd temporarily stayed
the suits by filing both business and personal bankruptcy petitions. At the time of his death, Prather had been holding his
enemies at bay for months. When the bankruptcy trustee finally arrived at the hand-carved door of Prather's hillside

mansion to take possession of his books and records, Alan had pleaded for just a little more time and bolted the door in her face. Associates reported that he'd begun sobbing in public and talking openly about killing himself.

What the hell can all of this have to do with Sam's father and mother? I glance up at the second-story deck, where Angie is squatting in front of my new banister to get a better look at the bubble in her carpenter's level. She's so tiny and her tool belt is so laden that some of the junk bangs against the deck floor. I know that she's been watching me read, but she doesn't want to rush me so she looks away. When I catch her eye anyway, her lopsided, toothy grin is melancholy. I find myself grinning back up at her. I like Angie; I like her a lot.

But Angie herself has not been the primary source of my pleasure over the past few months. That would be Sam. Sam is, at the moment, sitting on his sitting box and leaning forward at a steep angle resting his elbows on his writing box. Having completed my name, he's taped up another sheet of paper and, with upper lip sucked securely under his teeth, is printing his own in a rainbow of colors. Reluctantly, I tug my attention away and back to the newspapers.

The final Prather article is buried in the midsection of yesterday's paper. Even the most horrific events in life are eventually buried in some midsection somewhere. Debris-sifting is complete, the story says. The bodies have been positively identified. The fire inspector is satisfied *to a reasonable degree of scientific certainty*, that the manifold of the idling engine would have been sufficiently hot to ignite a stream of gasoline. And given the position of the manifold relative to the fuel line, he'd concluded, *a loose gasket or a hole in the line would have allowed just such a stream of gasoline to drip in just such a way.* The service records on the Prathers' Cadillac led authorities to a mechanic who claimed to have warned the couple that a gasket needed replacing.

Alan and Denise Prather were blown to bits in the midst of sucking in carbon monoxide. Was it suicide? Accident? Both? The papers began to have fun with the names: *accidental suicide,* they tried, and *suicidal accident.* However bizarre their deaths were, the authorities initially appeared to think the precise cause was a nicety of timing that didn't change the result.

But the last paragraph of the article before me suggests that closure may not be so near at hand. Denise Prather had apparently been a practicing psychologist at one time. *Sources close to the investigation say the police have now asked bankruptcy trustee Francesca Jones, to turn over the dead woman's patient records.* This detail was apparently an afterthought that dawned on detectives subsequent to turning the keys to the mansion over to the trustee.

The bleat of my cell phone somewhere under the hammock jars me. I groan and look hopefully at Sam. Obligingly, he scoots off his box, falls to his knees, wriggles beneath me, retrieves the phone, pushes the button, and says suspiciously, "Who's this?" He listens, nods, says "uh-huh," and "uh-huh" again, then hands me the phone and climbs back up on his sitting box. To me he says dismissively, "It's only Max."

Honest to God, I wish this kid were mine.

The voice of the man I sleep with when I sleep with anybody is slightly breathless. "Good morning, Matty . . . Listen, hon, two patients canceled this morning. I was wondering, what if I just showed up on your—"

"Good morning, yourself."

"—doorstep?"

"Can't. I'm expecting—get this—a client."

"A paying client?"

"Let's not get carried away. I'm guessing Angie has a proposition to make about exchanging services."

"Well, as it happens, I was thinking of making a proposition to you myself . . . an exchange of services of sorts."

"Angie says their proposition is urgent."

"I cannot begin to tell you how urgent my proposition is."

Max is a busy shrink. He rarely has the time for "urgent propositions" in the middle of the day.

"How about dinner?" I laugh. "You could cook. We could examine your urgent matter."

"Weigh its magnitude."

"Shrink it down to size," I suggest.

"Stop already."

"Speaking of shrinks, I'm sitting here with newspapers up to my knees. I'm rereading the accounts of the Prather deaths up at Irongate. The paper says the wife was a shrink. One of your tribe. Did you know that? Did you know her?"

"A little. Denise gave up her office practice a few years ago, after she was diagnosed. Huntington's disease, I think it was. I heard it really wiped her out. But before that she had a pretty good reputation; did a lot of pro bono work."

"Like what?"

"Family counseling at the free clinic, some volunteer work with local gang kids, court-ordered therapy for probationers— stuff like that."

"Ahh, the scales begin to fall from my eyes."

"Huh?"

"Jimmy Abeyta."

Sam looks up inquiringly at the sound of his father's name. Sam almost certainly doesn't know that he comes at the end of a long line of gang punks, so I swallow my speculation. Instead, I invite Max to figure out what he's going to cook for dinner tonight. Max's only recreation, unless you include me, is imagining and preparing and eating food. He thinks green-chile stew; he thinks maybe flan for dessert and . . .

As Max talks, I sense Sam's growing excitement. I follow his gaze to the spot in the compound yard. Someone is getting out of an old GTO painted with dull gray primer. When Angie bought this car for her husband, it had been a barely drivable wreck. Today it's running like a top and every dent has been hammered or Bondo'd out.

"Daddy!"

TWO

❧❧❧

I SIT UPRIGHT AND USE MY TOES TO PROBE FOR SHOES somewhere beneath the hammock. Unsuccessful, I pull my bare feet under me like a yogi. My prospective client is trying for a strut as he approaches me but settles for a stagger, and it's painful to watch him.

Jimmy was probably a good-looking kid once. When he was little, he probably looked like Sam. According to Angie, in Jimmy's two and a half decades on the planet, he's worked as a roughneck on oil rigs, a grease monkey, and a laborer on construction crews. He's not only permanently stooped from crushing two vertebrae in a fall from a scaffold, he's been stabbed more than once and hit with enough force to dislocate his shoulder. Now there's no cartilage in his nose. His face is scarred and his arms are tattooed: the ubiquitous dagger-with-blood-drop and the words *Mi Familia* and *Gangster*. Angie says he promises to get his tattoos removed if he ever gets a few extra bucks together.

Jimmy has a rolled-up newspaper in his hand; he uses it to wave up to his wife, who calls that she'll be right down.

"Hey, babe, no rush. I got to say hello to my little man here."

Sam is jumping up and down. "Daddy, Daddy!"

"Samson! *M'ijo!* How's my boy?"

Father and son shadow-box for a few seconds. Then Jimmy drops carefully to one knee and draws the child to him. Sam is careful too. He's been taught how to hug without hurting his father's back. But once he is safely in Jimmy's embrace, Sam squeezes hard like a kid. Neither lets go quickly.

Eventually, Jimmy rises, pulls a lawn chair over, and flicks his chin at the drift of newsprint under me. "So you read these already, right?"

I nod.

"None of that shit has anything to do with me."

"So Angie tells me."

"Hey, Sambo, I'm thirsty, man," Jimmy tells his son. "You think you could help me out, get me a drink of water, maybe?"

"From the hose?"

"No, little *vato*, from the kitchen. If it's okay with Ms. Donahue."

I glance at Sam's eager face and instantly capitulate. "You have to get a chair and pull it up to the counter. You know where the plastic glasses are?"

Sam wipes both hands against his shirt and nods with vigor. "Try not to spill too much," I say.

As Sam tears off toward the house, I look at Jimmy and laugh. "This is likely to take a while."

"He's something else, *que no?* I gotta thank you for being so good to my family, Ms. Donahue. Should I call you Ms. Donahue or Miss Donahue?"

"Matty is fine."

"Hey, look at Angie up there. She doing a good job for you?"

"She's doing a great job."

"I taught her, you know—framing, carpentry, finish work—everything, man. I used to be the best. But that was before my accident, you know. I shoulda got comp, but Eloy never signed up, so . . ."

"Jimmy, if an employer isn't paying into the worker's compensation fund, you can sue him and collect damages for your injuries. In addition to which, your employer was in violation of state law. If he's still in business, I'd say your chances of a decent settlement are pretty good."

"Yeah, well, Eloy's family. He's going to make it right as soon as he gets a few bucks together. But, hey, it's good to know all my rights and shit. Good to know an *abogada* . . . a lady lawyer," he explains to me.

"Angie tells me you *need* an *abogada;* that you have a legal problem?" I pick up the top newspaper from the pile. I fold it so the paragraph about the police asking for Denise Prather's patient records is faceup.

"Is this the problem?" I ask, handing it to him.

"Hey, that's pretty good. How'd you guess that?"

"It's not rocket science: One, Denise Prather took court-referred patients; two, Angie tells me you've had some . . . trouble with the law. I take it counseling was a condition of your probation?"

He nods.

"When? Recently?"

"No, man, that shit was fuckin' years ago. Before I even married Angie. Sam was only a baby. The judge gave me six months for some shit and said I could spend it in county or I could agree to counseling. Denise Prather was next up on the freebie list, so she's what I got."

"And you told her something. And now you're worried that someone is going to find out what it was. Did she record your therapy sessions? Is that it?"

"Jesus Christ! What the hell are you, some kind of detective, or what?"

"I've had a little experience with psychologists."

"Oh, yeah. Angie says your boyfriend or whatever's a shrink, right?"

"He is . . . but, I've been a patient too."

"No shit!"

"No shit. And I know therapists sometimes tape sessions. I'd be surprised, though, to hear Dr. Prather had done that without a patient's permission."

"*Client*—that's what she said we'd call it. . . . I wasn't a *patient*. I wasn't all crazy and shit."

"Okay," I concede. "Client. But you knew she was taping?"

"Yeah, but she said it was like if I was talking to a priest. It was a 'sacred trust'—that's what she fucking said. I could tell her anything and it wouldn't leave her office. Sure, at first I was all worried about the tapes, but she said they could help her—help me too. She even played the early ones back to me later, you know, so I could hear myself and see my progress and shit. After probation, when the free sessions ended, I quit. I figured she burned the tapes or whatever. Now she fuckin' dies . . . and the cops want to listen to those goddamn things!"

Jimmy's eyes narrow menacingly, and a vein pulses on the side of his neck.

"That can't happen, Ms. Donahue!" He draws his hand into a fist. "*THAT IS NOT GOING TO HAPPEN!*"

Sam is moving like a processional across the patio, fiercely concentrating on holding a china plate steady in both hands. Atop the plate is a red plastic glass filled to the brim with water. He reacts to the sense of crisis in Jimmy's voice and trips, sending plate and glass into the air. Jimmy lurches sideways to catch the glass in one hand and the plate in the other. The save is over in an instant, but the sudden move has cost Jimmy: His face is distorted by pain.

"Daddy!" Sam screams, then freezes in fear that he's caused his father more hurt. Quick tears hover. His next voice is so small, it is barely audible.

"Daddy . . . I'm sorry . . . I'm sorry . . . I'm sorry." Sam's tears spill over and his words break up into little chipmunk sounds. "Sor . . . sor . . . sorry."

Jimmy's belligerence evaporates instantly. "You better not be sorry. Me and you got ourselves something here. We got us a circus act. We can take it on the road, *que no?*" He tickles the boy until Sam dissolves in laughter.

"You're good with him," I say.

"*Cómo no?* He's my son. He's the one who's good for me."

Angie joins us. She stands behind her husband's chair with her hands resting on his shoulders like a turn-of-the-century bride posing for the wedding photograph.

"What is it you want from me?" I ask them.

"You're a lawyer," says Jimmy. "You can keep the cops from getting my tapes, no?"

"What's on the tapes?"

"You don't have to know what's on my tapes. Nobody has to know."

One of Angie's hands drops. It begins to slowly twist into her stomach.

"Do you know what's on them?" I ask Angie.

She shakes her head. "I know it's something that'll get him in trouble if the cops get 'em. But I know Jimmy, and so I know it couldn't be too bad. Anyway, Jimmy has a right to keep his tapes private, doesn't he?"

"Yes, he does. Anything he said to Dr. Prather in therapy is privileged communication. All Jimmy has to do is come forward and claim the client-psychotherapist privilege. He doesn't even need a lawyer to do that. But, sure, if you want me to, I guess I could contact the D.A. or, better yet, the bankruptcy trustee who's holding all the Prather property. If we need to get a court order—"

"I'm not coming forward." Jimmy interrupts flatly.

"Uh-huh," I say, my voice even flatter.

"You got to do this without using my name."

"Why me?"

Angie looks contrite. Jimmy shrugs and his eyes wander until they settle on Sam. "Sambo, here"—he laughs—"thinks you're a great lawyer."

"Sam doesn't even know what a lawyer is."

Jimmy shrugs again, eloquently.

Angie reluctantly explains. "We don't have any money right now, Matty."

"Uh-huh."

"But I was thinking, you know how you can never find your shoes? Listen, Matty, we could maybe put radiant heat-ing in your office floor before we close it up. You'd like that, wouldn't you? Next winter—snow on the terrace ledges outside, you inside your office, brick floors warm as toast."

"Uh-huh."

"I wouldn't charge you for the labor," she entreats, "and I've got my license now, so we could get the contractors' discount on materials and—"

I interrupt. "So, let me get this straight. The reason you want to hire me as your attorney is that your five-year-old son likes me, and because I'm willing to barter for my services?"

"Pretty much." Her face says she wishes it weren't so, but there you are. "That and, you know, like Jimmy says . . ."

"What does Jimmy say?" I put this question to Jimmy, who shrugs a third time.

"This thing don't take no Perry Mason or whatever," he explains. "All you got to do is just go say, 'This guy who ain't coming forward has a right or a privilege or whatever to keep his shit private,' and then you get my tapes back, and we burn them, and that's all there is to that."

"Un-huh."

"How hard can that be?"

THREE

DESPITE THE COSMOPOLITAN VENEER, IN MANY WAYS
Santa Fe is like any other small town where everybody
knows everybody. As it happens, I know both of the principal
players in the dispute over Denise Prather's patient records.
The detective who requested the records is Daniel Baca. Detective Baca and I have had occasion to develop a tepid mutual respect, and I expect him to be as rational as a cop can be
about honoring a citizen's rights to privacy. And I've known
Francesca Jones (Frankie to one and all), the trustee in the
consolidated Prather bankruptcies, since law school. When
my license to practice was suspended for a time, Frankie was
one of the few who kept leaving messages (quick, chirpy messages) on my machine, despite months of bottomless silence
from my end.

This morning, Frankie is happy to take my call but typi-
cally distracted by the buzz of chaos in her office. In the first
couple of minutes she interrupts the old-girlfriend catching-
up no fewer than six times. It's only when I tell her that I represent one of Denise Prather's former clients and want to talk

to her about the dead psychologist's audiotapes that she gives her secretary the order to hold her calls.

"There is a God," Frankie says into the phone.

"What?"

"And She answers prayers."

"What?"

"Not two minutes ago I asked Her to deliver me from my own busybody instincts about those frigging session tapes. Now *you* call. Matty, it's enough to send me back to church."

I'm not surprised that so far Frankie has refused to hand over Denise Prather's confidential records to Detective Baca. Refusing has probably been a pain in the ass and she has nothing to gain by it. But, like me, Frankie has been on a shrink's couch a time or two herself. The thought of having her darkest secrets made public would send a chill down her spine. Protecting such secrets is the right thing to do and, up until now, Frankie has been the only one in a position to do it.

On the other hand, I'm also not surprised that she's seizing the opportunity of my phone call to shift the pain from her ass to mine.

"Terrific!" she cheers. "Now *you* can figure out how to keep confidential tapes out of the hands of the police. I can put this hot potato in your capable hands, Matty. Not a minute too soon to suit me."

And perhaps least surprising of all, Frankie has additional agenda of her own. Frankie is habitually full of agenda.

"You want me to *what*?!" I squawk into the mouthpiece when she tells me her scheme.

"To live in the Prather house," she answers coolly. "Work there, sleep there—live there. The fire department is out now and, prematurely or not, the SFPD released the scene to me two weeks ago; all the recovered bones have been shipped to the Office of the Medical Investigator; Health and Safety has removed their red flag. Nobody has an interest in the house itself anymore except us. Well, the heirs and us. Don't you see, Matty, it's the perfect solution."

I sigh and move the phone to my other ear as I pace my

small kitchen. Frankie practices law (and life) like a conjuror on speed; for Frankie, every setback ushers in an opportunity. Problems are mere harbingers of newer and better solutions.

"Okay, okay, hear me out," she insists, "this can work out great for everybody. On the one hand, you can protect your client's interests and take the onus off me: I'm not fond of being crossways with the SFPD. At the same time, you can make a little money from the trustee's fund. And, best of all . . . you solve my mundane problems."

Frankie's mundane problems involve getting Alan Prather's business and financial records analyzed and organized for closure of the bankruptcy cases. The high cost of even moving those massive business files from Prather's home office to some neutral setting is compounded by the post-explosion requirement for round-the-clock security at the mansion.

"With all the publicity, the place has become a target for vandals and the morbidly curious," she says. "The creditors want somebody physically living there yesterday."

While seeming to listen to my earnest preaching about the psychotherapist/patient privilege, Frankie's fevered brain has been concocting a novel proposal. Now she's pitching it hard.

"Ideally," she continues, "I would have hired a lawyer or an accountant right from the get-go to analyze Prather's business practices. We've got a mare's nest of shifting assets from accounts and companies, moving money from Peter to pay Paul. But I haven't enough money in the kitty to hire—no offense, Matty—a regular lawyer. We barely have enough to hire both a paralegal and the security guard. And our first priority is security. I've been going crazy scouting for the right people. And then you call! Matty, this deal is *perfect* for you!"

"Frankie, I don't know. I've got my own practice. . . ."

"Right," she says in a monotone, the sarcasm just under the surface. Frankie has met Mickey the Mick so she knows just how much of a practice I have.

"Look, Matty, I'll have my secretary messenger over the bankruptcy files this afternoon. Read them, see what you think. And, Matty, wait till you see the Prather place: You'll love living in a mansion!"

"Frankie, I have a house."

"You said you're having it renovated. That means noise, dust, mess. Am I right?"

At this moment Angie is running a table saw on the other side of my now permanently open front door. Every piece of downstairs furniture is shrouded in plastic. The only place with enough room to pace is the kitchen. I've moved my desk into the kitchen. There's an inch of sawdust and a lizard on it.

"Matty, I could ask the bankruptcy judge to approve a couple thousand a week for the combined service. We'd have had to pay more than that if we farmed the jobs out separately. But it's as much as we can swing. How would that suit you?"

Two weeks at that rate would pay my mortgage for a month. In two months, Angie will have finished the renovations and I'll have a renter in the main house. I could put off getting a real job more or less forever. At the thoughtful silence on my end, Frankie hoots triumphantly.

"Good, then," she says. "Why don't you go up to Irongate and take a look at the Prather mansion this afternoon and . . . pack a few things."

"Ahh, but . . ."

"Oh. And I'm supposed to meet this detective—somebody Baca—at the D.A.'s office early next week to discuss my lack of cooperation. You'd want to be at that meeting, anyway, to protect your client's interest. So you could go with me. Better yet, *instead* of me. You'll get a chance to meet Raskin there too."

"Who's Raskin?"

"The bankruptcy court has granted permission for the frigging creditors' committee to continue. The committee's basically made up of a lot of pissed-off, suspicious creditors who believe Alan Prather stashed some of their money someplace. They dog my every move and generally make nuisances of themselves. Claude Raskin, who is the most suspicious and pissed-off of all, heads the damn thing. And he's somehow wrangled an invitation to this meeting in the D.A.'s office, so you'll be meeting him soon. . . . That is if you're willing to take all this on . . . ?"

"You don't think there could be a conflict of interest? I already have a client with a very different agenda, you know."

"Piffle," she says.

Neither of us speaks as I contemplate this paradigm shift.

"Matty? Are you there?"

"Have you finished the inventory of the property that has no monetary value?" I ask.

"I'm about done with it. When I am, I'll give notice to the creditors and, if nobody objects, I'll formally abandon whatever's useless, like always. That junk will go to the probate estate—I guess to the relatives. Why?"

Into the pause, I lift my eyes heavenward. What I'm about to suggest is no absolute violation of law. But it is precisely this tendency to manipulate and twist procedural rules that has gotten me in neck-deep shit in the past.

"Who are the relatives? Do we know anything about them?"

"Not much. The husband's brother is in Seattle, I think. The wife's mother is in a nursing home somewhere in Kansas. No kids—"

"Draft a Notice of Abandonment today, Frankie! Get telephone approval from the creditors if you can and file it with the Bankruptcy Court as soon as possible. Today, if you can."

She takes a second to comprehend the implications of this suggestion.

"I see what you're getting at, Matty, and it's no skin off my nose, I guess. But getting rid of the trustee's legal rights to the tapes won't keep the hounds at bay for long, will it? And in the long run, won't this maneuver leave your client's secrets even more vulnerable?"

"It depends."

"On what?"

"How far I want to stick my neck out."

Deep into the foothills, I reach the main entrance to Irongate Estates and downshift to begin the steeper climb ahead. Despite the shriek of publicity over the suicides, the steep winding dirt road is nearly empty. Each of the long gravel drives behind these gates leads to a substantial mansion hidden in the hills. You won't find old adobe haciendas at the ends of these drives. It's all pickled vigas and lap pools and gleaming walls of glass. Yet another incarnation of Santa Fe style.

"Hello ... hello ... Is anyone up there?" My voice sounds hollow as I call into the speaker box. "This is Matty Donahue ... I'm down at the gate. Could someone buzz it open?"

A bleep of static; the iron bar swings aside. As I maneuver my Toyota up the steep curve, I open the window to suck in the fresh spring air. Immediately, I smell it—the lingering stench of an old fire.

The fire department's yellow tapes lie on the ground around what's left of the Prather garage. I park behind a pile of debris about ten feet from the back of the house and head for the wicked-looking little man in the gray uniform. He unholsters his gun and points it at me.

"Hold it right there, missy!"

Frankie had messengered over a bulky batch of bankruptcy files, which I now place carefully on the ground. The guy looks to be about eighty and weighs maybe a hundred pounds. His arm, held straight in front of him, keeps dipping from the weight of the gun at the end of it. Feeling more ridiculous than scared, I hold it right there.

"I'm Matty Donahue. I'm the lawyer."

He doesn't lower the gun. "You're the lawyer? They sent a lady lawyer? Jesus H. Christ. This here's a job for a security man. Not some damn lady lawyer. That explosion left a hole in the kitchen wall you could drive a truck through." He eyes me with disdain and shakes his head. "Till you get that hole boarded up, lady, anybody can just walk—or crawl—right in." This last he adds slowly, making his voice crawl like the vermin he invites me to imagine plundering the Prather abode in the dead of night. "You're not planning to sleep here all by yourself, are you?" he oozes.

"I am." I smile, inviting a truce. "Would you show me around before you go?" I ask sweetly. "Show me which keys fit which doors, how to turn the alarm system on and off?"

The old man shrugs, then reholsters his weapon. "There ain't no damned alarm system. The owners just stuck stickers up all over the place saying there was alarms. Cheap! Cheap! Cheap! This place must of cost about a million bucks and *they* fake the alarm system."

I scoop up the files and follow him along the flagstone path around to the front entrance. As he ushers me through the door, I stop dead.

"Wow!"

"Hell of a view, ain't it?" he says proudly, as though it were his own.

I stare across the expanse to a towering bronze statue of an Indian in full war-dress. I recognize the artist and know the approximate price tag. This statue of Short Bull, once chief of the Lakota Sioux tribe, cost more than I paid for my whole house on Canyon Road. The chief is centered on a broad circle of terrazzo at the far end of the immense living room. Beyond him, outside the two-story wall of glass, sloping rock walls dotted with piñon frame the blood-red sunset a hundred miles away.

"Wow!" I say again, in awe.

"There's no damage at all here," says my guide apologetically. "You want to see some damage, foller me, sister."

He likes my reaction to the kitchen, which is more awe. The far kitchen wall, like the one in the living room is made of glass. Most of the kitchen, though sodden from fire hoses, is still intact. The wall between the kitchen and garage is adobe on this side, concrete on the other. But where a double door once separated the two, there is now nothing at all. Like the aftermath of some blast in a Road Runner cartoon, part of the wall has vanished. To cover the hole, heavy black plastic is sloppily tacked and taped over it on the garage side.

"See," the little man cautions, dangling the ring of keys at me. "See, anybody or anything can just walk right in on you anytime of the day—or night."

FOUR

━━━◦◦◦◦◦━━━

A LONE IN THE PRATHER LIVING ROOM, I KICK OFF MY shoes and stand before the wall of entertainment devices. I press play on the pre-loaded CD player. Vivaldi fills the house. I flip it off, pour myself a brandy from the sidebar—Courvoisier—and warm the pony glass in my hands as I begin to prowl.

I am a natural and unrepentant voyeur. Not in the vulgar, obscene sense, but in the vulgar, nosy sense. It's nearly impossible for me to pass a window without peering inside or to lay my coat on a guestroom bed without pausing to take in the age of the carpet or the quality of the lamp light. It's not the the rug or lamp that interests me, but the imagined lives spent vacuuming it and reading by it. And I like best observing without being seen observing. I've discussed this shameful little flaw in my character with Max. Max says, "Hmmm."

Being alone in someone else's house is a snoop's bonanza, and I get right to it. Down the hall to the master suites, I enter what I guess to be Denise Prather's bedroom. The walls are barren. No pictures or art objects anywhere. The spacious white room is made to seem more so by its sparse furnishings:

plain wooden bed topped with a simple white coverlet; one wooden nightstand and one wooden dresser; a rocking chair facing the window. The expensive Oriental rugs were her only extravagance. Denise Prather's bedroom is more commodious than a monk's cell, but a monk would feel right at home here. Did she sleep with her husband in here, I wonder.

Beyond her bedroom is a smaller room that must once have been a working office. One door leads to a modest waiting area and then directly to the outside, presumably to permit *clients* to enter without passing through the house. Though far from cozy, at least I can imagine a real human being working here: typing at this computer, pulling a file from one of these cabinets, reading from it as she sits in one of the armchairs. Would Denise curl her feet up under her? Would she be so casual?

A couple of abstract paintings (which look suspiciously like inkblots) are in direct line of sight of what I take to be the client chair. There to invite free association, I surmise, since the blobs don't look at all like the rest of Denise's taste. Floor-to-ceiling bookcases fill two walls. The books are arranged alphabetically by subject matter and within each subject, by height.

I browse, picking up volumes at random. Many are psychology texts and case books; a few of these have ambiguous religious overtones, titles like *Pagan Archetypes and the Christian Soul*. There are how-to books on gardening and journal-writing. One shelf is devoted to audiotapes, unlabeled except for handwritten sets of random letters and consecutive numbers; next come journals and photograph albums. Each has a date printed neatly in felt-tipped pen on its spine.

Among the photographs, I recognize Alan Prather's white-blond hair, wire-rimmed glasses, and sharp facial features from the pictures that were on television hourly in the first days after the explosion. Denise is slender and pretty in the early pictures—gaunt and angular in later ones. The date on the last album is more than three years ago.

I hike back through the monk's cell, across the hall and into the north end of the wing. The contrast is stark: The eclectic impact of Alan Prather's personal lair is overwhelming. Colors, textures, antiques, and treasures of every variety. On the wall above a Paul Bunyan-sized slab of petrified tree used as a table is nailed an array of Apache snake-dance skirts. An ancient East Indian panel made of jungle-iron screens a Victorian settee placed atop a Navajo rug. I try to reconcile Alan Prather, the suicide, the failed entrepreneur, the con-man, with this eccentric and wondrous room.

The far door of Alan's bedroom leads to a huge office annex complete with desks, tables, filing cabinets, and library-stack shelving heaped with apparently unsorted sheets and bundles of paper. A closet-sized steel vault stands open, and inside are more shelves and more stacks of paper. On each of three desks is a computer monitor and keyboard and, before each, a swivel chair. According to Frankie, Alan Prather had long ago fired his bookkeeper, secretary, lawyer—even maids—everyone who demanded payment for services.

It is in this room that the records of his chicanery or incompetence or bad luck reside. Here is where I will settle in and make order and earn my keep. There's no time like the present, so I spend the next three hours getting acquainted with Alan Prather's idiosyncratic filing system.

As evening passes into night, I turn on a light. The bank of control buttons on the wall seems elaborate. Absently, I flip one of the switches from the off position to the on position and silently the vault door sweeps closed. I flip another switch—a sudden crash of music from deep in the house assaults me. Not the tripping, sewing-machine music of Vivaldi, but the clash and thunder of Beethoven. The same button won't turn the CD player off. Shit.

I hasten into and across Alan's opulent bedroom and down the hall to see what's wrong with the entertainment center, flipping on lights as I go. When I reach the living room, the glass is rattling in the windows.

Whenever I hear Beethoven booming like this, I think about his deafness, imagine him standing hunched over his pianola, ear slammed down hard on the lid and his fingers pounding the keys, forcing more sound than the instrument can produce, more emotion than ordinary mortals can stand. I reach the light panel and touch the switch. A single spot illuminates Short Bull. The rest of the immense space remains in shadow. I make my way to the CD player and hit stop just as another crash splinters the air.

This one didn't come from Beethoven's Third. I stand perfectly still, waiting as the ripples of noise die. The silence seems complete for a second or two. Gradually, I hear crickets outside. And then something else, a bumping—no, a rustling kind of sound. I realize that with my car parked behind the house and no lights, an intruder would have no way of knowing someone was inside. Until he heard the sudden crash of Beethoven, that is. Now, if somebody's here, he knows he's not alone.

I'm at once mindful of macabre deaths—not only the ones that happened here in the crematorium beyond the kitchen—but the ones from my past that jump up sometimes when I pass the tripwire into sleep. A flash of memories: dead lover, dead friend; the I-don't-want-to-be-dead-too panic. My heartbeat accelerates. I picture the kitchen with its gaping hole covered over by black plastic . . . but the new sound isn't coming from the kitchen.

Reminding myself to be sensible, I force deep, even breaths. I orient myself until I can track the sound. Then, moving as quietly as I can, I tiptoe back across the polished brick floor of the hallway and into Denise's bedroom. The source of the sound seems to be just beyond that door to her adjoining office. I inch nearer and listen. No question. Someone or something is on the other side of this door.

My finger moves to the bedroom wall switch. I snatch it back. Illumination will only backlight me and make me a target. My eyes search for anything that might help. I can make out two irregular shapes sitting on the bedside table. One is a telephone. I know that it will take the police too long to get here. According to the papers, the fire department didn't make it all the way up these dirt roads to face the garage inferno for an hour after neighbors called them.

The sound on the other side of the door is now a kind of

scraping, like a drawer closing. My eye begins to twitch, as it does these days when I'm unnerved. Cautiously, my hand closes like a vise around the other item on the bedside table, a heavy candlestick. I turn the knob, push, and reach for the light switch with my improvised bludgeon, but . . .

. . . There is no light switch! For one sickening second, everything is blackness. Then I begin to make out shapes: file cabinets to the right bathed in moonlight, desk to the left, take a step forward . . . chair . . . second chair . . . third . . .

No! There is no third chair.

The shape is crouched like a bear in the center of the room. Suddenly, like a bear, it rises up to its full height and lumbers a step toward me . . . then a second step.

This man, if it is a man, is as wide as he is tall. The lumbering, I realize, even in my terror, is the waddle of a very, very fat man. *Get around him.* How? No way. *Back through the house?* He will be slow with all that fat. *I can move faster, get through the house, out the front before he . . .*

The swing comes toward my ear in slow motion. I can feel it coming, hear it. I think to duck, but before I move, the blow explodes on my cheek, knocking me sideways. Bile rises in my throat, my knees buckle, and I stagger backward. He presses forward. I can smell his underarm sweat as he raises his ham-hand and I brace for another punch.

This time I'm faster. My arm swings up, then down. When the candlestick, held tight in my fist, strikes the fat man's skull, I feel the reverberation all the way to my elbow. The two of us are in such close quarters now that when he slumps, he pins me against the door frame.

And I feel him.

He is wearing a tank-top undershirt damp with sweat. His flabby bare arms are slick. His curly hair, surprisingly as smooth as silk, brushes my face. He stabilizes himself against the wall, then groans and pushes himself away. I imagine he's considering his options. I still have the candlestick in my hand. We are still in darkness.

"I haven't seen your face," I whisper like a conspirator, hoping he will understand that I can't describe him to the cops—as though my description of the fattest man anybody's ever seen wouldn't be enough to identify him. But he grunts a kind of affirmation, staggers again, and, panting, picks up the edge of something he drags along the floor toward the French doors.

A light spring breeze wafts through the open doors as he exits. I let my back slide down the wall behind me until my butt reaches the floor. I hold my breath staring into the chill darkness. I don't breathe again until I hear the crunch of tires on the gravel drive, a car moving away from me.

After a few seconds I get up, flip on the lights, and survey the damage. Denise's office, hours ago too orderly, is a jumble of open and spilling drawers. This break-in doesn't have the feel of a souvenir hunter seeking tokens. Nor was this a burglary. The fat guy didn't come in the easy way through the kitchen plastic. He didn't go for any of the valuables in the house. He came here, to this room.

So, I sit on my instinct to call the police and instead examine the files strewn on the desktop and across the floor. I have a pretty good guess as to what the fat guy was after. But he missed the mark. What he was looking for is still here.

FIVE

~∞∞∞~

NEXT MORNING, IN ALAN PRATHER'S VANITY MIRROR, I see that my cheek and temple are discolored where the sumo wrestler-intruder bashed me. I search Denise's bathroom for something to conceal the damage. No luck. Eventually, I find a forgotten cosmetics bag in the drawer of what had been Alan's secretary's desk. Fifteen minutes with the thick Pan-Cake makeup and I look like an uninjured floozy. Not exactly the look I usually aspire to, but better than blotches of yellow and purple.

The visible remnants of last night's terror disappear under layers of matte finish, and with them, most of the emotional traces too. It's hard to stay spooked on such a bright spring morning. The sky stretches cloudless as far as the eye can see. It's Friday, and I have three days to secure this place and sort a few things out before my meeting in the district attorney's office.

First things first. I make some calls and get lucky. A bonded crew with a good reputation can squeeze in a weekend job. They arrive before ten o'clock: four men and two boys, with saws and shovels, a bobcat, and a mammoth construction

Dumpster. The crew boss assures me I can leave for a few hours and, with some misgiving, I do. I do because I must. Frankie said the meeting on Monday is to be a "discussion," about her (now, I guess, my) cooperation in the police investigation. Before I attend any such meeting, I'd like to know just what I've gotten myself into.

So I leave Irongate, driving down and out of the socially rarefied air of the Santa Fe foothills. I stop at the main post office downtown to mail a package. Then I head south until I hit the ragged end of Santa Fe. Here the working-class neighborhoods spill, one into another. Everywhere, flat brown roofs are etched against the sky as sharply as a draftsman's pencil lines. The sky here is beautiful too, but tourists don't see this side of Santa Fe. Chamber of commerce brochures never feature these stuccoed, cinder-block cracker boxes on postage-stamp lots. I pull into the driveway of one with no garage, no porch, and a tiny lawn of mown weeds. A gray GTO is parked in front.

I knock, then knock again. The blare of a television commercial ceases, but no one comes to answer the door. No one calls from the other side.

"Jimmy, it's Matty Donahue, are you in there?"

No answer.

I twist the knob, push the door open, and step into a living-dining room the size of Alan Prather's Jacuzzi. The odors of stale beer and fresh cigarette smoke are entangled like old lovers. Jimmy Abeyta is lying flat on his back on the floor. An overflowing ashtray and the TV remote are on the floor next to him, and next to the ashtray is a large sheet of plywood covered in AstroTurf upon which an elaborate train set has been constructed complete with switches, bridges, stations, and mountains of papier-mâché. A wee hand-painted sign reading "Samsonville Station" is glued to a toothpick on the depot building.

Except for his hand holding the cigarette and his mouth launching the fleet of little Os, Jimmy is completely immobile.

"Sorry, I can't get up," he says flatly without looking at me.

"Jesus, what happened to you?"

"Shit happened." He gives me a sour look. "Life *happened*, *Esa*. What you doing here anyway?"

"Can you move at all?"

He turns his face to the wall.

"Jimmy, tell me how to help you!"

After an audible sigh, he flicks his chin toward the wall. "Next room—closet, a harness and a strap. You'll see it."

On the wall at the end of the closet hangs a contraption resembling horse tack. I heave the leather and metal straps over my shoulder, return to the living room, and, as best I can, follow Jimmy's instructions. By the time the harness is under his back and fastened in front, we're both sweating and his face is screwed up with pain.

"Now what?" I gasp.

"You'll need a chair." He points to a metal hook near the center of the ceiling. "Use the exercise hook."

Once I've securely attached the broad strap to his harness and threaded it through the ceiling hook, I pull hand-over-hand and he begins to rise off the floor an inch at a time. But Jimmy is flopping from the harness like a marlin in a net, and we have to stop every few inches to let him adjust to the new position. At one of the stops I ask, "Does your fat friend think he found what he was looking for last night? Or have you had a chance to tell him he waddled off without the tapes?"

"What . . . the fuck . . . you talking about?"

Feeling like an opportunistic sadist, I pull him another notch higher. "Denise Prather's records, Jimmy. There was a break-in at the Prather mansion last night. Her client file-folders were taken. Most of them. But he didn't get what he was after."

"What?"

This last "what?" is in a higher register, making his innocent ignorance even less convincing.

"I said, he didn't get"—I raise Jimmy's body another notch toward vertical—"what he was after. You should at least have told him what he was looking for," I say sarcastically. "The audiotapes of Denise Prather's therapy sessions . . . you ignoramus."

Another weak "What?"

Notch by notch, I explain the stupidity. "The paper files Fatso stole are irrelevant ... nothing more than biographical data, billing records, and bureaucratic reports. Why"—I give the strap a savage yank—"didn't you tell your friend he had to get the tapes?"

"What friend, *Esa?* What the fuck you talking about?" Now he's just testing me.

"The fattest man I've ever seen. Ring a bell?"

All at once, as he lets the pretense go, Jimmy becomes dead weight.

"...Ahh ..." I say. "I take it you do know what the fuck I'm talking about."

No answer.

"You came to me to use the law to protect what you said to Denise in therapy. You've got a legal right to protect those secrets. But you didn't trust me to do it, did you? You thought you'd be better off getting some stupid thug to steal them."

"No, I didn't get him ..."

"... too stupid yourself to even instruct ..."

"... to steal them. It wasn't like that."

"... him properly. He stole the wrong records, for christsake."

Dangling just one notch short of vertical, Jimmy repeats, "It wasn't like that!"

"Then, how was it, Jimmy? You're hanging by a thread with me in more ways than one."

He struggles free and limps off to the kitchen. When he returns pulling the cap off a bottle of Modelo, he demands, "Who asked you to come here anyway?"

"This is instead of what? 'Thank you, Matty, for dragging my sorry ass up off the floor'?"

"Yeah, okay ... okay. I just ... you can't do anything about this ... and I don't like people coming in here ... seeing me like that."

"Not liking something doesn't mean you have to act like an asshole."

"... I said okay, *Esa.* Okay, all right? *Muchas gracias.* Is that what you want to hear?"

"What I want to hear and what I need to hear aren't the same things, Jimmy. If I'm going to go on with this, and especially if I'm going to keep my mouth shut about last night's break-in, I need to know what's on these tapes you're so desperate to protect."

He lowers himself into a chair, eyeing me over the neck of the Modelo bottle. "I told you, that's my private shit. Like you said, I got a privilege. I don't have to tell anybody, *que no?*"

"Jimmy, I'm sticking my neck way out for you. I didn't report the breaking and entering . . . yet . . . but I'm due in the district attorney's office in three days to argue about those very same tapes. The cops believe that somewhere in those session-tapes they might find a guy with a very strong motive to murder Denise Prather. I don't know that they're wrong. I don't even know that someone isn't you."

"Oh shit . . . you really think I could have killed Denise and her old man? This is so fucked up. It was only *after* she died . . . only *because* she died and I didn't know what would happen to her records . . . who would see them, that I got worried. I told you all this."

"Then, make me *believe* it. Tell me what's on the tapes. And while you're at it, tell me who your corpulent friend is."

Jimmy lights a Camel and smokes about half of it, taking his time, thinking it over.

"Okay," I say, losing my patience. "forget it. I can find out both without your help. I can go back up to Irongate right now. I can listen to those tapes this afternoon. I can call my detective friend, I can describe the man who broke in last night. Let's see how long it takes them to find a four-hundred-pound Mexican bad guy."

"How do you know he was a Mexican?"

"He had great hair."

Jimmy suppresses a laugh and sucks on his beer. "Three thirty, three fifty tops. Four hundred pounds is too much."

"Who is he?"

"Fat Boy."

"How apt."

"His real name is Ernesto but everybody calls him Fat Boy.

He's my first cousin on my father's side. He's been a *gordito* since we were little. And you're right, he's all proud and shit about his hair. But you're wrong about me telling him to swipe Denise's records. I didn't know he was going to do that. Fact, I didn't even know he *had* done that till him and Chatto showed up here this morning. See, I didn't only tell Denise about me—I fuckin' told her about all of us; me and Chatto and Fat Boy. And that was only the *first* stupid time I opened my stupid mouth. It was the second time that's causing all this trouble, now."

"And the second was?"

He sighs. "I told Fat Boy that I told Denise about us. Ernesto's never been to a shrink, so he must have figured she just wrote things down, that what I told her was in her notes or something. So he goes over there like some ignorant *puta* and steals the wrong shit. And now both of them, Chatto and Fat Boy, come over here this morning all pissed off and tanked up and start threatening me and—"

"That's how you ended up on the floor?"

"Yeah."

"Jimmy, you'd better weigh your options here. You don't want to tell me what's going on, that's fine. We part company."

He smokes another cigarette all the way down to the filter before either of us speak.

"Shit . . ." he says finally, "you got your car here? Grab your keys, *abogada*, we got to take a little ride."

Agua Fria Street is one of the last Hispanic hold-outs in a city which is increasingly anglofied and so precious you could puke. As we travel farther into the old neighborhoods, the individual lots get deeper. Most were once small truck-farms. Even now a few crops flourish beside a maze of unnamed by-roads. The dirt road Jimmy motions me down leads to a cluster of dusty pink and turquoise and unfinished mud houses. The common yard in front of us is a hard-packed circle of dirt that serves as playground, gathering place, parking lot, and open-air garage for a couple of junk cars.

"Okay, here," Jimmy instructs. "Drive by slow but not too slow. Check it out. See . . . that's where it happened. *Dios mío,* I haven't been in this barrio since that day."

I drive past the compound and down the road, then circle through the neighborhood and back again to the common yard, where I park the car with the engine idling.

"We were messed up that day," Jimmy tells me. "We'd like *borrowed* this ride off a car lot and we were all smoking shit and drinking. I was what—nineteen, maybe? We were only looking to show *Los Duranes* they couldn't fuck with us, you know? They'd been in our neighborhood showing colors. It was a sign of weakness if we let that go. But nobody was going to get hurt that day because nobody was supposed to be here that day. *Los Duranes,* everybody who lived in this compound, were all gone to their patron's funeral—showing respect and shit.

"Anyway, when we drove in, it was quiet as a grave and Chatto starts yelling some shit out the window and then me and Fat Boy are yelling too. If somebody had been in one of these houses, they would've heard us, no? They would've come out, no? And, if somebody had come out . . . if we'd known somebody was here . . ."

He takes a ragged breath, then continues. "The gun was Chatto's and Chatto was driving and he shoots out of his window at this piece of crap, old broke-down pickup sitting up on blocks, you know, to make a statement. But see, the yard is like real small and Chatto, he starts skidding around in there like some *loco cabrón* and shit. He almost lost control of the wheel. That's when I grabbed his piece and I shoot a couple of times at the pickup truck too. Then Fat Boy says give him the gun and then he shoots at the truck till he don't have any bullets no more. It's just some empty, old fucked-up pickup in the yard; it don't even have wheels on it. It's nothing.

"And then we heard one of *Los Duranes'* cars coming, all glass mufflers and shit, and we split. That's all. That old truck is all shot to shit by this time anyway. That's all! We were out of there before *Los Duranes* got around the corner. Nobody even saw us."

"So you got away with the vandalism?"

"Yeah, but there's a catch. Later that night, we get picked up for car theft and illegal substances and some other shit. I think it's going to go down bad. *Cómo no?* But that's not what happened. It was a busy week, or something, for the D.A., and the car-lot guy doesn't press nothing because we'd dumped the ride we took back close to his lot. So charges get reduced to joy riding and less than an ounce."

"And you were convicted on those charges? Sentenced?"

"We pled. Chatto got like a month because he had a prior, and Fat Boy got nothing because, except for being so fat, Fat Boy's lucky. Me, I had only one arrest after some juvie shit and it was for some piddling shit, so I got probation on condition I go see some shrink on the freebie list.

"And the shrink turned out to be Denise Prather."

"Nobody even questioned us about shots being fired here. Nobody ever asked, 'Were we here?' Nothing. See, *Los Duranes* had a lot of enemies—still do—and *Los Duranes* themselves never knew who shot up their place." He shakes his head.

"And so nobody says nothing to us about the old man who was sleeping off a drunk in the bed of the pickup. We found out about that later."

SIX

"I DON'T BELIEVE THE SUMBITCH IS DEAD."

Claude Raskin is a bandy-legged, burly, mid-life cowboy with some oil money. It's been years since the jacket of that gabardine suit closed, so when Claude hits the table, the saucer-sized turquoise hanging from his bolo tie flops up and down against his belly. Raskin is not only the head of the creditors' committee, he also holds the largest claim by a single individual against Alan Prather and his companies—somewhere in the million-and-a-half-dollar neighborhood. Through his political connections, Claude has managed to get himself invited to this meeting in the district attorney's office. Claude's pretty much dominated it since he walked in and took an empty place at the head of the table.

"Y'all mark me," he instructs, standing and hiking up his trousers, "Alan 'Slick' Prather is sitting on some goddamned beach somewhere sippin' Cuervo Gold."

I'm watching that bouncing turquoise and Claude's red face and the spittle flying out of his mouth. I'm wondering if he's going to hurt himself.

Evidently, our host is wondering too. "Now, Claude . . . ratchet yourself down a notch, will you?"

As he speaks, W. P. Skyler's eyes never leave the small rubber ball he is methodically tossing and catching. "The evidence is pretty damned convincing, Claude, what with the wife's head and all." The ball goes *whish* and *thwack*.

Skyler's amused composure is fake. He's the assistant district attorney responsible for prematurely turning the Prather house over to the bankruptcy trustee. He's been ordered by his boss to deal with us. *Us* is a prominent and very angry citizen; a police detective who knows Skyler made a mistake; and me, who is refusing to cooperate by turning over evidence. Four people in this room and a Gordian knot of conflicting purposes. It's enough to make a young A.D.A. nervous. But apparently W. P. Skyler's life pose is nonchalance. In order to toss the ball, Skyler has unbuttoned his pin-striped vest and loosened his Pierre Cardin tie.

". . . sippin Cuervo Gold," repeats Claude, his eyes bulging, "which Slick Alan bought with *my* money, and he's making a date with tonight's whore who he's gonna pay for with *my* money. And you notice I didn't say his *wife* was on a beach, Mr. Skyler. No sir, the wife's dead all right. The sumbitch killed her and some other poor bastard too and turned them into crispy critters and skipped the country."

Whish—thwack goes Skyler's little ball.

Raskin gives the carved conference table another good rap with his fist and surveys the three of us.

"*You* know I'm right, don't you, Detective. You gotta at least leave room for the possibility that Slick's still alive."

Detective Daniel Baca and I had greeted each other a half hour ago outside this conference room. Dressed, as ever, in sport jacket, pastel shirt, and knife-creased jeans, he'd nodded to me.

"Ms. Donahue . . ." he'd said, and the quick nod. Not "Hey, Matty, it's been a long time." Not "How've you been, Matty" or even "What are you doing here?" Only "Ms. Donahue," the way, if you were a cop, you might address a witness or perhaps

a suspect—terse and just to the chilly side of neutral. I'd nodded back.

"Detective," I'd said.

Now, as he listens to Claude Raskin rant, Baca takes a sip of
coffee and is slow to answer. It's not in his interest to make the
assistant D.A. look bad.

"Mr. Skyler made a reasonable call, Mr. Raskin. The fire
department had declared the event an accident, the probable
result of gasoline leaking on the hot manifold of an idling engine. The medical examiner is satisfied that the bodies are
those of Alan Prather and his wife, Denise."

"Bullshit!"

W. P. Skyler chuckles. "Mr. Raskin is a skeptic. . . ." *Whish—
thwack.*

"You're damn right I'm a skeptic!" Claude fumes. "And you
jackasses in the district attorney's office ought to be skeptics
too. Have any of you seen that low-life skunk's body? No, you
have not! They had to *spoon* it out of the ashes. Is there a de-
finitive DNA analysis? No, there is not! All the flesh and blood
and hair were burned away. You mark my words, Alan Prather
killed his wife and some other poor nameless fucker and he
walked away with millions of hard-earned goddamned dollars that rightfully belong to poor saps like me!"

"Excuse me," I interrupt. "Didn't the medical examiner af-
firm the identity of the remains?"

Denise Prather's body was identified immediately because
so much of her head had escaped the ravages of the fire. But
her husband's body was a different matter. In the first hours
after the blaze, the identification had been tentative, made
only on the basis of body size and reasonable presumptions:
Prather's garage, his car, his wife. DNA analysis isn't possible
when the bones are completely charred and there is no flesh
at all.

"I read that there was a delay in identifying the husband," I
continue, "but I thought that was conclusive now too. Isn't it?"

"Yes, Counselor, it is," W. P. Skyler answers. "The bone fragments were shipped to the O.M.I."—*whish—thwack*—"the

Office of Medical Investigations—and thoroughly analyzed. Alan Prather's body was identified in several ways: the pattern of sutures between the plates of the skull and the size of the oxipital"—*whish*—*thwack*—"protuberance. And there were the teeth."

"Shitheel," Raskin breaks in, "the skull and the oxything only showed he was a possible—a white male over thirty. And a couple teeth ain't enough...."

Daniel Baca stands to face Claude Raskin: He doesn't speak until Raskin falls silent.

"With respect, sir, the remains were positively identified against dental records. And there were not a *couple* of teeth. Eight teeth were still firmly embedded in the jawbone. They were compared to Alan Prather's dental X rays. The match is absolute, Mr. Raskin: the shape of each tooth, the position within the jaw, the fillings, cavities, even a root canal. There is no doubt."

That at least sits Raskin down. "But . . . then, why?" He wobbles his head like a dog trying to work his way through or over or under this hard blank wall. "Aren't you the one," he asks Baca, "who wanted this case opened back up? If you're so sure the skunk's really dead, what's your story, Detective?"

Frankie had explained Baca's story to me. He'd been the on-call homicide detective the night of the fire. He'd gotten the call and he and his partner were the first members of the SFPD on the scene. But Baca's vacation was set to start two days later, so the following morning the case was turned over to a new team who had taken the investigation to its conclusion. When Baca got back, it was all over but the shouting.

But, for whatever reason, he hadn't been able to let it go. He retraced the steps of the second team. When he discovered they'd basically closed up shop on the basis of the arson investigator's report and had neglected such SOPs as canvassing the neighborhood, Baca took those steps himself. He'd come up with two potential witnesses: a young couple taking a late evening stroll in the foothills. They were about a mile below the Prather gate when they heard the whine of a motorbike engine behind them. They barely turned, barely glimpsed the dirt bike as it passed them at breakneck speed in the darkness. They might have noticed more, but at that precise moment, the sound of an explosion shattered the air. The woman said later she'd thought it was an earthquake. She and her husband hit the ground and waited to die.

Eventually, they'd recovered their wits and their nerve, run home and called 911. By that time others had already called. The couple mentioned the bike and the 911 operator told them they might be contacted. They gave the operator their names. But nobody called them back. They'd thought about the bike since that night but figured since the police hadn't called, it must not have been important. Then, one day they were contacted by the detective in the sport coat and knife-creased jeans. The case, which was slipping slowly toward the dead files, is being resuscitated.

"Mr. Raskin, I appreciate your skepticism," says Baca gently to the suspicious cowboy. "If I were in your position, I'd feel the same way. But, the fact is, sir, we know *who* are dead. What we don't know for sure is *how* they got that way. It could have been what the arson investigator concluded—a double suicide with a crazy twist that didn't change the result. But the physical evidence is sufficiently ambiguous that we can't rule out murder. And that's where you—you and Ms. Donahue here—are in a position to help us. We're looking for people who may have had motive to harm either Mr. Prather or Mrs. Prather."

"All you got to do is look at Prather's bankruptcy petitions. There's thirty-seven creditors listed. Every single one of 'em had motive to beat the shit out of the creep."

"Yes, sir, we are doing just that. Of the thirty-seven, fourteen are institutional creditors like Citicorp and MasterCard—implausible candidates. Of the remaining twenty-three, twelve have airtight alibis for the night of the explosion. The remaining eleven are substantial businessmen, most former partners of Alan Prather . . . like yourself."

Raskin is a little nonplussed by the insinuation that he might be a suspect, but he recovers. "Good. Good. You look for a money motive, young man. Greed's the thing that twists a man's mind. Mark me."

"Yes, sir. Be assured we are pursuing those avenues. But to be thorough, we want to look at others as well. What we haven't been able to do yet is to identify persons who may have wanted to harm Mrs. Prather. She'd told a friend, a Genevieve Moreno, that someone had threatened her life. The friend didn't know who exactly—only that it was a former patient."

It's my turn to be nonplussed.

"And that brings us to the point of this meeting. Ms. Donahue"—Baca turns to me—"I understand that you're sitting in for the trustee this morning?"

"Yes."

"Did you bring Denise Prather's case files with you?"

"No."

"Are you planing to turn over those files?"

"No."

W. P. Skyler pockets his little ball and buttons his vest. This is his cue to enter the fray. Both men had advance notice that I was going to refuse to turn over the patient records and Skyler was content to laze around until that happened. Now that it has, it's his show.

"Ms. Donahue, are you familiar with the concept of obstruction of justice?"

"I am indeed, Mr. Skyler. As I'm sure you are aware of the concept of privileged communication between psychotherapist and patient."

Skyler smiles. "Dueling concepts."

"Uhmm."

"Correct me if I'm wrong," he says, folding his pin-striped arms, "but isn't there case law that holds that the only person who can claim that privilege is the patient?"

"You are not wrong," I say.

"The shrink herself couldn't have claimed the privilege. Sure as hell, the assistant to the trustee in a bankruptcy action has no right to claim the privilege." There is an edge to Skyler's voice.

"I'm claiming the privilege on behalf of a client, a former patient of Dr. Prather's."

"And the client is . . . ?"

"John Doe."

"Of course it is. So, let me get this straight. You're acting both on behalf of the bankruptcy estate of the Prathers *and* on behalf of a mental patient."

"On behalf of a client of a psychotherapist."

"You don't see a conflict in this situation?"

When I don't answer, W. P. Skyler cocks his head at me and grins like an entomologist who has just spotted a new bug.

"I'm told that your license was suspended a few years back," he says.

These moments aren't as bad as they used to be.

"That's right," I reply.

"I'm told you were representing a nut case then too. And that the conduct leading to your suspension was failure to recognize a conflict of interest."

"That and neglecting clients."

"It just gets better and better."

I never know when this issue is going to come up. Some people know these things about me. Some don't. Detective Baca does, and he sits impassively looking down at his hands.

Skyler is smiling. But he's the opposite of cheerful.

"If you refuse to cooperate now, Ms. Donahue, we'll just have to see you in court. And, if that goes as I think it will, the disciplinary committee will soon be receiving yet another complaint about your conduct. Some people are cursed with chronic bad judgment, Ms. Donahue. The legal profession isn't really the best place for those people."

"Okay, that's enough of this!" Daniel Baca stands. He nods to me once again, and leaves the room without another word.

SEVEN

———◁◦◦◦▷———

T HE CLEAN-UP CREW HAD WORKED LIKE DEMONS FOR TWO days, making shorter work of it than I would have imagined possible. By the time they'd cleared out late this afternoon, the site was clean and neat. Sheets of plywood now separate the kitchen from the great black ruin on the other side, floor-to-ceiling pipe jacks support the connecting roof, and heavy-duty spring locks festoon all the doors. The new alarm system will be installed next week.

Although the workers had proven themselves trustworthy, I'd decided to hang out at the kitchen-end of the house on both days and pretend to oversee the operation. Once the worst of the mess had been moved out, I began to sweep and mop and putter in the kitchen like a housewife. This kind of physical work—washing the gooey ash off cans of peas and putting them in order between the cans of beans and the cans of corn, wiping out drawers and refilling them with clean forks in the fork slot and clean spoons in the spoon slot—is not what I was hired to do.

But nearly always when I have a decision to make, I clean my mind by cleaning my physical space. Now, as I toss out spoiled food and spritz the inside of the dead couple's refrigerator, the image of Jimmy Abeyta sobbing in my car on Friday fills my mind. On the drive back from *Los Duranes* barrio, Jimmy had told me the rest of his story.

Seven years ago, fifty-year-old Augusto Santiago was sleeping off a drunk in the bed of the junked pickup, when Chatto and Jimmy and Fat Boy drove into the common yard. What Jimmy learned later was that three of their bullets had entered Santiago's body: one in the arm, one in the large intestine, and one in the colon. In the following months, Santiago underwent several operations. He lived the few years left to him with a colostomy bag. Two and a half months ago, he died of complications from the gunshot wounds.

"I only saw him once," Jimmy told me. "After the second operation, I went to the hospital to look at the old man. He don't even know anybody's there. He's got tubes and shit running everyplace. I'm just standing at the door, staring at him. All at once I get sick and start vomiting on myself and on the floor in the hospital hall, and then I get some paper and try to wipe it up and then a nurse comes and pulls my arm and I get up I run.

"I was supposed to be seeing Dr. Prather for an appointment that afternoon. She was in this little office in town then, and I ran all the way there. When I get there, I still smell like puke, I start choking snot and all at once I'm telling her about the old man. She gets a cloth and tells me to wipe my face. She gives me an old sweatshirt of hers and she lets me sleep on a couch in the back for a while. After that day, you know, I mean, I talk to her some more. I never talked to no shrink before. I can't believe I'm doing it; my *carnales* wouldn't like it if they knew. But it helped, you know.

"What we did to that old man," Jimmy continues, "it got to me. I tried to find out sometimes what was going on with him. I heard he was using one of those shit-bags and staying drunk most of the time. He was probably staying drunk most of the time before . . . but . . . you know? Anyway, I kept seeing

Denise Prather till my free time was used up. Then, after Sam was born, me and Angie got married. I stopped getting messed up all the time and we had it real good for a couple of years, Angie and Sam and me—until my accident. And I was even coming back from the accident. And now this shit!"

After Jimmy's finished his story, the two of us sit silently in the front seat of my car parked in his driveway. I asked: "You never told Angie about any of this?"

He shook his head.

Finally, he'd said tentatively, "I don't know for sure what it would carry . . ."

"The sentence?"

"Yeah . . . I mean, if I woulda just gone to the cops right off. I mean the old guy wasn't dead then; it couldn't of been murder, right, *Esa*? But now . . . how long would they put me away now, you think?"

I'd started with a lawyerly answer. "It's not a black-and-white question, Jimmy. There's a wide range of—"

"Worst case!" he interrupts viciously.

"Worst case? If you knew the truck was occupied, it would come under the drive-by statute. You could be charged with depraved-mind murder."

"I told you we didn't know."

"We're talking about what they could charge you with. Even if they believed you didn't know Santiago was in the vehicle, they could still charge homicide during the commission of a felony. Felony murder carries a possible death sentence."

"I figured."

"But this wouldn't be worst case," I'd argued. "There are a lot of extenuating circumstances here. The district attorney would have charging options. This thing could be pled way down—"

"How low?"

"Manslaughter . . . I'm almost sure. Possibly involuntary, if you were to cooperate—"

"Meaning give up my home boys?"

"That would go a long way."

"Well, that's not in the cards, *Esa*."

"Jimmy, don't be stupid! Your loyalty is to your wife and child, not to some scum—"

"Fuck you! You don't understand nothing."

I count to three silently. "Then, explain it to me."

A strange thing happened then. Jimmy began to cry. He didn't make any noise and he didn't look away or squeeze his eyes shut. He just sat there and let the tears run down his cheeks and curl under his chin.

When the tears finally stopped, he said, "They told me they'd kill him. Chatto said before they go to jail for the rest of their lives, they'd kill him."

A chill shoots through me. "Kill who?"

Jimmy didn't answer.

"Kill who, Jimmy?"

"I'll do whatever it takes to protect my boy."

"That's what this morning was all about?" I ask. "You on the floor?"

He nodded. "They paid me a little visit. They made their point."

"Do you believe them? Chatto and Fat Boy are supposed to be your friends. Fat Boy is your cousin, for christsake."

He shrugged. "They're both my cousins. Maybe I could plead this down, but they never could. They both got other felonies since this one. So this one would *bitch* them—make them habitual criminals. What do *you* think they'd do to make that not happen?"

The chill spread. "It wouldn't do any good"—I'm talking to Jimmy, trying to convince myself—"for them to hurt Sam after the fact. They're trying to scare you."

"Maybe so," he said, "but I don't see calling their bluff, do you?"

"Jimmy, I want you to tell them the tapes are no longer at the mansion. I put them in the mail on my way over here this morning."

"Sure you did."

"Jimmy, the tapes are gone. Tell them that."

After a long time more, I told him I thought he had to tell Angie about everything. "She has a right to know."

Jimmy rocked and hugged himself. This wasn't a new thought.

"It wouldn't change anything for Sam," he said, choking back tears, "but if I tell Angie, I lose her. I lose them both. Telling her changes nothing for nobody except me—I would lose everything."

"Maybe. But it's what you have to do, anyway."

I say it with more certainty than I feel.

EIGHT

W HAT'S LEFT OF MY BRUISED FACE IS EASILY COVERED with a light touch of makeup, so I meet Max for lunch at the Three Sisters on Canyon Road, just down the street from my home. The waiter seats us at a linen-draped table on the hundred-year-old porch hanging precariously from the side of the building and brings us two complimentary thimblefuls of sherry.

"Mmmm," Max approves. "Who knew I liked sherry?"

"If you didn't, you should. Sherry is your kind of drink."

Why do I say things like this? I'm pretty sure I love this guy, but there's something slightly persnickety about him that brings out the bully in me. Especially when I'm feeling stressed.

"Is it?" He asks this question with a raised eyebrow in a way that makes me certain he isn't inquiring about his taste in sherry. He's familiar with my cranky moods and he's asking if I'm all right.

"Sorry," I admit with a shrug. "I've got a problem."

"Want to talk about it?"

I hate this question. Still, I capitulate and tell him what's been going on, in strict confidence and minimal detail, and disguising identities. Fat Boy and Chatto become Thug #1 and Thug #2. As usual, Max listens without interruption.

"So, you see the problem? I have to figure out how to protect Sam."

"I see that there's a problem," he answers mildly. "But, are you sure it's Matty Donahue's problem?"

"Damn it, Max, don't give me that insipid, shrinky crap. Sam is in danger."

"Yes. Apparently he is. And I know how you feel about the boy, but . . ."

I hope Max doesn't really know how I feel about Sam. In the past few months, I've known what it means to be enchanted. And, like the enchantment of fairy tales, bliss mingles with something slightly sinister. In such a tale, I think I would be the villain: an unmarried thirty-four-year-old woman who has, quite simply, fallen in love with a child who is not her own.

". . . but he's not your child." Max echoes my thoughts.

I haven't come to terms with my feelings for Sam, much less spoken them out loud to anybody. But Max isn't anybody. He sees a lot.

"Whether the police should be brought into this situation or not," he chastens gently, "has to be a decision for Sam's parents. Neither the child nor the choice is yours, Matty."

I look across the crisp linen tablecloth at my lover: dark, receding, hair tinged with gray over a face you just naturally trust. I settle on the eyes behind his steel-frame glasses. Somehow those steadfast eyes manage to convey how much he loves me without giving me an ounce of hope for an easy answer or a pleasant outcome. It's a look I'm familiar with. Long before Max was my lover, he was my shrink. But that's a story for another day.

To resist acknowledging his mild rebuke, I look away. The table is in sunlight dappled through the new spring greenery of an ancient cottonwood a few yards away. When the tree sprouted, this building, like all the original structures on Canyon Road, was a Spanish family home of mud bricks and blood-cured dirt floors. And, like all the original structures here, this one has gone through many incarnations in the past century, the last of which are a succession of trendy restaurants in this decade. The Three Sisters is merely the latest of those fashionable eateries and, like its predecessors, the food and service and ambience are superb. A great Santa Fe mystery is the breakneck turnover of restaurants and galleries so good that they deserve to grow roots and thrive but which last only a season or two, to be replaced by another with a new motif and a new appetizer.

"All right, Max," I admit as plates are set before us. "Sam is not my child. But he *is* a child. And two thugs have threatened to murder that child. Who's going to protect him? Jimmy doesn't know how to defend himself, much less his son. Angie doesn't even know, yet, that Sam's in any danger."

Max picks at his food and shakes his head ever so slightly. He has urges, Max does, to protect me from myself.

"Look," I press gently, "if I'm required to relinquish Denise's session tapes, the thugs go to prison for a long, long time. But before they do, they may try to harm a little boy. So, Max, whether I want to be part of the Abeyta family crisis or not, I *am* part of it."

He doesn't respond and we eat in silence, each lost in our own thoughts. When the waiter places coffee and a real silver pitcher of real cream before us, Max finally says, with clear misgiving, "I take it you have a plan?"

"I do." I smile. "Actually, I have three plans. First one is obvious. I'm going to do what I've been hired to do: do my best to make sure the tapes are given the legal protection to which they are entitled as privileged communication."

"And the other two plans?"

My other two plans are a little murkier, and I have no doubt that my dearly beloved would not approve of either. So I change the subject.

"It's a beautiful day. Let's walk up the hill to my house," I say. "I told Frankie I'd be in the neighborhood and she left a message that she'd be dropping something off there. Besides, I'd like to see what Angie and Sam are up to."

Walking up Canyon Road in the middle of a spring day is

easier said than done. The tourist season is in full swing and this narrow road, originally designed for burro traffic, is crowded with cars moving at a crawl and walkers and bikers darting between and around them. Max hooks his thumb into my belt so we can wend our way up the street without getting separated. I catch a glimpse of our reflection in a gallery window and I think that if I met that couple, say at a party someplace, I'd probably want to get to know them.

Although I've only been away from home for a few days and the construction is making a hellacious racket, I feel like the returning prodigal daughter. Max pushes open my cedar-pole gate and, mess be damned, I'm glad to be home. The racket stops abruptly and Angie calls down from the deck, "Hey, Sam! Look who's here!"

A curly head pops up from the hammock. Sam rolls sideways, spills himself onto the ground, and heads our way. He starts out grinning and loping but, when he gets nearer, something like embarrassment takes over.

"Where have you been?" he demands, enthusiasm replaced with reproach.

"I've been going crazy because I didn't get to see you for days!" I grab Sam's hand and head back to the hammock. "It's a darn good thing you're still here, or I would have missed seeing you today too."

I pull him onto my lap and we sink low into the hammock. We've had a bit of practice sharing this hammock, Sam and I. So we sort ourselves out by lying flat side-by-side looking up into branches until our string bed settles into a gentle sway.

"Where have you been?" he asks again, less accusatory now.

Out of the corner of my eye I notice that Max is making his way up the ladder to the loft where Angie is working. He's giving me some time alone with Sam. The man is a prince.

I don't answer Sam's question immediately. Instead, I put my palms together and slowly twist them.

"Here's the church and here's the steeple ..."

Sam watches, imitating the moves as best he can. Teaching and learning this hand-trick preoccupied us mightily several weeks ago.

"...open the doors and..."

He keeps letting his index fingers go limp too soon, making the maneuver impossible. Just at this moment, he's concentrating on keeping them stiff and twisting his wrists at the same time. I used to reach over at this point and hold one or two of his knuckles up until his hands could fall into proper place for "...see all the people." This assistance wasn't appreciated, so I stopped giving it.

"I've been staying at another house," I tell him, finally answering his question. "I have to work there in the daytime for a while, so I'm staying at night too."

"What kind of house?"

"Do you know what a mansion is?"

"It's like a palace. Princes live there."

"Yeah. Well, the place I'm staying is a mansion. It has lots of rooms and the rooms are big and—"

"Aren't you going to live here anymore?"

"Not for a while. But I'll be here sometimes even while I'm staying at the other place."

"At the Mansion?"

"Right."

"Can I come to the Mansion?"

"I don't see why not. You and your mom can come for a visit."

"My mom's mad at me."

"Oh?"

"She's mad at me and Daddy and Uncle Eloy and everybody."

"How come?"

"Some of Daddy's friends came to our house and Daddy told me and Mommy to go away."

"Ahhh."

"And Mommy got real mad at us."

Max and I hang out for a while, checking the renovation progress and oohing and aahing and asking Angie annoying questions. The exterior is complete. All the remaining work will be done on the inside. The newly created room just under the balcony, the one we're tentatively calling my new "office" (always said with quotes around it) is coming along nicely. It's a story and a half of panes of glass; from brick floor to beamed ceiling, the outer wall is nothing but French doors and windows.

This room is becoming a very serious room, and that's beginning to worry me. A person working in this room might actually have to wear grown-up clothes and keep time sheets. So far, I can't even see where such a person might take a nap. Would I still drag my lawn chair out to dig through Mickey the Mick's trunk? Or would I invite him into this very serious room? Would he come? Would I care?

As Max and I are thinking about leaving, Francesca Jones arrives.

"Hi, strangers. Glad I caught you." As she walks, Frankie is absently searching through open files in an open purse the size of a weekender suitcase. She gives it up as a lost cause as she reaches us.

"Well, well, well," she says, "this is quite something. Who's the contractor?"

I introduce Frankie to Angie, and they hit it off instantly. It is my mother's contention, one of her many unverified—but nonetheless firmly held—notions about the human race, that the more similar two individual's body types are, the better they will get along. Both under five feet two, Frankie and Angie are eye-to-eye when they speak and shoulder-to-shoulder as they turn. Both are muscled like gymnasts and they spring along a half-step too fast for me as Angie shows off her job site. I drop out and head back for more conversation with Sam. But Sam, too, is otherwise engaged.

He and Max are in deep conversation, sitting cross-legged on the ground. I find myself wondering what kind of father Max would be—make that what kind of father Max *is*. The truth is, Max is already a father. He has a much-loved daughter, Sarah, from a previous marriage. Sarah and his ex-wife live in New York.

At the moment, Sam is explaining something with customary solemnity and Max is paying exquisite attention. I plop myself down next to them and lean back against the apple tree. So Angie got a whiff of Fat Boy and Chatto when they came to warn Jimmy; and she got pissed at Jimmy when he told her to get Sam out of there. So much for how Jimmy is entitled to keep secrets from her. What will she do when she finds out how desperately dangerous the situation is?

"You know," I tell Max when Sam has bounced away to find his mom, "the Prather mansion might actually become the safest place to be in Santa Fe. The creditors are not only springing to close up the damaged garage, but Frankie's already hired somebody to put in an alarm system, as well as bars on the windows and doors."

"Good."

"It might even be the best place for Sam for the time being."

"Except that it's apparently a target."

"Not anymore. I told Jimmy to tell the thugs that the tapes are no longer at the house."

"Is that true?"

"I figured that if the tapes were physically gone, they would be safe from everybody . . . including even from the district attorney."

"Yes, but is it true that the tapes are gone?"

Frankie and Angie round the corner like boon companions, full of animated conversation. As they approach, Frankie encircles us in that conversation as naturally as water running downhill envelops any obstacle.

". . . great. And you do have your contractor's license, don't you?" she asks Angie.

"Sure."

"I've made requests for proposals on the construction up at Irongate," Frankie complains, "but it's Santa Fe and it's summer when all the licensed contractors turn into goddamned prima donnas who can *maybe* get to you in a month to *maybe* talk about submitting a bid."

It's pretty clear that Frankie is in the grip of a brainstorm involving my contractor.

I groan. "Not another idea; I beg you."

NINE

~~~

Y OU'VE REACHED PATRICK PRATHER'S MACHINE. LEAVE A
message and I'll get back to you.

"Mr. Prather, my name is Matty Donahue. I'm calling
from Santa Fe. I'm helping the trustee with your brother's
bankruptcy estate and I also have . . . another role. If you
could give me a call at—"

"—Hello, this is Patrick . . ." The voice is friendly and
slightly sexy. "Sorry, I didn't get the whole name . . . Matty?"

"Donahue."

"Like the talk-show host?"

"Exactly like the talk-show host."

"And Matty? Is it short for something?"

"Unfortunately, Matilda." What am I saying to this stranger?
It's been years since I confessed my real old-lady name to anyone. I don't even use it on my tax returns.

"Wow, Matilda, huh? Want to know my middle name?"

"Oookay."

"Ignatius."

"You're making that up."

"And my initials spell . . ."

I laugh out loud. "And are you one? A pip?"

Jesus Christ, I'm flirting. With a total stranger. A second's reflection tells me that part of what is going on here is that the spoiled brat in me is mildly pissed at Max. Prince or no, he's cutting me no slack these days. But that's not all that's going on. I *like* this guy's voice.

"No"—Patrick laughs—"but I guess I was one once, because Pip was my nickname growing up. Now I'm just an old boat captain, more of a poop than a pip."

"Boat captain? Frankie, the trustee, told me she thought Alan's brother was some kind of a computer wizard."

"More like a computer grunt. I spent five years turning one or two good software ideas into a business. I was lucky and it was enough to let me move here to Seattle and retire. For the last eight months I've been living my boyhood dream. Just me and this boat and the sea. People tell me I'm crazy—too old to play around like this—too young to retire. But I think it's important to take a time-out every once in a while—get your bearings, you know what I mean?"

"An intermission."

"Yeah."

"I know exactly what you mean," I say. "I've spent the last six or so years on intermission myself."

"What can I do for you, Matty?"

"Well, since you're the executor under both your brother's and your sister-in-law's wills, you and I need to coordinate the disbursal of some assets to the heirs and the sale of some of the mixed property."

"Mixed property?"

"Ummm. Like the house. Everyone in America who owns equity in a home has a homestead exemption. Some of what their home is worth is exempt from being taken by creditors in a bankruptcy. So, when the house is sold, the proceeds will be split between the creditors and the heirs."

"Yeah, I guess I knew that, but I don't really know how it works and . . . this is going to sound odd but, the truth is, I don't much care."

"Even if you don't, you have an obligation to the other heirs, don't you?"

"Matty, the only heirs are Denise's mother and myself. Denise's mother has Alzheimer's. She's in a very good home in Kansas but she's pretty much vegetative. Her bills are being paid by a trust set up by her late husband, so she's not going to need another dime as long as she lives. And as for me, well, like I said, I've been lucky. My ideas paid off . . . it's almost embarrassing how handsomely they paid off."

"So you don't care about Alan's money?"

He laughs again. "Well, there isn't much of it left to care about anyway, is there? And what there is will be fought over by the vulture creditors who hated my brother. It's not a battle I have any enthusiasm for."

As Alan Prather's next-of-kin, Patrick had been telephoned by the authorities the morning after the fire. It was he who made long-distance arrangements for the burials of the remains.

"Toward the end, Alan was getting death threats from them, did you know that?" he asks me. "Not serious threats. Vultures don't kill, they just consume the carcass. I didn't even make arrangements for memorial services in Santa Fe. I was afraid the vultures would desecrate the ashes."

"I . . . uh . . . you know, in a roundabout way, I work for the vultures. The creditors will be the beneficiaries of most of my work here."

"Yeah. I'm sorry. I didn't mean to get carried away. But those people added to the pressures that drove my brother to do what he did."

I find myself trying to picture Patrick Prather's relationship with Alan. I'm also trying to picture what Patrick looks like.

"You may be interested to know," I volunteer, "that one or two of the creditors don't believe Alan is dead."

"Well, I can't say I'm shocked. Those people lost a lot of money. It's natural for them to hope they can get it back."

"And . . . uhh . . . the police are also considering the possibility of murder, now."

"Are they?" He asks it sharply. "That's a surprise. I thought that avenue had been closed."

"I guess it's reopened."

"Well, the police are wrong too. Like I say, vultures don't kill."

"So you don't have any doubt? I mean about how they died. You believe it was a double suicide?"

"My brother and his wife were living in a tragedy of Shakespearean proportions, Matty. There was no sane way out. Do you know what Huntington's disease is?"

"I know it's a kind of wasting away. Victims lose more and more control of their bodies. It must have been very difficult for Denise."

"Difficult, yes. She couldn't stand or even sit without support. Later, she couldn't swallow even soft food properly. The disease renders the body worse than useless. Arms, legs, head—the body is incapable of the most basic things like laughing or feeding itself or wiping its own ass."

"I didn't really understand. I—"

"But the mind . . . her mind remained as clear as a bell. Denise understood everything. Drop by drop, she watched her dignity evaporate. The disease would have killed her body eventually, but not until every ounce of her soul had been murdered."

"I'm so very sorry."

"But that isn't what you called about, Matty. You had some estate business to discuss. If I have to sign something or . . . whatever, to make your job easier, I'll be happy to oblige. Just let me know."

"I won't take any more of your time now, Patrick. But I've sent you some things and intend to send you more. Will mail reach you on the boat?"

"Did you send it to the address I left with the trustee? Sea Door Marina, Slip Number Forty-five?"

"Yes."

"I'll get anything that arrives within the next couple of days. After that, I'm out to sea for a while, but they'll hold it at the marina until I get back."

After we hang up, I brood some that I never got around to explaining my "other role" to Patrick. Maybe later. Later, for sure.

I spin the chair under me slowly, taking in the neat piles of paper on the library stacks lining Alan Prather's office. I've managed to organize the relevant documents for three of his companies—one work station for each. Prather named each of his companies for high-desert vegetation. So far I've located fairly complete records for two partnerships: *Tumbleweed* and *Sagebrush*, and one corporation: *Piñon Inc.* On a long folding table I've arranged index cards into a matrix of linking assets: by documents, by company, by reference to other documents and other companies. And, of course, there are the white dry-erase boards that are like adjunct brain cells for me. I can barely think without them. I bought a few and tacked them up in here. Upon them I've diagrammed the certain connections. So, for instance, I can see where the medical building purchased by Tumbleweed was sold to Sagebrush and mortgaged to Piñon. This particular set of transactions is fairly straightforward and open. Others are less so.

TEN

---❦❦❦---

I'VE BEEN SLEEPING AROUND. THE FIRST COUPLE OF nights after I moved in up here, I tried out each of the three guest bedrooms: the pink one, the yellow one, and the blue one. There is absolutely nothing wrong with these clone rooms (apparently furnished with the help of a Holiday Inn consultant) and no sensible reason for me not to sleep in them. But I reject them out of boredom.

And Denise's bedroom is out! One night I'd dented Denise's pure white coverlet with my backside for about a minute before I jumped up and fled the room. I had to dig into my subconscious to know what that resistance was all about. I grew up in Santa Fe in a household with one man and two women. The man, my grandfather, was rough and funny and wondrous and my favorite person on the planet. One of the women, my mother, was pretty funny and wondrous herself. The other woman was my grandmother, and she was another matter altogether. She informed me, when I was little, that she was my "second mother" and that I should call her that.

It was from Secondmother that I inherited my two drops

of New Mexico blood in the sea of Irish. One drop Hispanic and the other Jicarilla Apache. I loved her, but Secondmother seemed always in the grip of something otherworldly. In her presence, Grandpa and Mom became calmer, less boisterous, and, without knowing why, so did I.

Secondmother's bedroom was off-limits to me as a child, and so, naturally, it acted as a magnet. I would sneak into her room when she wasn't there and rummage through her things: voyeur even at age nine. But sometimes she'd surprise me; she'd be lying in the dark atop the coverlet. A sound, deep and continuous, somewhere between a groan and a chant, would escape her lips, and I'd jump nearly out of my skin. Once in a great while she wouldn't shoo me out. On those occasions I would lie down with her. There, in the dark, in the crook of her arm, I would tell her things I never told anyone else. When I was old enough, they told me Secondmother had cancer. After she died, I stopped going into her bedroom.

Denise's room brings back old feelings I don't wish to revisit. Which leaves, of course, only Alan's exotic mishmash. And this is where I am this evening, writing the third rough draft of a Motion to Quash the Grand Jury Subpoena. I settle on the bed and scooch around amid a pile of Moorish pillows with a yellow pad balanced against my knees, feeling like a secretary in a harem. I try to find just the right words to convince the court that neither the cops nor the grand jury are legally entitled to see privileged communication between a patient and psychotherapist. Just as I put the pencil down and settle in for the night, the godawful scree of the front gate squawker jolts me nearly out of bed. I fumble on the nightstand for the right button, and when I flip it, the voice on the other end says "Howdy up there."

"Mr. Raskin?"

By the time Claude Raskin makes his way up the driveway and arrives at the front door, I've thrown on a pair of jeans and a sweatshirt—though I haven't yet managed to find my shoes.

I turn on the outside light and peer around the edge of the door at my late caller. The turquoise in the center of this bolo tie is even bigger than the previous one and this gabardine jacket is just a tad smaller than the other gabardine jacket. Raskin brings one arm out from behind his back and displays a bottle of red wine held by its neck in his ham-hock hand. "I figured this might be what lady lawyers drink."

I take the bottle and cradle it against my sweatshirt, neither opening the door wide enough for him to pass through nor closing it. "What can I do for you, Mr. Raskin?"

"You and me got something to talk about."

"We do?"

Twenty minutes later, on the back patio with a sky full of stars and with glasses full of what does turns out to be what this lady lawyer likes to drink, Claude finally edges toward the real purpose of his visit.

"I sat on this here porch many a night. Me and Slick and some others, lookin' at those stars and drinkin' Scotch whiskey and plannin' how we was all going to get rich together. Them days, we all thought the sonofabitch was smart; which, maybe he was. Hell of a lot smarter than the rest of us. But we . . . I, anyway, thought he was a friend too. And that, he wasn't."

"No, I guess not."

"I never really hated a man before Slick come along. Never seemed worth the effort. But it gets under your skin, being taken for a fool . . . by somebody you trust."

"Probably the only kind of person who can take you for a fool."

We contemplate the stars some more. This far from Santa Fe, the night sky is as clear as if you were camping in the wilderness. As usual, I can locate not a single constellation. I think those shepherds in ancient times who spotted Orion's belt were high on something.

"You been looking at Slick's files, bank records, and so forth?"

"Umm."

Claude reaches down for the bottle on the floor, then stretches across to pour me another dollop. "You find any hanky-panky yet?"

Normally, I would only put the answer to that question in

a formal report to the Bankruptcy Court. But it's just possible Claude can fill in some blanks for me and I don't see the harm in telling what I've discovered so far. Which is that Alan Prather had been skimming money for years before he died.

He'd used his management role in each of six real estate partnerships to make sure they did business with other companies he controlled. His property management company, Tumbleweed, was the flow-through company for all billing and paying activity between the real estate partnerships and outside vendors, bankers, and other companies Alan owned personally. The first part of the scheme was pretty simple.

"Here's what he did," I explain to Raskin. "Say Tumbleweed had performed some remodeling work on the office building that Sagebrush, one of the partnerships you belonged to, owned. Tumbleweed's invoice to Sagebrush was usually for twenty-five percent more than the work was worth. Your Sagebrush partnership, whose checkbook was also handled by Alan, would pay his Tumbleweed management company this inflated amount. Tumbleweed, in turn, would subcontract the work out to a third, legitimate, party for the proper, lower, amount. When it was time to pay this third party, Alan would pay this legitimate company the lower amount it had bid, but then Alan would also present Tumbleweed with another invoice for the twenty-five percent marked-up difference. This second payment would go to yet another company Alan owned, say Yucca Materials and Supplies."

"So, what you're saying," says Raskin, "is that if we don't catch the overcharging in the first place—when Sagebrush paid Tumbleweed—we'd never see the rest of it 'cause we weren't owners in Tumbleweed or any of Slick's other companies."

"That's about it; Alan Prather ran a mini money-laundry. Your books for Sagebrush and even Tumbleweed's books were always in balance. And as for Yucca Materials and Supplies, it didn't exist except for stationery, invoices, and a mailing address. All fake. Yucca used Alan's social security number for banking, and kept small balances in non–interest bearing accounts. In short, all money paid to Yucca went directly to Alan.

"With the six real estate partnerships that Tumbleweed

was managing, Alan was skimming off upward of half a million each year. And I think this was just the tip of the iceberg. I think he was taking even more through the financing end of these deals, but I haven't figured out how yet."

"See, now, this don't surprise me one little bit. And it's our own damn fault too. There just ain't no help for how stupid we were in the early days. Stupid and greedy."

I get a sweater from the house and bring out a couple of wool throws for our laps to ward off the night-chill of the high desert. When I toss one to Claude, he reciprocates by pouring the last of the wine into my glass.

"Tell me about those early days," I invite.

"Well, when we all first started putting money in these deals of Slick's, I was wary as a virgin's daddy. But then, he was always giving us these meticulous financial reports. Goddamn things weighed a ton. Take you a week to wade through them. But they always seemed to be in order, every penny accounted for. So we began to relax, you see."

"And the reports stopped coming?"

"Not all at once. And when they did, it seemed it was our idea, not Slick's. We'd actually complained he was burying us in paper. So, he 'obliged' us by giving us pared-down versions of the reports: *synopses,* he called them. They got thinner and thinner over the years. But every time one of us would ask a question, Prather would call a meeting and heft up another ton or so of papyrus and we'd all groan. Got to be a joke, kind of.

"When he stopped reporting altogether, we were genuinely relieved. Then he stopped calling regular meetings; he'd just call each of us up on the phone and tell us how things were going. Every once in a while, he'd invite us all up here to this fine house to discuss business but, like I say, we'd end up out here on the porch drinkin' Glenlivet and talkin' about whether we'd rather spend that just-around-the-corner money on a private jet or a hunting lodge in Wyoming. 'Bout two in the morning, he'd have us sign somethin' or other."

"But, surely you were expecting a return on your money. When none came . . . ?"

"See, but some did come early on; the yield was downright bounteous, in fact. It was that early fat return that made us so simple-minded."

"Hmm. I think that may have come from some diddling with the financing-and-refinancing angle I'm working on."

"Who you might want to ask about that is Gene Saavedra; he was the banker on mosta Slick's early deals. All I know is when Slick explained how much more we could realize if we let it ride, visions of sugar plums danced in our heads." Claude laughs bitterly. "Now, this here crap you say he was pulling—the village idiot should've seen that coming."

"The question now," I muse, "is what Alan did with all that cash. It's not in any of his accounts. Did he just spend it on . . . all this?"

"Could be. Just look around at this goddamned house! Have you seen his bedroom? Until about a year ago, when he started firing people and filing his bankruptcy petitions, the man lived like a maharajah."

"It's possible," I concede. "But the legitimate checks going out of his personal accounts seemed to cover even his profligate lifestyle."

"So, you think there was a stash somewhere, just like I suspected?"

"I haven't found a hint of a trace of one so far. . . ."

"But cash money don't just evaporate, Ms. Donahue."

"No, Mr. Raskin, it don't."

My eyes don't close for another hour after Raskin leaves. But, by midnight, I'm deep into a dream spun off from the mounds of Moroccan pillows under my head. A serving girl with a jewel in her navel is trying to wake me.

"Wake up! Something's wrong!"

She's calling to me from far away. But the girl with the fancy belly-button sounds increasingly like Angie Fox Abeyta. It takes another second to realize Angie isn't some variant on the dream. She's here . . . somewhere.

I find my jeans once more and stumble through the darkened house. The shouting becomes louder. Now it's punctuated with thumping raps on the front door.

"Matty! Matty!" Angie's voice is urgent.

Half of my brain is still in Morocco. I open the door and, for the second time tonight, stand barefoot squinting at an uninvited guest. Make that two guests. Angie sails past me with a duffel bag on one shoulder and Sam on the other. I peer out into the darkness, silently cursing my failure to reset the gate after Raskin's departure.

"Can we sleep here tonight?" Angie says.

"What, huh?" I mumble decisively.

Angie sheds her burdens in the middle of the foyer as I turn on lights and, for the first time, get a look at Sam. Eyes red but dry, breath coming in shallow puffs, little body tense and still, tucked in like a small animal in a windstorm. His mother doesn't look much better. "Come on," I say, scooping Sam up before he can protest, "let's see if the kitchen works yet. I saw some cocoa mix in the cabinet."

The kitchen is functional despite the fact the ceiling is being held up by tall pipe-jacks. I set Sam on the Mexican-tile counter while I begin to search for midnight libation. Silently, Angie and I discover cups and cocoa and even an old package of miniature marshmallows, hard as diamonds.

Sam follows his mother with his eyes. When the cocoa is ready, she tries to move him to the table, but he stiffens so she sets the hot chocolate and melting marshmallow goo on the counter beside her son. She takes her own to the table and slumps over it.

"You look like you could use a little something with that cocoa," I say, searching the small stash of what must have been cooking liquors.

She doesn't answer. I reject two kinds of sherry and settle on peppermint schnapps, pouring a generous shot into her cocoa and another into mine. I figure when she's ready she'll tell me what terrible urgency has brought them to my door tonight. We drink and gradually begin to talk about the work schedule on Canyon Road. Sam has begun to droop. I bring a pillow to the kitchen counter. He hugs it.

"We left Daddy for good," he declares, staring into my eyes and waiting to see whether I have anything to add. I don't.

Eventually, Sam falls asleep. Angie carries him and I put fresh sheets in the pink room.

"Okay, what happened? What's going on?" I demand when we're back at the table. Angie pours herself a cupful of peppermint schnapps and combs her orange hair with her fingers. In the bright light, her freckles stand out and her skin looks bleached. Like Sam's, Angie's eyes are red.

"Jimmy said you told him to tell me the truth. That I'd forgive him."

"I didn't say you'd forgive him."

"No, huh? Well, that's what Jimmy heard. He had to get his nerve up. So he drank all day, then did some dope." Angie sips the schnapps, breathes deep, and studies me over the rim of her cup. "Then he told me everything . . . the old man they shot . . . Fat Boy breaking in here . . . you catching him."

"Ummmm," I say.

"He told me if I was any kind of wife I would stick by him now. He said he would have told me about Augusto Santiago a long time ago if I wasn't such a cold, unforgiving bitch. That I could have helped him, but all I ever did was threaten to leave and that a man can only live with that so long."

Tears stream down her face as she tells me this. She scrubs at them with her fists.

"We need a place to stay, Matty. If we can sleep here tonight, tomorrow I'll try to find—"

"Angie, it's fine, really. I have to be in court tomorrow morning, when the alarm system is being put in. I'd be grateful to have somebody in the house while the installers are here. And, after that, this place will be like a fortress. You and Sam can stay here as long as you want to."

"He's a murderer, Matty. How can I live with him? How can I raise my child with him?"

"It was a long time ago. He told you the truth about it."

"Only because he was afraid *you* would! And how do I know that he's told me everything? How do I know what else he's done? Or will do? How do I ever know?"

Not long after Angie has fallen asleep in the room next to Sam's, there is yet another pounding on the door. This is becoming a very busy night, and I keep forgetting to close that damn gate.

"You fucking bitch; fucking . . . fucking bitch," Jimmy flings in my face as I once again stand staring out the front door. "I did it. I told her, just like you said, and look what happened. I want to talk to Angie. Let me in. *ANGIE*," he screams like Stanley Kowalski. *"ANGEEEE!"*

"Jimmy, this isn't the way. Take a minute and decide what your next move ought to be."

Jimmy very slowly folds in the middle like wet cardboard. I turn away, meaning to close the door, but something interferes. The something pushes back . . . and sticks its head out.

"Daddy . . . shhh. You'll wake up Mommy." It's Sam.

"M'ijo," Jimmy croaks.

Jimmy reaches for his child and I move to stop him. But he stops himself first. Stops himself cold, straightens up, and gets control of his voice.

"Right, Sambo; hey, you're right. We don't want to wake up Mommy. It's just the way we left things, you know. I just came to say good night so you wouldn't worry. You worried, *m'ijo?"*

Sam nods.

"Well, you got to stop that, no?"

Sam nods again.

In the next heartbeat, Angie is at the door, pain showing sharp in her face. Without saying a word, she grabs Sam up and away. When they are gone, I hear the breath catch in Jimmy's throat.

We walk to his car in silence.

"I'm sorry," he says wearily.

"It's okay."

"It wasn't your fault."

"No."

"She would have found out someday anyway."

"Yes."

He gets in his car and hunches over the wheel.

"Did you tell her about the threat on Sam's life?" I ask.

"I was going to . . . that's why I told her about the rest; so she'd understand—you know—how it came down. But she went crazy. She wouldn't listen . . ." He shakes his head. "What do I do now, *Abogada?*"

"Go home," I say.

The next step is up to me.

ELEVEN

—◦◦◦—

"OYEZ, OYEZ, OYEZ, ALL RISE, THE HONORABLE ELLEN Cuthbert presiding."

The Honorable Ellen Cuthbert is about fifty with a wad of reddish-gray hair stuck into a messy bun that teeters on the collar of her black robe like a pet mouse. The judge is a very sharp lady with bullshit-detector eyes. When a lawyer appearing before her begins to shade the truth or, God forbid, put one over on her, Judge Cuthbert's eyes do a remarkable thing. Her eyes widen so that a ring of white surrounds the big hazel irises while, at the same moment, her black pupils begin to shrink just as though she were walking toward a bank of fluorescent lights. If the poor shmuck shyster isn't watching those eyes, if he continues in his puerile pursuit of prevarication, the little dots of black in the center of the judge's eyes become smaller . . . and smaller still. Before her pupils disappear altogether, the lawyer is on Cuthbert's permanent shit-list and is threatened with contempt of court. Occasionally, Judge Cuthbert metes out teaspoons of jail time to unprincipled attorneys.

Of course, Santa Fe lawyers call the phenomenon the *evil*

eye and, of course, a kind of local legend has grown up around it, the gravamen of which is "Don't fuck around with the evil eye. When you see it coming, your next sentence, no matter what, is, 'Sorry, Your Honor, I believe I may have misstated . . .' "

Just at this moment, Cuthbert is looking hard in my direction and her eyes have just begun to flicker ever so slightly.

"I think you'd better explain yourself, Ms. Donahue. Who exactly do you represent here?"

Now, that's the question, isn't it? The problem is that the very thing that gives me—or, more precisely, my client, *John Doe*—legal standing to protect the tapes is the very thing that puts me in a potential conflict of interest. Do I represent the bankruptcy estate (the creditors of Denise and Alan Prather) or do I represent *John Doe*—Jimmy, Denise's unnamed patient? Can I represent both? Skyler has asked the judge to tell me I can't, and this question must be the first issue of the day.

"Well?" The pupils are holding steady.

"Both, Your Honor."

"Both?"

"Each of my clients is aware that I am also representing the other, and neither has a problem with this. Although it seems unusual, there is no actual conflict. There are no mutually exclusive interests. Not even any interests in common."

"Your Honor," Skyler interrupts wearily like a man at the very end of his patience, "we can't *possibly* know how these convoluted interests of Ms. Donahue will intersect. This is extraordinarily irregular!"

"Let's save our indignation for problems we can see, Mr. Skyler. So far, I don't see how Ms. Donahue's dual representations are hurting anybody."

Who they're hurting, of course, is Assistant District Attorney W. P. Skyler himself. But for my representation of *John Doe*, I would not be interested in keeping evidence from the district attorney and, but for my representation of the bankruptcy estate, I would not be in a position to do so. But the law doesn't speak directly to Skyler's problem and the judge isn't going to interfere with my attorney-client relations for him.

"You can't let her do this!"

"Mr. Skyler, put your ball away."

W. P. Skyler hasn't actually been tossing his little ball in the courtroom. He's just been fingering it and rolling it around on the table in front of him.

He looks sulky as a twelve-year-old but, taking a gander at the judge's eyes, pockets his ball and sits down.

"Okay, then," says Cuthbert, "let's get to the real issues at hand. I've read the pleadings. Ms. Donahue, your Motion to Quash the Grand Jury Subpoena is based on New Mexico Statute 61-9-18; in effect at the time you allege *John Doe* made certain communications to Denise Prather. The threshold question is, does this statute give *John Doe* the right to deny the grand jury access to audiotapes of his therapy sessions. I can tell you both right now, on the face of it, all things being equal, the privilege would, indeed, give him that right.

"But the second-tier question is: Are the circumstances in this instance so compelling that the privilege should be overcome? This is the people's argument, right?"

Skyler nods.

"Yours is strictly legal argument, Ms. Donahue. You bring no witnesses. But I understand you, Mr. Skyler, do have a witness on this issue?"

Detective Baca is brought in. He tells the judge why murder is suspected. And he tells her that a threat had been made against Denise Prather's life by a former patient. Without the patient records, the police cannot pursue that avenue of their investigation. I cross-examine.

Skyler rises again. He sighs. He looks at me with disdain. I can see his hand in his pocket manipulating and massaging something. I presume it's his little rubber ball.

He asks the judge to require "at the very least" that I turn over all of the *other* tapes in my possession, the ones featuring the *rest* of Denise Prather's patients. Surely, *John Doe* can only claim the psychotherapist privilege for himself, Skyler argues. This is a nice point.

I counter-argue that it is possible to tell from old court records which probationers were sent to Denise Prather for therapy. If I turn over all of their records but one, the police will be able to easily identify my client by process of elimination. I argue that the other patients don't even know their privilege is about to be violated and that the judge, on her own motion, should act on their behalf. I argue lots of things.

The judge nods and listens to arguments, reads the statute to herself a couple of times, skims through the copies of legal precedents that Skyler and I have piled on her desk. Eventually, she says she wants to think about it some more and she'll take the matter under advisement. But we aren't done here. Not by a long shot.

"All right, Ms. Donahue," Judge Cuthbert says cursorily. "You turn the tapes over to the court this afternoon. We'll provide protection in the court's safehold while we sort all this out."

I know as soon as I open my yapper that her pupils are going to start shrinking.

"Your Honor, there is a problem."

"Yes?"

"I don't actually have the tapes in my . . . uh . . . possession at present."

"That's all right," she says, tidying up her desk, ready to wrap this up, "you can get them to the bailiff this afternoon."

"Well . . ."

"Well?"

"When I say I don't have the tapes, I mean I don't actually have access to the tapes. You see, the tapes were Denise Prather's personal property. They had no monetary value to the bankruptcy estate. Technically, they belong to the Prather heirs, so they were legally abandoned by the trustee to Prather's personal representative."

"Where precisely are those tapes now?" Muscle twitches around the eyes.

"Ahem . . . I don't know precisely, Your Honor. Somewhere on a . . ."

The judge's pupils are in full retreat.

". . . boat . . ."

They are mere pinpoints, those black bullshit filters of

hers. And the rims of white around the hazel circles are widening and narrowing in a kind of hypnotic pulse.

"...out to sea."

The courthouse lockup is a temporary holding facility, just a couple of boutique holding cells at the end of the main hall in the courthouse. Since it's not a real jail, there isn't a cafeteria and so the bailiff brings me a Lottaburger and large fries from across the street. There's nobody in here with me for the moment so, as I consume my lunch, I stretch my feet out along the bench, brace my back against the concrete-block wall, and chew on my options as well.

I think I'm technically right on the law. "Property," we learn in law school, is a bundle of rights. I now consider this particular property—the tapes. In the beginning, Denise Prather owned blank tapes, she had the exclusive right to possess the physical tapes. Then, with Jimmy's permission, she had a right to tape their conversations and the right of possession stayed with her. Now somebody has a right to the content of those tapes. Judge Cuthbert will decide who that somebody is. There may be rights to make copies, maybe even sell copies. But right now no copies have been made. Right now there are only the originals and Denise Prather still has the exclusive right to possess them, or would have if she were alive. Since she isn't, her heirs have inherited that right.

Patrick Prather is the executor of her estate and thus the only person on earth entitled to possession of the tapes. Until, of course, a court of a competent jurisdiction orders him to give them up. Hard to do when he's a couple of hundred miles out to sea.

I know I'm not here for long. The day is late; Cuthbert won't hold me overnight here in the court lockup. So, either she cuts me loose in the next hour or so, or else she ships my sorry ass out to the county jail for a spell. No Lottaburgers at the county jail, I'll bet.

My immediate future seems to be hanging on the question of just how *much* of a fast one Judge Ellen Cuthbert decides

I've pulled. By my Motion to Quash the Subpoena, I invoked the court's jurisdiction over the question of what will happen to the session tapes, which are potential evidence in a criminal case. By the time the judge asked the bailiff to escort me down the hall here, she'd ascertained that I had also, quite deliberately, shipped that potential evidence out of her jurisdiction. It's the kind of stuff that pisses judges off.

So the question she'd put to me a couple of hours ago was the only relevant one from her point of view.

"When, exactly, Ms. Donahue, did you do this? Because if you moved those tapes out of this jurisdiction *after* you received the grand jury subpoena, then your contempt for the judicial process is beyond my comprehension. And, I assure you, dear girl, you will pay for it. And"—there were no pupils visible in her eyes whatsoever—"I should never have to warn an attorney in my courtroom not to lie to me, but I will mention that the only one who ever did so is no longer an attorney. Do I make myself clear?"

Skyler was sitting over there smirking like the Cheshire Cat.

"Yes, ma'am," I answered. "I ... uh ... thought the question might come up. If I may approach the bench?" I flashed a yellow receipt the size of an index card at Skyler before I placed it on the judge's bench.

"This is the Certified Mail Receipt from the central post office in Santa Fe. As you see, the package was sent to Mr. Patrick Prather, Slip Number Forty-five, Sea Door Marina, Seattle, Washington. If Your Honor will please note the date."

Next to the receipt, I placed the trustee's Abandonment of Assets, which Frankie had rushed to file with the federal Bankruptcy Court. The date stamp on top of this document was the day before the date on the mail receipt. And the date on the mail receipt was three days before the meeting in the district attorney's office and four days before I received the subpoena. I'd mailed the tapes to Patrick Prather the morning after Fat Boy had broken in and smacked me, two days before I'd even spoken to Patrick Prather himself.

I'd done it because predicting that the D.A.'s office would take some action to get the tapes was a no-brainer. I thought they might actually have a subpoena waiting for me when I opened the door to the meeting to "discuss my cooperation." And I'd already discovered how valuable and vulnerable those session tapes were to at least one fat tough guy.

All in all, at the time, getting the tapes the hell out of Santa Fe seemed, well, clever. Dangerous to the threads of my meager career, no doubt, but probably not fatal. When I came to believe that Sam's life might depend on keeping those tapes away from everybody, I wished I'd destroyed them altogether.

I hear the bailiff rattling a ring of keys; the main door to the holding cells opens.

"You're wanted in chambers."

I follow him down the hallway and around the corner to Judge Cuthbert's outer office. In one of the reception chairs, Detective Baca glances up from a clipboard on his lap and nods as I cross toward the judge's chambers. It's nearly five o'clock and Baca hasn't even loosened his tie. Unless I miss my bet, Judge Cuthbert has been using the detective here to stretch the long arm of the law all the way up to Seattle, Washington, to see just what's what at Slip No. 45 of the Sea Door Marina.

As I pass through the door to the judge's inner chamber, I try to read Baca's face to guess what he may have discovered in the past few hours. Fat chance.

Inside, Skyler is already seated across from the judge, who has shed her robes to reveal a rust-colored suit that is indistinguishable from her rust-colored hair. She's busy with something on her desk and motions me to the chair next to Skyler. He's looking a shade less satisfied and doesn't even bother to say hello.

"Okay . . ." Cuthbert says, gazing at the two of us, eyes nearly in the normal range, "three things. *First,* the officer outside has made some informal inquiries. According to the marina office in Seattle, the brother of the deceased *did* receive a certified package a few days before he set sail. If Prather's following his itinerary, he should, at this moment, be somewhere off the coast of Mexico. He's expected back in

Seattle in about three and a half weeks. In the meantime, the marina office agreed to forward messages to the two or three most likely stop-over ports requesting that he contact Detective Baca immediately. For now, I don't know what more we can do on that front. Any ideas?"

Skyler mumbles something under his breath. I think I hear the word "mockery."

"All right then, *second* . . ." continues the judge, "I intend to proceed on the assumption that Denise Prather's session tapes are still in existence and will be in this jurisdiction within three to four weeks. We might as well use this time to our advantage. Therefore, having taken Ms. Donahue's Motion to Quash under advisement, I want you two to educate me more thoroughly on the law.

"You first, Ms. Donahue—brief in ten days. After that, Mr. Skyler, you will have seven days to answer. And three more days will be granted you, Ms. Donahue, if the movant wants to respond. By the time you've got everything to me, the brother-in-law and his boat should be back in Seattle. We will know whether the tapes have been recovered and if I need to exercise my brain about all this, or if the tapes are gone and the question is moot.

"Now then, *third*. Ms. Donahue, what shall we do with you?"

"I apologize to the court, Your Honor."

"Do you now?"

Out of the corner of my eye, I spy Skyler's hand slip into his pocket. It emerges with the ball. He slumps back into his chair, barely suppressing a grin.

"Your actions, Ms. Donahue, appear to have been technically within the letter of the law," Cuthbert says.

"Yes."

"But your intent was quite obviously to circumvent the orderly process and spirit of the law. Lawyers have been suspended for such things."

Skyler forgets himself in his merriment and tosses the ball about an inch.

"We'll go off the record for a moment," the judge tells the court reporter who's been tapping away at the machine from her stool in the corner.

"The detective out there," she says, motioning to the waiting room, "says he knows you, Ms. Donahue."

"Yes, ma'am."

"He told me informally that he'd guess you must have a good reason for doing something as stupid as this."

"Did he?" I ask.

"Did he?" Skyler asks in an altogether different tone.

"Detective Baca says you're unorthodox but, in his experience, you are, I think his exact words were . . . 'a thoroughly honorable person.' "

Will wonders never cease?

Cuthbert leans forward, locks the pre-evil eye on me, and demands, "Are you? A thoroughly honorable person?"

TWELVE

—◦◦◦—

"I OWE YOU ONE."

"No."

" 'Thoroughly honorable person?' Yes, I do."

"Okay, you do."

Detective Baca and I left the courthouse and have begun to walk toward the center of town together, leaving a rather dismayed W. P. Skyler in our wake.

"It must have cost you," I tell Baca. "Cops need the cooperation of assistant district attorneys."

He shrugs. "Not as much as assistant district attorneys need the cooperation of cops."

"But still . . ."

Daniel Baca is one of those Hispanic males who start out life in profoundly beautiful bodies but abdicate their birthright in their late teens. You see the little kids, like Sam, running around: huge, soulful eyes; long lashes; silken hair; perfect brown bodies, and spectacular smiles. But as they grow up, some go the way of Jimmy Abeyta, and others, like Baca, get buttoned down. Today, Baca's eyes hide behind tinted glasses, his hair is shorn and shot with gray, his smile seldom in evidence. But he flicks me a bit of one now.

"Never mind," he tells me. "I've spent a lot of time testifying before Cuthbert over the years. We've gotten to know each other. Today, when I mentioned that I knew you, she asked me, off the record, what I thought of you. So, I told her. That's all."

"So, I owe you one. If there's ever anything I can do ..."

"Well, now that you mention it. ..."

"What?"

"You hungry? Want a Frito pie?"

We've reached the plaza and find an iron bench to sit on. Across the street, between a couple of pricey galleries, is what's left of an old Woolworth's store. A window of the store is open to the street and, out of that window, they sell Frito Pies (a small bag of Fritos which the server opens along the top so she can dump in a scoop of hot Texas chili and some cheese). They give you a plastic spoon so you can eat right out of the bag.

"Sure."

While he's fetching dinner, I watch the plaza life. There are, as usual, a bunch of purple-haired teenagers hanging around the Häagen-Dazs Ice Cream Shoppe, goofing on tourists and flirting with each other. Across the plaza in the other direction, the Indian vendors are closing up for the day, getting up from their low-slung folding chairs, rolling up their sidewalk blankets and tucking about a quarter million dollars worth of silver and turquoise back into velvet cases. The benches around me are full of people of every conceivable ilk, chatting and eating and taking in the early evening air.

"Here," Baca says, "hope diet Coke is okay."

"Perfect."

You've got to eat a Frito pie at just the right speed: slow enough so that the Fritos reach the just-this-side-of-soggy stage but not so slow that they actually dissolve into mush.

"What," I ask between bites, "is it you want me to do for you?"

"Matty, this is the second time you've landed in the middle

of one of my investigations. Last time, you were a pain in the ass; pardon me for saying so. But, I must admit, in the end it was you, not the department, who solved the case. And you did it at no small expense to your own life. I haven't forgotten that."

"Thank you, Detective."

"Daniel."

"Daniel. Thank you."

"As it happens, you're in a position to do me a favor in this case."

"I've already told you everything I know about Denise Prather's session tapes."

"It's not about that."

"What, then?"

He takes the Frito bags and empty cups to the trash bin on the corner and returns sucking his eyetooth and considering precisely how to say something or other.

"This is a murder investigation, Matty."

"So you've completely excluded the possibility 'suicidal accident,' as the newspapers call it?"

"I've spent hours with the fire inspector, and we've got a guy in-house, an expert on combustion engines. Our in-house guy insists that for the explosion to have done so much damage, there had to have been a second ignition source. Somewhere around the Caddy's gas tank is the most obvious place."

"Oh?"

"It seems that while it's possible for the initial fire to have traveled through the fuel line or along the floor to the gas tank without help, our guy swears the initial fire would more likely have burned itself out before it reached the tank. For the tank itself to explode, he says, there would have to have been something like a pinpoint leak to wick the fire up into it. The fire inspector says now that he doesn't really disagree."

"I see."

"Does that seem probable to you? That there was a leak in the gas tank too?"

"Well, it seems like a lot of coincidence."

"Exactly. First, there is the one-in-a-million shot that in the midst of a suicide attempt, the fuel line leaks gasoline onto a hot manifold and ignites. Now, add to that another completely separate leak in the gas tank. What are the odds?"

"So, you conclude that the Cadillac had to have been tampered with?"

"I do. That's why we want those tapes. But the session tapes are only one avenue of inquiry. Not the only avenue."

"No?"

"Claude Raskin is dead right when he suggests we look at Alan Prather's enemies: former investors, partners, other creditors. And it would help if I could get a better idea of how all those transactions worked. I asked the chief to spring for a forensic accountant." Baca gives a bitter little chuckle.

"Guess not, huh?"

"Which brings me to you. The favor."

"You want me to tell you what I'm coming across as I examine Prather's business practices. I'd be happy to."

"Well, that was sure easy."

"Daniel, you're not the only one who wants to know how the Prathers got dead."

It's been dawning on me for a long time. But, during my little stint in the holding cell today, my short-term life objective suddenly became crystal clear. Through legal avenues, I've got about a sixty-forty shot at keeping Jimmy's secrets out of the hands of the law. That's not close to good enough. In four weeks, the cops could have the tapes and Jimmy could be charged with the murder of Augusto Santiago. In five weeks, Sam could be dead. So, as I see it, I've got no choice. I've got to find out who murdered Denise and Alan Prather, and I've got to do it in less than thirty days.

"It is in my client's best interest," I tell Daniel Baca, "to have the Prather case solved *before* Judge Cuthbert rules on the motion. So, for the next four weeks, my goal is the same as yours. You betcha I'll provide you with information. All you've got the patience to listen to."

I tell him about the skimming and money-shifting I'd described to Claude Raskin. Daniel takes notes and nods and asks questions.

"But this is a two-way street," I say as he pockets his little notepad. "You tell me what you learn too."

"I can't tell you everything I know, Matty. I'm a cop."

"On the other hand, you want information from me. More than information. You want thoughtful analysis of books and records..."

A teenager passes in front of us, bouncing a couple of hackysack bags off his knees and ankles with precise timing.

"You see that kid?" asks Daniel. "That's how I experience life these days. I'm juggling a jittery captain and a pissed-off D.A. That kid just has to screw up by a quarter inch to lose the whole game...."

"Sometimes life is a balancing act."

"I'll give you what I can, Matty. It'll probably be less than you'd like."

"Beggars can't be choosers. I'll take what I can get, Detective."

THIRTEEN

❦

A S I ROUND THE CURVE AT THE TOP OF THE PRATHER driveway and get a full view of the front door, I see Angie. She's looking edgy and hugging herself tight. Sam doesn't know what they're waiting for, but he's standing close and leaning against his mother's legs the way kids do when they remember they're utterly dependent on some adult for everything.

Since mother and son showed up at that door two nights ago, they haven't gone back home. And the morning following that dreadful night, Jimmy announced he couldn't stand being alone in *their* empty house and he couldn't stand doing nothing while he waited to know his fate. He's had a standing offer of work on a construction site in the Jemez mountains, from his scofflaw uncle Eloy. So, Jimmy'd taken off.

Angie hasn't forgiven him for lying to her, yet, but there have been twice daily phone calls and I can hear her tone gradually mellowing. Jimmy's problems are becoming, once again, *their* problems.

This morning, before I left for court, Angie'd wrung her hands and wished me luck and I'd wished her luck and, I guess, we both got what we wished for. At least, for the time being, we didn't get what we feared.

"The judge took the matter under advisement," I tell her matter-of-factly as I reach the door. She and Sam dog my steps across the foyer, down the hall, through Alan's bedroom, and practically into the bathroom.

"What does that mean?" she demands at the bathroom door.

"Thirty days," I answer, "more or less. That's how long we have to figure out what happened to Alan and Denise."

"What are you talking about? I'm talking about Jimmy. What does 'taking it under advisement' mean?"

I busy myself at the sink and talk to Angie in the mirror. I explain the effect of the judge's ruling to her reflection. I explain that our chances of winning the motion are less than perfect. I splash water on my face and watch hers in the mirror as I explain the rest of it—why I (we) have no choice.

"We've got two ways to save Jimmy," I tell her as I move back into the bedroom. "One, the judge could rule in our favor, and if she does, I don't see any way Jimmy is ever tied to the shooting of Santiago. But if she rules against us, it'll only be a matter of days before the cops arrest Jimmy."

Angie fishes in her pocket, pops two antacids into her mouth, then another two.

"Why can't we, you know, just burn the tapes? Everybody always says that's what Nixon should have done."

"Look, Angie, first, I don't even have the tapes. Second, if and when I get my hands on them again, I can't very well destroy them. I'm skirting the edge already. If those tapes end up destroyed now, I lose my license to practice law. I'm not willing to do that for Jimmy."

"And not for Sam either?" She probably wishes the whine wasn't there in her voice. I stare at her without speaking. This is not a question I'm going to answer out loud.

"Like I said, there are two ways to save Jimmy. The second is we build ourselves an insurance policy. You see, Angie, if the Prather mystery is already cleared up by the time the judge rules, nobody will care about Denise's session tapes anymore."

"But how can we do that—solve the Prather mystery?"

"First, we've got to know them—to know Alan and Denise Prather—better than we do now. We put ourselves in their shoes, walk through their days. You start here, in their home. Much of the evidence of how they lived is right here. Surely, some of the evidence of how they died must be right here too. I'll give you a list of things to look for."

"Me? What do you mean, *me?* What about you?"

"I'm going on a little trip."

"Huh?"

"Angie, it's not only the victims we have to understand. I have to take the measure of their enemies too. I need to put faces to the people Alan Prather cheated."

The trip to Albuquerque is about an hour as I drive it; a little more with Max at the wheel. Max's Continental is the latest entry in a line of conservative cars. When I first met him, Max drove a Porsche. Even that Porsche he drove prudently, obeying all existing traffic laws and inventing some. But the very fact that he once owned such a thing suggests a rakish disposition that is rarely in evidence now.

"What ever happened to the Porsche?"

"You remember, I sold it."

"Yeah, but why did you sell it? I can't recall."

He sets the cruise control precisely at the speed limit and studies the vast horizon. "Hell, the bloom was off the rose about two months after I bought it. And God forbid you should need a new part for one of the damn things—you can wait six months. But, mainly, I guess, it was Sarah. When she'd come for her summer visits, I'd be afraid to take her anyplace in it. Who needs the worry?"

"Speaking of Sarah, July will be here before you know it."

"Sarah's not coming this year. Enid's taking her to Europe."

"Wow."

"Mmmm. I'm sure it'll be a great experience."

"But . . . ?"

Max flicks me a you-caught-me glance. "But I'd planned a

fishing trip and a hike through the Pecos. Truth is, I'm feeling a little cheated."

"You ever think you might want another child, Max?"

"Where did that come from?" Momentarily throwing caution to the winds, Max takes his eyes from the road and looks at me full in the face.

"Oh, Sam, I suppose. My brain is full of Sam these days."

The tires of the Lincoln skitter briefly along the edge of the asphalt before Max brings his gaze back to the highway. In unspoken complicity, we let the subject of children drift away. There's the little feel of a test about this two-day trip. When Max and I sleep together, it's always in his bed or mine . . . well, once on his kitchen table . . . but this will be our first motel experience.

The real test, though, is more about the fact that this is a working trip for me. It's going to be hard for Max to maintain his customary remoteness from what I have begun to consider my avocation and he considers my folly.

He dips a toe in now. "Tell me about this guy we're going to see. He's a doctor?"

"Dr. Phillip Rosenbloom, a radiologist, is one of many doctor-investors Alan Prather collected along the way. These doctors are still paying off partnership debts on a couple of medical centers and will be for the foreseeable future. They're pissed."

"Who could blame them?"

"Some of them were downright obscene on the phone. Rosenbloom seemed a tad more sanguine and philosophical than the others."

"He's the only one who agreed to take time out of his busy schedule to talk to you about Prather's machinations, right?"

"Machinations, huh?"

"Schemes, devices . . ."

"I know what the word means, Max."

"So?"

"Never mind. Turn off at the next exit. Rosenbloom's office is about fifteen minutes from here."

Twenty minutes later, we pull into the parking lot of Albuquerque's Northside Medical Complex. After that, we wait
another forty-seven minutes in the cafeteria for the good
doctor to join us. I use the time productively, making scallops
in the top edge of my Styrofoam cup with my thumbnail.

"Ms. Donahue? Sorry to keep you folks waiting."

Dr. Phillip Rosenbloom looks like I'd like my father to
look. Since I have zero recollection of my own father, who disappeared before I was three, I started (probably around age
four) to separate males who were older than me into various
categories around the subject of paternity: looks like a solid
sober father; looks like a fun pop, looks like a mean sonofabitch. This one would fall into the droll-uncle category, I
decide. Nearly six feet; curly gray hair; a wide, natural smile,
and amused eyes, Rosenbloom slumps into one of the plastic
chairs and drags another over to rest a foot on.

"So, you want to know if any of us blew Alan Prather up?"

"Well, my objectives were a little more modest," I reply.
"But if you've got an opinion on the subject . . ."

He laughs. "Too many good possibilities to choose from.
We all got stung by him, and stung bad. But we weren't the
only ones who got stung, and Alan Prather wasn't the only
one doing the stinging. Physicians in general are a pretty
chastened bunch these days. You mention a new investment
scheme to a guy in a white coat today and you're lucky he
doesn't use the prospectus to cut out your liver."

"I've been going over Prather's records, but the medical
center deals are difficult to follow. Could you tell me a little
about how it all worked with your group?"

"Well"—he takes a sip of iced tea—"we have to go way
back to the salad days. The good years for us were the seven-
ties and early eighties; M.D.'s were pulling in a couple, three
hundred thousand per annum. But—and it was a big 'but'—
Uncle Sam was taking over half of it. It killed us how much we
paid in taxes. The holy grail in those days was *shelter*. We
talked about tax shelters on the golf course, at conferences, in
surgery. 'What are you into? Did you hear about George? He
hooked up with this new guy who put him into a silver strad-

dle.' And some of the schemes were luscious." Rosenbloom
shakes his head.

"Alan Prather, for instance, had some of our guys in medical buildings with component depreciation. Meant they
could write off every floor tile and faucet washer on a separate
schedule. They ended up sheltering more income than they
had. Ahh, those were the days, my friend," he sings.

"And then the tax laws changed in 'eighty-six."

"Exactly. No more big write-offs. So we tried to sell these
white-elephant medical complexes and surprise, surprise, there
were no takers. We'd never cared before that they weren't turning a profit. Hell, we *wanted* the loss. Suddenly we had nothing
but loss. And, almost simultaneously, the insurance companies
began to seriously dictate to us, and the medical establishment
embarked on the slippery slope of HMOs. So, now we have no
shelters; but what the hell, we have no income either."

"Sounds grim." I try to sound sincere. "But I take it that
wasn't the last act. I mean, most of the money you lost with
Alan Prather came *after* the golden age, didn't it?"

"Right. It's humiliating when you think about it. We'd already been fleeced like spring lambs and had a debt structure
that brought tears to our eyes. But, like addicted gamblers who
can't leave the table until *all* their money is lost, we yearned to
come out whole. That's all we wanted, just to come out whole.

"In the early nineties the RTC, the Resolution Trust Corporation, was taking over savings and loans everywhere from
Little Rock to San Bernardino. And with the savings and
loans the RTC ended up with all of their assets—generally,
real estate holdings that had been mortgaged to the hilt. Stuff
that had 'gone south.' That stuff included our property.

"The RTC was selling this savings and loan property off at
thirty cents on the dollar. Problem was, you couldn't buy your
own property back at those bargain-basement prices. That
would have been collusion.

"You guys want anything more to eat? They're closing up
the kitchen and I have to be getting back to my office pretty
quick here."

Max suggests that Rosenbloom and I walk back while he

gets the car gassed, so we agree to meet in half an hour and the doctor and I stroll together across the medical campus. Albuquerque is a thousand feet lower and ten degrees hotter than Santa Fe, so instead of daisies and hollyhocks, the vegetation hugging this sidewalk is sage and mesquite and yucca. A counterfeit stream flows down a little incline over smooth river rock, the sound of the hidden recirculating pump barely discernible.

I pick up Rosenbloom's last line. "It would have been collusion; I take it Alan Prather had a way around the problem?"

"And his way around it seemed feasible. Simple and feasible and only slightly felonious. We would simply buy *each other's* property out of hock. There were about ten of us docs and maybe half as many of the dentists who were willing to take the next plunge.

"All each of us had to do was bring in just enough new blood to form a new partnership or corporation. Alan set up about six new companies that way. Each was a mixture of some old guys and some new guys. Enough new names in each group to pass muster on the RTC guidelines. Sure, there was a lot of confusion about just who was going to be entitled to what when the dust settled. But, at thirty cents on the dollar, we'd soon have this golden goose to lay enough eggs to make golden goddamned omelettes.

"After we got the properties back from the RTC, Alan refinanced each of them locally. We had to guarantee these new mortgages, but we actually got some of our cash back at refinance time. It was the proof we needed. Everybody would be fat again; there'd be enough profit to cancel out most of those little inequities."

"Cool."

"Yeah."

"How badly did it go?"

"First, we all got sued. It was a civil suit, but criminal charges were in the air. My brethren bailed like they were on the *Titanic,* and they grabbed at exorbitantly costly settlements as though they were life rafts. Second, Prather had sucked up most of the 'little inequities' I mentioned. We found out later he'd actually sold some of these deals out from under us at a profit we never saw. So today we've got none of the new profit and all of the old debt, we're paying off settlements, and we're still too rich to file bankruptcy ourselves. So we're stuck."

"Damn," I say, letting the sarcasm show just a little.

"See, nobody outside the medical community ever has any sympathy for this story." His tone is equal parts self-pity and self-mockery.

"Tell me, Doctor, did any of you get more damaged than the others? Anybody get hurt beyond repair?"

We've reached the back entrance to Rosenbloom's office. He leans against his own door and smiles down at me. He shakes his head.

"Nobody lost so much, they didn't have anything more to lose, Ms. Donahue. These doctors aren't desperate enough to risk a day of billable time, much less years in jail, for the sake of revenge. Well, there was this one dentist . . . David Drake. He's the only one I can think of who went off the deep end. But he had a heart attack about six months ago. Heard it was massive, that he's a vegetable. May even be dead by now. Either way, I can't see him planting a car bomb or whatever it was."

"Who profited by Alan Prather's death or . . . ?"

"Profited? Have you been listening? We lost our shirts."

". . . or might have been threatened by Alan Prather alive?"

"Not our guys." He turns his key in the lock, then faces me. "You do know that I was just joking about one of us blowing him up?"

"Well, it looks like maybe somebody did."

"I'll tell you who you should talk to . . . Gene Saavedra."

It's the second time his name has come up. "The mortgage banker."

"Mortgage banker—ski bum? With Gene, it was always a toss-up. In the old days, Gene Saavedra conducted a hell of a lot of business on the chair lift and in the bar. He used to charter planes and fly some of us up to Taos on Wednesdays for three or four runs. Then we'd talk money on the flight back. It was on one of those ski Wednesdays that Gene first introduced

us to Alan. Gene was placing all Alan's loans in the early days.
But he bailed out of Alan's deals a long while back, so maybe
his information is dated. He used to know a lot though; maybe
it's worth your while to talk to him. I don't even know if the
man's still in Taos."

"The man is still in Taos," I say. "And he's next on my list."

Back on the road, Max asks more about where we're spending
the night. I've decided to make the big loop through the Jemez mountains to Valle Grande and then on up to Taos.

"We should get to Jemez Springs before five . . ." I tell him.
". . . I've made reservations at a new B&B, The Hummingbird.
Supposed to be good. I told Angie to forward any calls there."

"How are Angie and Jimmy taking the news from the
courthouse?" Max asks.

"Angie's called Jimmy to tell him that the court took the
privilege question under advisement. But I'd like to see him
in person to explain the rest of it. That's why we're stopping in
Jemez Springs."

Without a word of protest or question, Max makes the
turn onto New Mexico 44. At the San Ysidro "Y," he veers
right and heads for the spectacular red-rock country of the
Jemez Reservation. Beyond the Jemez Pueblo and just before
we get to the village of Jemez Springs, I take out the map
Angie made for me.

"Turn left here, go back toward the river," I direct Max.
". . . Okay, okay, there at the big white rock, turn left again."
The big white rock is marked on Angie's map as "big white
rock." A hundred yards to the left of the big white rock is a big
yellow front-end loader, a big black wrecking ball on a crane,
two enormous and overflowing Dumpsters, and piles and
piles of apparently salvageable debris roughly divided by type
of material and size: short boards, long boards, toilets and
sinks, bricks and flagstone. The only visible movement is the
front-end loader heading our way.

"HEY, EXCUSE ME," I scream over the noise, "I'M LOOKING
FOR . . ."

The driver leans out and yells back, "WHAT?" as he shuts his rig down.

"Jimmy Abeyta," I reply at a reasonable decibel level. "You know where I can find him?"

"Abeyta? He's one of Eloy's nephews, ain't he?"

"Yeah, is he around someplace?"

"Eloy's got so damned many nephews, it's hard to keep 'em straight. Jimmy's the crippled-up one, right? I think Eloy's got him doing some sit-down job back at the trailer. I don't know if he's there though. Eloy let everybody go early again."

The driver points us in the right direction, fires his engine back up, and turns the loader. The wheels on one side are about a foot higher than the wheels on the other. I wonder if he knows that Eloy doesn't believe in worker's compensation insurance.

Max drives down a rutted path and parks near a house trailer set among the cottonwoods at the far end of the job site. The trailer door is open and Max steps up into it, then offers me his hand. Inside, the room is outfitted as an office with racks of blueprints and a couple of beat-up filing cabinets. Sitting hunched over a desk, Jimmy is scowling and chewing on a carpenter's pencil.

"What the hell?" he says when he sees us.

"And howdy-do to you too. We were in the neighborhood and thought we'd stop by. Jimmy Abeyta, meet Max Cortino."

"The shrink," Jimmy says flatly.

Jimmy motions us to a couple of molded plastic chairs. He dumps spoonfuls of instant coffee into plastic cups and, from the hot plate, picks up a glass pot stained the color of rust and full of water off which no steam rises. "Sorry, this is all we got."

I take my cup but have no intention of getting it anywhere near my mouth. Max drinks the stuff down like it's Starbucks Columbian Supreme. "This is a great spot," he says. "The cottonwoods really keep it cool in here."

Jimmy gives Max an indecipherable look, then turns his back on him. "Angie told me you might stop by," he says to me. "She says you're going to play private eye. What's up with that?"

My answer is preempted by the screechy sound of the

walkie-talkie on the desk. *"Jimmy, you there, Jimmy"* . . . static . . . *"Are you there? Chatto needs the new lumber order right away"* . . . static . . . *"I'll be"* . . . static . . . *"minutes"* . . .

I jump up so fast, the tepid crap in my plastic cup spills all over my slacks.

"Chatto?" I say incredulously.

"What? Who?" asks poor Max, to whom Chatto is still Thug #2.

"I can explain," yelps Jimmy, steadying his own cup and standing in an attempt to regain control.

"The hell you can!" I shriek. "You're up here working with the man who threatened to kill your son? I suppose Fat Boy is here too. There is no possible explanation for this."

"Look, lady, *mi abogada*, I know you won't understand this, but . . . they are . . . Chatto is Eloy's nephew . . . he's my cousin too. They're family."

"SAM IS YOUR FAMILY, YOU SONOFABITCH!"

"Look, Ms. Donahue, Matty." Jimmy pats the air with his hand like he's trying to tame a child. "What I did, I reached out to Eloy. He straightened all this out. It's like you said, Matty, they were just trying to scare me. Don't worry, we're not going to have any trouble from them now."

"Are you out of your fucking mind?" I fling my cup at Jimmy's head. It misses. I grab a roll of blueprints and use it like a machete across his shoulders. Max stays out of the way and Jimmy makes no move to strike back.

I scream at Jimmy: "I ought to volunteer those tapes to the cops right now. I ought to put the whole lot of you in prison for the rest of your sorry lives."

"No, please, Matty, I know you don't understand but, trust me; I'm doing what I think is best."

Outside, breaks squeal and tires skid to a stop. A moment later, hands appear on either side of the trailer door. Then a head . . . and a body.

"What's going on here?" the head demands. "Jimmy, you left your mike on and I heard the racket. Who are these people?"

FOURTEEN

HE MAN WHO FILLS THE TRAILER DOOR IS TOO OLD TO
be Chatto. He's in his mid-fifties, dressed in Levis, a
khaki shirt, and heavy work boots. He looks, for all the world,
like Edward James Olmos—right down to his pineapple
complexion.

"*No es problema, Tío,*" says Jimmy.

"Uncle Eloy, *ella es Senorita Donahue, la abogada.* The one
I told you about. And this is her *amigo*, Mr. uh . . ."

"Cortino, Max Cortino." Max offers his hand across to the
doorway; Eloy takes it and civility is restored. That is, except
for me. I'm panting hard and I've still got a stalk of mangled
blueprints in my raised fist.

"Ahh, *sí*, of course. *Yo comprendo.* Please . . . Miss . . ." Eloy
offers his open palm and I reluctantly relinquish the blueprints. He makes a small ritual of straightening them until I
regain normal exhalation.

"Won't you please sit, miss. I can see you are a woman of
strong feeling and I admire that very much. Please"—he gestures toward the plastic chair—"I think I may be able to explain to you some things."

Eloy orders Jimmy to wash the pot and make some decent coffee. He draws a chair near and sits facing me. He sighs; he shakes his head; he sighs again. He drags his hand down his scarred face. "My wife and I have no children of our own," he tells me.

I say nothing.

"I am the oldest of five brothers."

"Uh-huh."

"Two of my brothers are dead . . . and the other two are in prison—"

"Mr. Abeyta, do you know what's been going on here?"

". . . Each of my brothers had sons."

"Look, I can see where this is headed. Your nephews are all you have. They are family. Well, let me tell you something. Two of your precious nephews have threatened to murder a child! A child who is also your family!"

Eloy Abeyta clasps his hands together so tightly, they tremble. He leans in close and looks up to the trailer ceiling. I seize the opportunity to give him my "father-image" once-over. Probably a decent man, I conclude.

"*Dios mío*," he says to the heavens. To me he says, "I know what you say is true, Miss; my boys have told me everything. What Ernesto and Chatto have done is a sin and God will judge them for it. But, Miss, their crime is in the threat only. An *estúpido* and evil threat, certainly. But one they never would have carried out. I know them. My nephews are not bad boys."

This, I think, as I sit looking into the tortured face before me, is palpable horseshit. The monumental errors of my own past rest on precisely this same kind of blind faith—believing people are going to be better and saner than they've ever been before.

When W. P. Skyler reminded everybody that the state bar had disciplined me after my representation of a "nut case," this is precisely what he was referring to. Skyler knew I'd gotten a court to order the state mental hospital to release the "nut case" over the objections of the boy's own mother and the State of New Mexico. And he knew that a week later the "nut case" had shot and killed his own father before he turned the gun on himself. What Skyler probably didn't know was that I'd been engaged to marry the "nut case's" father at the time. I'm certain that Eloy is making a similiar mistake.

"If I had looked after my brothers the right way," Eloy continues, shaking his head, "maybe now they could look after their own sons. But I was a bad example. I was a *pachuco* and so these boys' fathers were *pachucos* and now they aren't fathers at all. It is all up to me." He sighs. "When Jimmy told me his cousins had threatened my little Samuel, I was full of shame for those boys. Someone had to step in . . . to mediate . . . to bring peace back to our family. You see how I brought them all up here to work with me. Ernesto confessed everything to me. And they have confessed to our priest now also. We pray together every evening for grace and forgiveness. All day they work together. Ernesto and Chatto have begged forgiveness from Jimmy and from me and from our Lord."

Eloy takes both my hands in his. "Miss, Jimmy needs his family. And, I promise you, as I promised Jimmy, these boys would never hurt a child. They would never hurt one of our own family. If they did, I would kill them with my own hands."

That night, moonlight streaming through the window, I lie next to Max and stare at the rough timbered ceiling of the B&B cabin. Near sun-up, I snuggle against his back and press my nose against his skin.

"Umph," he says.

"Umph to you too."

"What . . . time is it?"

"Dawn."

"Are you just waking up or just going to sleep?"

"Neither."

"Umph." Max yawns one of those whole-body-shudder kind of yawns, turns over, and nestles his sleepy face against my neck.

"You want to talk?" he asks.

"Huh-uh."

He raises himself on an elbow, kisses my forehead and my cheek, runs his tongue along the edge of my upper lip. "Make love?"

"Huh-uh."

". . . Want to go somewhere?"

"It's four o'clock in the morning, Max, in Jemez Springs, New Mexico. Where can we go?"

"You have a swimming suit with you?"

"Of course not."

"Never mind; come on, get dressed." He jumps up and starts throwing on sweats and rummaging in the suitcase. "Oh," he says over his shoulder, "you might want to wear underwear in case somebody's there."

"Huh?"

"Or not."

Just a little north of the village of Jemez Springs, the buttes turn into real mountains and the road is a ribbon through a steep, rugged canyon. Nobody's out at this time of day. The one car behind us seems to have turned off someplace a mile or so back. Another five miles and Max pulls off the road. The sun isn't over the crest yet and the empty dirt lot he pulls into is still in shadow.

"Been here before?"

"It's the hot springs, isn't it? No. I've lived in New Mexico most of my life and I've never done this. Modesty, I guess."

"Time you got over it. Follow me."

We hop across the stepping-stones embedded in the creek at the far end of the lot and find the tracings of a path created by years of foot traffic. Max doesn't break a sweat during the steep fifteen-minute climb. Yours truly is another matter. As we round the last curve, I'm grateful to see the steam rising off the big pool, vaporizing in the cool mountain air.

"My God, it's beautiful," I exclaim.

The water is heated thousands of feet below by volcanic action. It rises and forms the big pool, then spills over the edge into a smaller pool below. Max and I find a flat rock to stand on and begin to strip. There is something both sexy and wholesome—practically Germanic—about getting naked on a mountaintop at dawn.

"My God, you're gorgeous," he says with such wanting in his voice, I know it must be true.

We sink into the bubbling liquid up to our shoulders. The algae slime of the rock shelf below the surface grazes the back of my legs, and I slither away from it, losing my balance and finding it again in Max's arms.

"It's been a long time since we made love," he says, holding me close. "You've been . . . preoccupied."

"I'm not preoccupied now. I am present occupied. You might even say"—my fingers move through the hot black water until I find him—"that I've got my hands full of this moment."

In my experience, men are so vulnerable when they make love that a grown woman could weep. Hard and eager and thrusting; then, afterward, spent and slack and trusting as a child with a fever.

Max leans back against the rocks, wanting to ask his after-sex question. "Do you love me?" he finally says.

I nod my head slightly in the dawning light. It is still often like this with me. Semi-darkness; semi-commitment.

I open my mouth to explain my hesitation and I hesitate even to start, and in the silence of that moment I hear or imagine I can hear a sharp crack above our heads. Before I can look up, Max pushes me aside. Something crashes into the pond between our naked bodies, sending geysers of hissing water into the air. As I struggle to regain my footing on the algae, somewhere up there in the dark, I hear another mammoth stone plunging toward us.

FIFTEEN

—◆◆◆—

I LUNGE OVER THE EDGE OF THE POND, FLOP MY NAKED belly across a slick expanse of rock, and claw for a handhold. I hear the second boulder hit the water inches from my foot.

"MAX!"

Max is a yard or so to my left, half out of the water; something dark is beginning to materialize in a jagged seam from his shoulder to his hip.

"Oh, shit, Max! Can you get out?" I cry.

I struggle to my knees and I'm yanking at his arms and he's scrabbling toward me, when I hear the rumble above our heads. We crouch impotently together as a third colossal stone crashes off an outcrop mere inches from Max's hand and careens downward like a giant pinball, splintering branches and bushes and small trees in its wake. Clothes forgotten, we follow the rock down the mountain, lurching headlong in its aftermath like naked flotsam. The boulder comes to a shuddering rest in the river just below the parking lot. We splash through the cold stream and actually reach the Lincoln before I realize that we can't go anywhere.

"No ... car ... keys," I gasp.

"I'll go back," Max pants, turning ... turning his back to me. I touch it, touch his slick spine.

"Jesus."

The seam down his back is now a deep, flowing gash. Max's back is slippery with blood.

"You're not going anywhere," I say.

There's a battered white van in the lot that wasn't here when we arrived. It could mean help—someone within the sound of a scream—could mean safety. Or it could mean something else altogether.

"Max, you're losing a lot of blood. You've got to stay here."

"You can't ... go back up there ..." protests my intrepid, mangled hero, "... by yourself."

"Stop prattling. Wait. I've got another idea."

I cross my arms across my breasts in a moronic attempt at modesty, then sprint across the lot to the white van. It's unlocked and I slide the wide door aside. Inside, the floor is a jumble of tools and horse tack and rags and blankets and empty McDonald's cups. On the front passenger seat is a greasy gray nylon jacket and a baseball cap; on the floor, a bunch of plastic CD holders and a player with a wire running up to the cigarette lighter on the dash. Hanging from the dashboard mirror is a St. Christopher medal and a rubber hula-dancer, overendowed and naked to the waist. The ashtray is overflowing with cigarettes smoked down to the filters. And, in the ignition, miraculously ... a key.

Honk the horn? Yell for help? Better think this through. If those boulders were shoved, the shover had to get here somehow, had to have transportation. Deciding the mishmash of junk in the van is a testament to its owner's character, I decide against calling attention to myself in favor of getting the hell out of there. In less than a minute, I've dressed myself in the greasy jacket and driven to Max. I dig through the blankets, help him arrange the cleanest one around his naked body, and put the van in reverse.

"My car," he says.

"We'll come back."

I check the rearview mirror one last time as I back out.

"Crap!"

A man in a black T-shirt and jeans is running toward the back of the van at breakneck speed, waving his arms back and forth like a semaphore.

"HEY! STOP! GODDAMN IT, STOP! THAT'S MY VAN!"

My mind races to recalculate the possibilities. Am I stealing some guy's van? Or am I fleeing with our lives from someone who just tried to kill us? How costly is the mistake going to be, either way?

I suck in air, press down hard on the accelerator.

I watch the racing, howling man become smaller in his own rearview mirror. As I top the shoulder of the road and speed across, I have a last glimpse of him, arms gone slack now, gaping openmouthed after us.

A couple of miles down the road, Max says quietly, "He didn't really behave like somebody who'd just tried to murder us, did he?"

I look over at him. No censure in his eyes, no accusation, just the question.

"Oh, crap," I say again.

In the village of Jemez Springs, just below the Bodhi Mandala Zen Center, is a circle of gravel edged by a couple of mineral baths and the Jemez Springs Police Department. Once inside the tiny station, our problem stated, it takes less than two minutes to pull on some borrowed clothes. Max is given a pair of oversized shorts; I get a fiesta skirt, a freshly ironed policeman's shirt, and flip-flops. Another ten minutes while the officer dabs at Max's back with alcohol and takes our statement. Forty more to pick up our stuff from the B&B cabin and get Max settled on the cozy screened porch of the local nurse-practitioner. After that, the officer who'd donated a spare shirt to me (Manuel Leyba, by name) turns on the salsa station in the Bronco cruiser and asks, "Ready to head on up there, Miss?"

By the time we pull into the parking lot at the base of the

hot springs, a young couple with three kids have joined the man in the black T-shirt and somebody has used a cell phone to call the police department and the dispatcher has radioed Officer Leyba here in the Bronco that a vehicle theft has been reported. Another officer has been dispatched with the "stolen" van to join us. "Looks like they're expecting us." Leyba nods toward the small group assembled. The man in the black T-shirt bounds over and slaps the Bronco's door as Leyba switches off the *Tijana* music and brakes to a stop.

"It's about time!"

Then he sees me. "*She* stole my van! Where's my god-damned *van*?"

The guy stays pretty hot under his collarless shirt until his van arrives, then he starts checking it out inch by inch. While he's at that, Officer Leyba and I make the climb up to the springs and, by the time we return with Max's and my clothes, Black T-shirt has shuttered down to an occasional "goddamn it to hell" under his breath. He points out, accusingly, that one of his blankets is missing.

"This is for the blanket." I hand the guy a hundred-dollar bill from Max's wallet. "I know I can't make up for the scare we must have given you—driving away in your van like that."

"I wasn't scared, lady."

"I thought someone had just tried to kill my friend and me. I thought it might have been . . ."

"Me?"

"I'm afraid so."

"Well, it wasn't."

"No, I guess not."

"I ought to press charges," he mutters. He looks to Leyba, who tugs at the bill of his cap and shrugs as if to say, *It's up to you, pal.*

"I'd understand if you did," I say.

"Well, I ought to . . ."

The couple with the kids are pulling out of the lot. The wife waves at my victim as they pass. He waves back.

"Somebody really tried to kill you?" he finally says to me.

"We thought so."

"Anybody hurt?"

"My friend was badly cut by a boulder."

"Well"—he turns to the officer—"I heard the rocks crashing just after I pulled in. I jumped out of the van, left the goddamned keys in it, and ran to see what was what. I figured it was a rock slide—natural, you know. Is she sure it wasn't?"

"Not a hundred percent sure," I admit.

"Anyways, I guess I went the wrong way—following echoes, you know?"

Surrendering his anger, he sighs. "I don't know if it amounts to a hill of beans but, after this one here"—he aims his thumb at me—"peeled a couple inches of rubber off my new tires, some guy comes crashing through the woods way over there." He indicates a spot about twenty yards on the other side of the lot. "Guy was running like hell toward the road, and just as he gets there, a car come down from the north, door opens, and this guy jumped in it and they took off."

"What did the car look like?" Officer Leyba flips his notepad to a clean page and poises his pen.

"Dark, I think it was a dark color. Maybe blue . . . or dark green . . . could have been black."

"Year? Make?"

Black T-shirt winces. "I'm usually good at cars, but I was so pissed. My van had just been ripped off."

"Can you describe either of the men?"

"Uh, the guy running, he had dark hair . . . about average height, I guess. His face was kinda mashed in like in the middle. He was wearing tennis shoes, I think. No, maybe not." He shrugs. "Sorry."

Leyba tells me it's not possible to get above the springs by car but that there's a forest service road up that way. "A four-wheel-drive could get pretty close," he says. "I'll check it out. But first, I guess we need to know, sir . . . whether you'll be wanting charges pressed?"

"Ah shit." The man tucks in his T-shirt and spits. "I guess the van's, like, okay . . . probably the blanket wasn't worth a hundred anyways. Shit!"

Before he leaves, he wants my address and phone number

and the name of my insurance company "just in case something turns up wrong with my van."

Minutes later, I get behind the wheel of Max's Lincoln and head back to town. From the walkway to the nurse-practitioner's house, I can see Max through the screening of her porch. Max is naked to the waist and hunchbacked from the wad of gauze dressing attached to his spine. But, all in all, he's looking quite recovered. He's smiling over his hump at the handsome woman who's pouring coffee into his cup.

They both turn as the screen door squeaks open.

"Morning, Quasimodo," I say.

The woman has a welcoming smile on her face. Max, as Paul Reiser would say, "not so much."

"I didn't stitch it," the nurse explains to me later. "I pulled the skin together and secured it with these." She displays a handful of tiny, transparent butterfly bandages. "The dressing is only to keep him as rigid as possible so he won't put pressure on the seam. But he'd be better off if he didn't have to move much today. I told Max, uh, Mr. Cortino, he's welcome to stay in the guest room here. . . ."

"Max?"

"You okay?" he asks me. "Apparently, you're not under arrest for auto theft?"

I step across the porch to plant a kiss on top of his head. "The victim decided to be a nice guy. A reluctant, pissed-off nice guy. But, nevertheless . . ."

"You're a lucky lady," he says, and there's a trace of "luckier than you deserve to be" in his voice.

"Well . . ." says the nurse, "I've got work to do inside. I'll leave you two for a while. Oh, you're welcome to stay here too if you'd like, Ms. Donahue."

When she has disappeared inside, I edge back a corner of Max's dressing. "I can't see anything. Does it hurt?"

He shakes his head. "Rachel gave me something."

"Rachel, is it?"

"Mmmm."

My fingers linger on his bare shoulder. Then, all at once, I'm starving. I help myself to the lone muffin from the wicker basket on the table and then to the crusts of toast on Max's plate. I press my fingertips onto the glass plate to embed any stray crumbs, then suck them off. It's all I can manage not to pick up the plate and lick it. With nothing else edible on the table, my eyes scan the room for nourishment. At the end of the porch is one of those four-gallon cans of caramel popcorn. I flip the lid and give it a taste. The stuff tastes five years old. I scarf down several fistfuls. I'm like a newly rescued concentration camp victim who can't get enough to eat. Sticky bits are clinging to my face and to the borrowed officer's shirt, and when I finally lift my head from the trough, licking my fingers and lips, Max is watching me like a tourist. Somewhat abashed, I wipe a few kernels back into the can.

"Wow," I say, "what do you think this is about?"

"Being alive," he says, "instead of dead."

I nod. I tell Max about the man seen jumping into a car. "The police department is contacting the forest service. They'll try to determine whether this could have been a natural avalanche."

"What do you think?"

"Hundreds of people come to the hot springs during the year. I would've thought somebody was making sure it was safe from avalanches. But I got the impression from Officer Leyba that we weren't going to know what happened up there this morning anytime soon—if ever."

"If it wasn't that . . . wasn't a natural rock fall . . . somebody deliberately pried those boulders loose."

"Yeah."

"For kicks?"

"Could be, I guess."

"But we don't think so, do we?" Max says it sarcastically.

I don't answer. If this trip was a test of our relationship, I can see how Max is grading it. Being too cowardly to cope with his censure, or my reaction to it, I avert my eyes.

"Matty, these things are too dangerous."

"What . . . *things*?"

"These . . . cases. These . . . clients."

"One case," I point out. "One client! Max, Jimmy Abeyta

came to me. I admit, the case has moved beyond a strictly legal arena, but—"

"No! This isn't the first time. These things don't happen to ordinary lawyers. Look, Matty, these things don't happen unless you're, somehow, seeking them; you deliberately court jeopardy."

My jaw tightens and Max sees my resistance. He shifts his ground slightly. "Matty, you're hardly even trying to practice law anymore. Ever since the last time you played private eye, you've been bored to tears with ordinary legal cases. And the first thing to walk into your life with a promise of peril, you embrace like a lover."

"What kind of psychobabble is this, Max? What I'm doing is for a five-year-old boy . . ."

"Partly." He says it flat and keeps his eyes steady on me.

"You're afraid," I say to those eyes. "You were injured and now you're afraid, that's all. It's understandable."

"You're damn right I'm afraid. It's *rational* to be afraid. You must admit your behavior has been other than rational."

That was the remark that did it. When a shrink tells you you're irrational, there's pretty much nothing to do but storm out and slam the screen door and prove him right.

Continuing along on my new career path—car thief—I throw over my shoulder: "I'm taking the Lincoln. You can rent a Jeep at the garage when you're finished vacationing with *Rachel.*"

SIXTEEN

---∞∞∞---

I HAVE NO CLEAR THOUGHTS DURING MY TWO HOUR drive through the Jemez canyon. I barely heed my passage along the rim of the Valle Grande volcano crater. Normally, that sight gives me pause. From the rim-edge road where you first view the cup-shaped cauldron to the rim on the other side is over fifteen miles. In the cup today this season's elk and cattle herds, tiny in the distance, placidly munch lunch in what was once an inland lake of molten lava. The only break in the vast hollow of grass are hundred-foot-high volcanic cores. When this place blew thousands of years ago, it was with a force five hundred times that of Mount St. Helens. That reflection usually puts a little proportion back into my life. But not today. Today, I'm other than rational.

Insensible to nature's wonder, I round the Valle Grande rim and drop down from the Jemez canyon through Los Alamos down to the Rio Grande canyon, then climb upward again along this river's gorge. The next thing I'm aware of is Max's Lincoln floating effortlessly up to the stoplight at the top of the hill next to the Taos plaza.

The Taos Inn is only a block away, but the odds of getting a room in this town in the middle of tourist season with no reservations are about as good as the odds of my looking at Max's recent evaluation of my motives coolly and . . . you know . . . rationally.

The address Claude Raskin had given me for Gene Saavedra, the mortgage banker, is north of town. So I creep along the narrow main street that carries all of the north-south traffic through Taos, making it perpetually gridlocked with bumper-to-bumper traffic.

North of town, I locate a dusty narrow street that leads to another dusty street and another. One of the permutations of Taos's relentlessly *anti-chic* sensibilities is its aversion to asphalt. Eventually, I pull into a long, rutted driveway that cuts through an acre of pastureland to my right and, to my left, an orchard overgrown with summer grass. The grass is being attacked by a close-shorn teenager with a fine set of yellow earphones around his nearly bald head and a weed whacker in his hand. He sees me, shoulders the whacker, and waves me to a stop. I touch a button to bring the window down and he sticks his face through the opening. Rap beat throbs thinly from his headset.

"You the bankruptcy woman?" he says too loudly. "The one who's been leaving phone messages?"

"Matty Donahue."

"Whatever." He murders the noise with a flip of a switch on his earmuffs. "Dad's gone."

"You're Gene Saavedra's son?"

"Yeah, Dad's away on business. Probably be gone a month. He says tell you he'll call you when he gets back. Says he's sorry you had to make the trip for nothing."

"Oh . . . that's too bad. Is that your mother there in the garden?"

"Huh?

The house and garden are a couple of yards ahead. I'd almost missed the woman sitting there on an iron bench, hidden as she is in a rampart of shoulder-high hollyhocks. Her head protrudes in front of her like a turtle in strange territory cautiously considering its next move.

"No," says the kid with an unmistakable hesitation in his voice. "I mean, yes; but she's busy."

If my antennae weren't out before, the kid's awkward fib shoots them forth. Why should I be so unwelcome that excuses must be made? Or is it the woman he's concerned about? I hit the gas with my toe and the Lincoln shoots forward as the boy makes a futile grab for the window. As the tires skid to an ungraceful stop at the edge of the garden, I leap from the car and practically bound toward the woman. Out of the corner of my eye, I see the kid take off, running toward the back of the house, holding his weed whacker high. He puts me in mind of Paul Revere: "The Donahue is coming, the Donahue is coming."

The woman is middle-aged and doughy. She's wearing an embroidered peasant blouse and baggy shorts. Her fleshy knees jiggle nervously and her hands have gone to her mouth, her fingers pressing tight against her lips like the monkey who speaks no evil.

"Mrs. Saavedra? I'm so glad I caught you home. Your son told me your husband is out of town, but at least you and I will have a chance to visit." Though it seems inanely transparent, I occasionally have an intuition that this instant-chum routine will work. It's like diving into a pool that's empty as I leave the board but will fill miraculously while I'm in midair . . . usually.

I leap. "What a lovely garden. The hollyhocks are spectacular." Uninvited, I move to the bench and plop down beside her. "When I was a little girl," I say, plucking three blossoms from the nearest stem, "we used to make hollyhock dolls. . . . Do you mind?" I set to work attaching the skirt to the bodice, noticing that soon Mrs. Saavedra's hands have slid to her ample breasts and her eyes are on the emerging doll.

It's been a long time since I tried this toy-making, and it's going badly. The flower parts are supposed to stick rigidly together to make an upright, skirted lady; this one looks like she could use traction.

"It needs a bobby pin," the woman says. "I have one in the house."

"Great!"

Twenty minutes later, she's built a skeleton for our doll and manufactured a display platform out of a paper clip stuck into an eraser. We've had a Coke and we've begun to talk about her. She's told me her name is Gencie and that she uses her maiden name instead of Saavedra.

"Gene and me were separated for a time early on and I retook my family name; had it changed back legal and everything. All my credit cards and bank accounts are in the name I was born with. Why should I change them back again?"

She asks this with a dash of righteous indignation. I get the feeling this is a frequent, and not entirely settled, topic with her.

"You go, girl," I say, and immediately regret the levity when she stiffens. "I mean it," I add hastily. "Taking someone else's name is a little like taking someone else's brand."

"Like if you were a horse or a cow," she retorts. "I'm no feminist, that's for sure, but this is my own little stand . . . I guess. You want some more Coke?"

I nod and, as she pops the top, I ask where her husband is today and she drops the soda can with a loud, splashy plop. I grab a wad of paper towels and she joins me on my knees on the floor where, together, we go at the spill like a couple of scrubwomen.

"I . . . uh . . . don't really know," she says to the floor. "Gene got your messages but he couldn't stay. Something, uh, came up."

"Business?"

"Uh-huh," she says, still talking to the linoleum.

"Did he get my last message saying where I was staying in Jemez Springs? I'd hoped he could call me there last night to confirm a meeting today. I hated dropping in unannounced like this."

"Uh, I really don't know"—she takes a good deal of time wiping imaginary dust off her knees—"and I don't know when Gene'll be back either . . . if that's what you were going to ask me. There's no use talking to me about Gene's business. He doesn't tell me a thing . . . really."

I let her off the hook and she relaxes slightly when I ask about the *retablos* hung on her kitchen walls. These sheets of tin upon which saints and holy scenes were hand painted by amateur but passionate hands were once the only sacred art in these wild northern reaches of the Spanish empire. Gencie shows me her collection of Mexican folk art: hand-carved crosses and punched-tin mirrors and small papier-mâché skeletons dancing in a wooden box on the kitchen wall. On a shelf are a number of decorative items that seem culturally alien to the others. Small boxes of intricately inlaid wood. I gently lift the lid of one with the back of my index finger and the strains of "The Blue Danube" tinkle sweetly forth.

"Austrian?" I ask.

"Swiss," she replies. "Gene always used to bring me back music boxes from his ski trips to Bern."

"Your husband goes to Switzerland to ski?"

"He used to. He still complains that Taos isn't alpine enough for him. Gene likes variety," she says wanly, ". . . and excitement." I'm pretty sure Gencie's no longer talking only about her husband's preference in ski slopes.

"Did Alan Prather ski with Gene?" I ask.

"Oh sure, all the time."

"Here in Taos?"

"And in Bern too. Gene said Alan Prather was one of the few people who could keep up with him on the slopes. I never really knew Alan that well. Oh, we'd get together with him and his wife sometimes out at the Santa Fe Country Club. But him and Gene just talked business all night. Me and Denise were sort of stuck with each other. But I didn't really mind, she was real nice and easy to talk to. We became sort of like friends for a while there."

"Did you see her more recently, after she became ill?"

Gencie sinks into a chair and sits sideways, facing away from me, and bites the side of her thumb. "I drove down to Santa Fe about a month before she died. I know I should've gone before that, but I had no idea how bad off she was. Honest!"

"Pretty bad, I guess."

"She needed a full-time nurse but, when I got there, no one was taking any care of her at all. I had to let myself in the house and follow her sounds to the bedroom. Oh my God, I could barely understand the words coming out of her mouth. Nobody was around and I couldn't just stay there forever, so I phoned nine one one and they said call Human Services. I stayed until they showed up. Maybe I should have done more. Probably I should have, but I . . ."

Gencie tears up for a second, then starts suddenly at a faint jostling sound from the next room. She stands abruptly.

"Uh . . . let me walk you out, Ms. Donahue," she says tensely. I allow myself to be elbow-guided across the kitchen and back out the front door. At my car door, she swipes a smile and a hasty good-bye across her face and waves over her shoulder as she lopes heavily back toward the house.

One of the problems with fooling someone into thinking you're her chum is the person you end up fooling may be you. Now I'm worried about Gencie. I start the engine and let it idle for a moment, trying to figure a way to learn what's got this woman so spooked.

As I near the gate, I see the kid with the earphones glowering at me from the weeds, and I pull over. "Sorry," I call out the window, "but I really needed to talk to your mother."

"You leaving now?" he snarls, pulling the headset down around his neck.

"Yes, well . . . I mean, I was about to leave, but I just realized I left my purse in your house," I improvise. "I'll just run back and get—"

I'm halfway out the car before I feel the flat of his hand in the middle of my chest.

"You stay here," he orders. "I'll get your purse."

He heads for the house walking backward so he can keep his wary eye on me. Just before he turns, he says to me "Stay!" the way you would say it to a dog in training to become a good dog.

"Absolutely," I call back obediently.

And I do stay—precisely as long as it takes him to close the front door behind him. Knowing I have only a few minutes at best, I hotfoot it along the ruts and sprint through the garden, decimating a few hollyhocks in the process. Once on the porch, I hush my ragged breath while turning the knob as noiselessly as I can manage. I needn't have worried about the noise. The place is erupting with it.

". . . and all you had to do was stay in the fucking house, but . . . NO!" The angry voice belongs to a male. But not to the teenager.

"You can't do one simple goddamned thing I ask, can you?"

"GENE, DON'T!"

"Let her go, Dad, she says she didn't say nothing! Where's the fucking purse? Hurry, help me before that woman comes back to—"

SMACK!!

The unmistakable sound of a hand slapping flesh is followed by a little mewling sound, and that is followed by silence.

After a few seconds, I knock on the door, which is slightly ajar, and call loudly, "Hello . . . Gencie . . . I think I left my purse in—"

"How do you do, young lady?" Now that furious voice is deep and smooth as suede. "Please . . . come in."

The man who belongs to the voice is swarthy and sleek with a glossy black ponytail. He approaches with a fluid athletic walk and an outstretched hand. I take the hand and feel the strength of it and the heat of it.

"Ahh, Mr. Saavedra. Your business finished early, I see."

"You must forgive my family. I am a very busy man and they protect me from interruptions. Please, please, won't you come into my den?" He gestures like a courtier toward the hallway that leads away from the kitchen. I ignore his arm and march to the kitchen, murmuring something about my missing purse.

At the table, Gencie starts. "Oh, Ms. Donahue"—she wipes at her cheek—"we . . . uh . . . didn't find your purse. I'm sorry."

Gene muscles past me and snaps, "Genevieve, pour something cold for our guest, why don't you? Bring it into my den."

"Genevieve?" I ask. "I thought your name was Gencie."

"Nickname." She smiles weakly. "Short for Genevieve."

"And your last name? Your maiden name? Would that be Moreno?"

"Yes. How did you . . . ?"

"A woman named Genevieve Moreno gave a statement. To a detective Baca. Something about Denise Prather receiving a threat?"

"WHAT?" Gene Saavedra crosses the room like a panther. He's nearly in his wife's face now, and it's costing her something not to cower.

"I didn't say anything, really," Gencie protests softly. Her voice is low, meant for him. The moment hangs there. It could go either way. The kid stays well away from them. What a swell pop this guy would make.

With an effort, Gene pulls back and smiles grimly.

To me Gencie says, "Yes, you're right; Detective Baca got my name from the nine one one records. Naturally, I talked to him a little bit about my visit to Denise, how worried I was and so forth. Denise was so hard to understand that day. She kept saying . . ."

She looks askance at her husband, who is a study in composed distress, and says, more to him than to me, "I told the detective I thought she had been threatened by a patient—"

"Ms. Donahue," Saavedra interrupts with forced civility. "I'm afraid you've come at a bad time. But I will be in Santa Fe one day soon. Perhaps you'd be good enough to join me for a light supper at that time."

He takes a step toward me, his muscular arms raised and held wide in a kind of herding gesture.

"Sure," I say, and once more allow myself to be genteelly tossed out of the Saavedra household. Nobody says a word about the nonexistent purse.

.   .   .

As I negotiate the sharp curves down the steep canyon toward home, I find I'm drifting across the double yellow line. This traumatic and disturbing day is catching up with me fast. I pull over into a wide spot on the shoulder of the road. My eyes come gratefully to rest on the river below me. Here, the Rio Grande is still deep and fast from the high-country run-off, frothing over rock ledges and piling up into waves and dashing around boulders.

In my younger days, I did a fair amount of rafting down the Taos Box back upriver. Now, as I listen to the surging of the water, I drift into a reverie of river trips and the memory of white-water spray on my face. Maybe for a little while I can forget plummeting boulders and bankrupted relationships.

When I wake, the early dark of sunset at the bottom of the canyon is beginning to shroud the car. I yawn and stretch and get out and pee in the bushes. Back in the driver's seat, I turn, aim the car down toward home and my brain toward the mysteries of this dying day. At the north end of Espanola, I stop at a pay phone. Nurse Rachel informs me ruefully that Max left her care shortly after I did. I drop in another dollar's worth of quarters and, on Max's answering machine, I leave a one-word message: "Sorry."

Five minutes later, on the south end of Espanola, I find another pay phone and leave a longer message: "I'll be home in about an hour. Call . . . please."

When I get back to Irongate, Angie and Sam appear to have gone to bed. On the kitchen table, Angie has left a long, detailed description of her survey of the house and a list of events of the past two days. Terminating the list is a bunch of phone messages. The last one is from Max. The message: "Please drop his car off at the garage he uses. He'll pick it up later."

Nothing else.

The call came in about a half hour ago. Presumably *after* he got my apology.

SEVENTEEN

DESPITE MY ROAD NAP, I'M BONE WEARY. AND STALE caramel corn notwithstanding, I'm ravenous again. So I leave Angie's missive on the entry table and head to the kitchen. From the limited options, I settle on pancakes made with powdered milk. For syrup, I soak a box of rock-hard brown sugar in a half cup of water and set it on the stove. Moving around the two tall pipe-jacks still holding up an edge of the ceiling, I put on a pot of water for tea, set the counter with a good china plate, then squat to rummage for a skillet in a lower cabinet.

A light tap on my shoulder scares the pee-waden out of me, and I yelp and end up splay-legged on my butt on the floor with the skillet in my lap.

"Why are you wearing a policeman's shirt?" he says.

Sam is dressed in too-small summer pajamas. His legs stick out about six inches from the hems, one bare foot crabs toward the other and then back again to where it started. "What are you doing?" he says.

"Making pancakes," I answer, lifting him onto the counter. "Want some?"

He takes a gander at the bowl of goo and picks up the drippy wire whisk. He touches it to his tongue.

"This tastes icky."

"Have patience. Good things can come from icky things."

"Like what?"

"Umm . . . like . . . penicillin. You know what penicillin is?"

"Medicine."

"Right. Medicine that comes from mold. Do you know what mold is?"

"Fuzzy stuff on bread. Icky things can come from good things too," Sam says. "Like poop from food. Did you know that?"

"Umm, yes, I did know that."

"Where have you been?"

"I had to go on a little trip. I saw your daddy, by the way. He misses you."

"Then why doesn't he come home?" Sam studies the pancake batter.

"Well, Sam, I'm sure—"

"I can pour that stuff in the pan," he interrupts, aiming the whisk at the bowl of batter. I'm way too tired for cooking with a preschooler, but I smile indulgently like a dotty spinster aunt, hand the kid a spoon, and start the skillet.

Over grainy syrup and pancakes the size of Frisbees, I ask what's been happening while I've been gone.

"Nothing," he says.

I ask how his mom is doing.

"Fine," he says.

I ask if there's anything new at all—if there's been anything good on TV—if there have been any visitors.

"Only Patrick. He's pretty nice."

I spit tea all over the table. "Patrick?"

"Mom told him he could sleep in the yellow room."

"SLEEP? HERE? NOW?"

"Um-hum. Wanna see?"

"You know, Sam, I think I better."

Sam takes my hand and leads me through the house to the

yellow room as though he is the homeowner and I the lost guest. He opens the door softly and I follow him in.

"See," he whispers, and points to the snoring lump swaddled in sheets. He tugs me forward for a better look. "See, there he is."

Indeed. At the top of the mound is a head in profile: tousled brown hair curling over his ear and about an inch of woolly beard shot with gray. What the hell is he doing here? He's supposed to be safely out to sea for three more weeks. If he's here, does that mean his sister-in-law's session tapes are here with him? And if they are, what's my obligation to inform the court ... or the cops? Oh shit.

This has been a very long day. Sometimes you just have to give yourself permission to not deal with one more frigging thing.

"Come on," I whisper to Sam. "Let's let Patrick sleep."

During the night, dreams masquerade as insights and I awaken no fewer than three times to scribble down bits and fragments that seem consequential. The next morning, I wake at six and find my notes incomprehensible. Still wearing the officer's shirt I put on in Jemez Springs and lay down in last night, I make my way to the bathroom and turn on the light. Big mistake. Sudden and harsh, illumination is no friend to the face looking back at me.

"Early ripe, early rot," the mother of a homely high-school friend had predicted of me. Yessireee.

I shower in water hot enough to boil lobsters, yank my too-short hair into a ponytail, swish and spit, pull on a clean pair of shorts, a T-shirt, and shoes I still refer to archaically as "tennis shoes," and head for the kitchen. None of my swelling list of houseguests appears to be up yet. I make a pot of strong coffee and, as it brews, let my fingers play with the coiled telephone wire.

Once or twice, I almost pick up the receiver to tell Daniel Baca about what happened to me at the hot springs. But how

do I make such a call without mentioning Chatto and Fat
Boy? And how would I talk about Chatto and Fat Boy without
talking about Jimmy and Augusto Santiago? I let the phone
cord and the instinct to call fall away.

When the coffee is ready, I take a cup of it outside with me.
The trees up here above the city are mostly juniper. The scrub
mostly piñon. From the back of the Prather patio, I pick my
way up a shallow ravine. Prairie dogs scurry as I pass. No
more than fifty yards from the house, a small spring inches
water up through the soil into a pool. I watch it turn into a
rivulet which runs fast then slows as it reaches sloping terrain
lower down and meanders past clumps of chamisa and wild
Russian sage. The early morning light silvers the thread of
water. I kneel and wet my fingers in the cold stream.

With my back propped against a boulder, I try to organize
the data accumulated on my two-day junket. The facts, such
as they are, only lead to questions. Did someone follow Max
and me from the Hummingbird B&B to the hot springs? Who
knew we'd be in Jemez Springs the night before last, much less
where we would be staying? Practically everybody, I decide.
But why would anyone want to harm me? Harm Max? What
was Gene Saavedra so afraid I'd discover? Did any of this tie to
the Prather deaths?

I butt my brain against such imponderables until I have a
headache and give it up to let my mind drift. To Max's appraisal
of the situation—dangerous; and to his analysis of me—
attracted to the danger and, therefore, *other than rational*. I'm
more than a little pained that he's being so stone-hearted in refusing to return my calls. Pained and guilty and worried.

A bearded man dressed in a pair of khaki slacks and a
brown shirt is striding up the hill toward me. The tousled
brown hair has been tamed a bit. As Patrick Prather nears, his
face becomes even more interesting: tan with curious eyes
and an intriguing grin.

"Matilda Donahue, got to be." He extends his hand. "I expected the green eyes and auburn hair, but your complexion
is darker than I'd pictured—not the milk-white skin of a
Limerick lass at all."

"Maybe we could keep the Matilda thing just between the two of us," I say, reaching up to take his hand.

Patrick drops to the ground beside me in easy familiarity.

"I apologize for crashing in without an invitation, but I'm afraid I didn't realize anyone was actually living here in the house."

"As executor of the probate estate, you have at least as much right to be here as I do. But I'm surprised. On the phone, you didn't sound anxious to come to Santa Fe."

"Well, when I talked to you, I sure didn't expect to be here anytime soon. I was about to make a long run down the Pacific coast. But when I got to Melaque, one of my scheduled stops, there was a message waiting for me from a detective here in Santa Fe. It sounded urgent, so I moored my boat in the bay, paid the harbor master's kid to watch it, and flew home. I drove a rental up here a couple of days ago. Apparently, I missed seeing you by only about an hour. When I told Angie who I was, she said you'd probably want me to stay. I hope it's okay."

"The, uh, detective who left the message . . . have you . . . talked to him yet?"

"No."

I fling a pebble into the stream. "Why not?"

Patrick sends a stone after mine. "I got your package. I figured you wouldn't have sent it unless you had a reason. Then, when I got the detective's message, I figured your reason had been to get the package out of the reach of the police. I figured you must have had a reason for that. I wanted to find out what the reason was before I did anything else."

"That's a lot of figuring," I say. "Not what most people would have done."

"No, probably not. But I'm not most people. And I gather that what I thought was a closed investigation"—he flings another pebble into the stream—"isn't closed after all. And if I've been wrong . . . if my brother and his wife really didn't commit suicide . . . well, I'm the only family Alan had. And, for all intents and purposes, I was Denise's only family too. I owe it to them to understand what happened here."

"That doesn't entirely explain why you're here instead of at police headquarters."

"Well, it struck me, Matty, that you're probably in a better position to uncover Alan's recent history than the police are. I know a little about that history myself, so I'm in a position to help you. But first, I'd like to know why the hell you're trying to hide what somebody must think is evidence. And why you're involving me."

"Did you open the package I sent?"

He tosses another pebble. "Yeah."

"And you listened to the tapes?"

"Some of them ..."

"And you made connections?"

"Some of them. I already knew that when my sister-in-law was still practicing, many of her clients had been convicted criminals. I listened to enough of the tapes to hear criminal activity discussed. It would seem that even the worst people feel it's safe to discuss their sins with a therapist."

"Mmmm."

"I gather that's what you're trying to protect?"

"Mmmm."

"And it's somehow your business to do that?"

"I represent one of Denise's former patients."

"I see."

I like this guy as much in person as I did on the phone, but I don't quite get him. Patrick is looking at me with his head cocked, trying, I think, to get me.

"I wanted the tapes the hell out of here before they were subpoenaed," I explain. "And you were the only one I could think of who had any right to possess them."

When he doesn't answer, I decide putting the tapes in the mail to him had been a bonehead move on my part. Reluctantly, I give him the rest of the bad news. "And now a district judge has ordered that the tapes be produced in her courtroom in three and a half weeks."

"Not much time."

"Presumably faster ... if I should *happen* to find out where they are ..." I leave the thought unfinished. "My job is to find out what happened to your brother before that deadline. And, of course, I'd be grateful for your help, but don't feel—"

He breaks in. "Okay."

"Okay, what?"

"Okay, you won't know where the tapes are until they're due in court. Okay, I understand what you're trying to do. Okay, I'll help any way I can."

"Really?"

"Really."

As the sun rises higher in the sky and the early chill of the high desert vanishes, I move from the details of the explosion to allegations of Alan's fraud and the fake accounts and the missing money and back again to the explosion. Patrick is easy to talk to. He listens well and asks smart questions. I also tell him about his brother's frequent trips to Switzerland with Gene Saavedra.

"Swiss banks may not be as fashionable as the Cayman Islands banks," I say, "but they're just as impenetrable."

"Did you find any Swiss bank account records among Alan's things? Odd account numbers, anything even suggestive of something like that?"

"No, but if he was hiding loot, I wouldn't expect to find evidence of it easily, would you?"

"The trips could have been just what they seemed, ski trips."

"Sure. But there's no question in my mind that Alan skimmed a lot more money than his lifestyle accounts for. So, where is it?"

"And you say Saavedra was nervous about your visit?"

"You'd have thought I was from the IRS."

Nearly half an hour later, I'm still talking and he's still listening, when we hear Angie yell a "hello up there." It's been helpful to work out recent events with Patrick.

"Thank you," I say as we walk down the hill together.

"Glad to be of help. By the way, I'm going to sort through some of Alan's things. Despite what I said earlier, there may be some personal items I'd like to keep . . . if that's all right."

"Sure."

"Then, if you like, we can talk some more this evening about your . . . shall we call it investigation?"

"I'd like."

Angie is waving up at us. Behind her, a cement truck is disgorging wet concrete down a long chute toward the floor of where the garage used to be, and a crew of two is raking the new pour. Sam is running back and forth along the edge like a line coach. I head for the activity and Patrick veers off, saying he'll see me later.

"What's going on?" I ask Angie. "Who are these guys?"

"Did you see Jimmy? Is he okay all alone up there?"

"Jimmy has his family to keep him company."

"What?"

"Who are these guys?" I repeat.

"They're mine . . . sort of. I hired them yesterday. After you left for Albuquerque, Frankie phoned. Said she'd really liked my work on Canyon Road and she had this great idea. The contractor she'd hired for renovation here had just crapped out and she wanted to know if I could handle a job this size. She'd pay me what she'd agreed to pay him if I could start like right now. I wrote all this in my note to you, didn't you read it?"

"Sorry," I say sheepishly.

"What do you mean, Jimmy's whole family?"

Apparently, Jimmy hasn't gotten around to mentioning to his wife that he's up in the mountains praying and bonding with his jackass cousins, the chief threats to her child's safety. Do I tell her? To what end?

"Eloy," I say lamely. "I mean I saw Jimmy's uncle Eloy. He's got a big construction job going on up there. Jimmy's keeping busy, looks fine. But speaking of big construction jobs, are you really in a position to take this on, Angie?"

"Oh, Matty, it's the kind of job that can put me in a whole different league. If I do well here, I can bid on this kind of work and they won't laugh me out of the water. And it's a lot of money, Matty. Is it okay with you?"

Crap. I rake my fingers through my hair. The accumulation of conflicting agendas in my life is beginning to overwhelm me. If I could think of any reasonable excuse to refuse permission, I would.

"Uh . . . I left you a list of things to look for in the house," I say instead. "Did you do that?"

"I started. But"—she aims a finger at the emerging concrete floor and manages to look at once shamefaced and energized—"I got a little sidetracked."

Angie is about a hundred percent happier than she was three days ago. She's probably right about what this could do for her business. And it will certainly take her mind off Jimmy's mounting problems. Oh, what the hell?

I spend the next half hour going over what Angie had gathered together: calendars, personal phone books, two months of telephone bills with the long distance numbers tagged and identified in Angie's own hand. I take a break to call Max. On his machine, I leave a contrite but spunky little message that makes me feel more pathetic than I did before I called. Screw this; maybe I'll call him again at bedtime.

For now, I toss the stuff I'd been working on in a box for further review and ask Angie to follow me into town to Max's garage so I can drop off his Lincoln. On the way back we stop at Kaune Market for some groceries. Kaune Market is a local jewel with everything from fresh herbs growing in flats to caviar so expensive it's kept it in a locked glass case. This is a gourmet's paradise and Max knows how to use all this stuff.

Unfortunately, Angie is no better in the kitchen than I am, so we buy lots of canned soup and four kinds of crackers. Sam drops junk from every aisle into the basket. Most of it looks no less nutritious than the junk we adults choose.

Tonight the three of us and Patrick dine on Campbell soup and Fruit Loops. Patrick pulls a bottle of wine from the newly reconstructed wine rack. He examines Angie's carpentry with approval. "The place looks even better than it did the last time I was here."

"When was that?" she asks.

"Must have been about three, four years ago."

"Long time between visits," I say.

"My brother and I didn't"—he hesitates, then smiles wearily—"do well together."

"Oh?"

He uncorks, pours, and hands Angie a glass. Then one for me.

"Alan resented me," he says.

"Why?" I ask with growing interest.

"I made some money. He ... lost some."

He lost more than some. If Alan had lived and let's say he had no ... hidden reserves, he'd soon be a very poor man. Alan had lost a lot—practically everything.

"Your success," I suggest to Patrick, "must have made his failure even more bitter."

"True. But Alan had been mad at me for a very long time. Not without good reason, I'm sorry to say."

"What do you mean?"

"There were only the two of us kids. Alan was older than me by two years. He was more everything than me: more popular, more talented, more interesting. I was the nerdy one who hid in my room with my calculator. And Alan was smarter than me too, in most of the ordinary ways."

"Yet you're the one who invented ... what was it? A computer program?"

"A way to integrate programs. True, but I was able to do that, in large part, because I had the luxury of time. Time and money. You see, our mother's family had always had a bit of money. For several generations they hadn't made it grow much, but they'd all lived by the adage *Never touch the principal!* So by the time I reached majority, it was still a tidy sum. Enough so that I could devote myself to fooling around with stuff that really interested me.

"When our parents died, they left everything to me, and I broke the family's cardinal rule. I took the money out of blue chips and put it into myself. All that principal was enough to start a little company which, for the first two years, couldn't have paid a single salary if it had to depend only on revenues. Ten years later, I sold the company for twenty-five million plus stock in the purchaser. So, you see, Matty, my success doesn't have to do so much with being smart as with having parents who favored me."

"They didn't love their other son?"

"Alan had borrowed from them heavily for some of his early ventures. He had bad luck and they finally lost faith in him. They had arguments. Then they cut him off and cut him out. They even stopped taking his calls."

"Seems harsh."

"Alan didn't deserve such parsimonious treatment any more than I deserved such advantage."

"And Alan hated you for that?"

"In a word . . . yes. But even more for what I did afterward."

As we rinse soup bowls and Angie wipes Fruit Loops from the floor under Sam's chair, Patrick explains that after their parents died, Alan had turned to him for financial help.

"I put him on a budget. Made him explain every deviation from it, made him justify every cent. Alan was a creative man. He couldn't live with those restrictions. That was eight years ago and it was the beginning of the end for Alan. And I've never forgiven myself. I was his brother, not his banker. What is a family for if not to help each other when times are tough?"

Angie is standing with a rag wadded in her hand watching Patrick as milk drips through her fingers. "That's what Eloy says."

I myself have been studiously avoiding the subject of Eloy and Jimmy's family since my first careless slip. Now I keep my mouth shut to see where she's going with this.

"Eloy is my husband's uncle," she explains to Patrick. "Eloy says families are hard, but life is hard too, and before you can do good in life you got to do good in your family. That we all have that responsibility first."

Having had a day to mull over Uncle Eloy's take on filial responsibility, I'm feeling a little sarcastic. "Eloy might do better by his family responsibility if he just carried workers' compensation insurance."

Angie's eyes shift to me and she blinks back tears. Patrick takes the rag from her hand. "Jimmy's uncle sound's like an interesting guy," he says. "Tell me about him."

So, we finish the after-dinner ablutions talking about our families. I haven't talked about my mother for quite a while and, later, when everyone has cleared out of the kitchen, I try to put a call through to the last number I have for her. It is for a spa in Romania. Trust my mother to go to a war zone to drink health-food puke and take the mineral waters. The call doesn't go through. She probably isn't there anymore anyway. It's over eight weeks; she will have moved on, to a new diversion. I've always felt simultaneously charmed and abandoned by Mother's peripatetic search for the new and exotic. Despite my peculiarities, I'm dull by comparison.

As if to prove as much, I spend the rest of the evening in Alan's office prioritizing and scheduling tasks for the next seven days. Researching and writing the brief on behalf of *John Doe*'s right to secrets—one that is sound and well-reasoned— heads the list. By using Frankie's account number, I can hook up to Westlaw and do the necessary case research right here on Prather's computer. Starting tonight.

Seven days would be plenty of time to do that job well if that were the only job. Unfortunately, there's still the work I was hired to do for the bankruptcy court. And perhaps most important of all, there's the insurance policy.

I continue to believe that the answer to how Alan and Denise Prather died lies either at the end of the money trail or somewhere within this house. With Angie distracted by her new contract, I can no longer expect much help from her on that score.

"You look like you've got the weight of the world on your shoulders." Patrick is leaning against the doorjamb. He's wearing Levis and his feet are bare. "You know, I meant my offer to help," he says, crossing the room and dragging a rolling chair behind him. He takes the list from me and scans it.

"What can I do?" he says.

"As I live and breathe . . . a gift horse."

We quickly divide up tasks. Patrick will continue where Angie left off. He says he can probably help with some of the dead-ends in his brother's bookkeeping as well. We work well into the night.

At bedtime, calling Max again doesn't seem so urgent. I make a mental note to do it tomorrow. Or maybe the next day.

EIGHTEEN

——◦◦◦——

"WE HAD A DEAL, REMEMBER?"

Detective Baca's tone is indisputably cranky this afternoon. Against his custom, he agreed to meet me here at this trendy *tapas* restaurant on Canyon Road and he's ill-at-ease. Daniel's restaurant comfort zone is pretty much limited to the third booth from the end at the Denny's near the station house.

"I'm sorry, but honestly, Daniel, if you hadn't called me, I'd have gotten in touch with you before the end of the day."

"Right."

"Just so the record is clear, our *deal* was that I'd give you a heads-up if I found evidence of cooked books—not that I'd report boulders falling from the sky. Besides, we don't have any proof that what happened to us in the Jemez was other than an accident, much less that it was connected to the Prather deaths."

"Right."

His crankiness is turning sarcastic. I survey the plate of tarts at length and inspect each one individually, hoping to wait out his exasperation. But when I finally pop a green tart full of pink stuff into my mouth and look up, there's been no change in Baca's expression.

"Okay, okay, you're right," I say through a mouthful of what might be red-pepper custard in a jalapeño crust. "I should have notified you about the assault as soon as I got back from Jemez Springs. I'm actually amazed you got the information from the Jemez Springs police department. You say it came through on a statewide criminal database?"

"We've got running water and indoor plumbing too."

"The computer actually named *me*?"

"You were briefly the subject of a criminal investigation, Matty. Auto theft is a felony, you know. We've got a program that'll pull up any name we have a tag on. When I phoned Jemez Springs, an Officer Leyba gave me the full story."

"You've got a tag on *me*?"

Baca shrugs. "Ever since you put your nose into my investigation. Now, stop stalling. Tell me what the hell the thing at the hot springs was about?"

"Daniel, all I know is that some very large rocks fell on Max and me. You remember Max?"

Daniel nods.

"Well, Max got hurt and I didn't know what the hell was going on, so I got Max into this guy's van and drove off to get help. I thought our lives were in danger. Turned out, I was wrong. Beyond that, I don't know any more than what you got from Leyba."

"Who knew where to find you that morning?"

"Unfortunately, about a dozen people. If you add anybody they might've told, probably twice as many."

"Names."

I hadn't called Baca because telling him about the assault would involve naming the Jemez Springs branch of the Abeyta family. Now, when I see him leaning toward me, eyes narrowed with professional interest, I realize I've started leaning away from him. So, before he completely decodes my body language, I begin listing the *other* people who knew or could have known about the Jemez Springs B&B: Angie, Frankie, Dr. Rosenbloom, Claude Raskin, possibly some of

Max's patients, and anybody who called the house while I was gone.

Daniel makes a list and when he's done, I add the one name that I'd personally like to have checked out—for reasons unrelated to the assault.

"You know who Gene Saavedra is?"

"Don't think so. Why?"

"For one thing, he's the husband of your witness; you know, the friend who told you that Denise Prather said she'd been threatened—Genevieve Moreno. Her married name is Saavedra."

"Oh?" He jots another note.

"For another, a few years back, Gene Saavedra and Alan Prather did a lot of business together. Saavedra is or was a mortgage banker who placed Prather's companies' loans. Supposedly, they parted company about the time Alan began the long spiral down the tubes."

"Supposedly?"

"Well, this morning I called several associates who knew them both. They all agree that Gene Saavedra stopped doing business with Alan a long time ago. As far as anyone knows, he and Alan haven't had anything to do with each other in years...."

"Am I hearing a *but* in there somewhere?"

"Yeah, *but*, these two guys were more than business associates. They were big buddies once, went on ski trips to Europe together. And there's no mistaking that Saavedra wasn't thrilled to see me when I showed up on his doorstep. I'd told his message machine that I was coming to his house to discuss Alan Prather. But when I get there, this grown man *hides* from me. Hides and tells his family to lie to me. And he was on the verge of kicking the crap out of his wife when he found out that she'd talked to you. Whether this guy and Prather were in cahoots or Saavedra's got his own secrets to protect, I don't know."

"Anything else?"

"Saavedra knew the name of the B&B where Max and I were staying."

"Be nice to know if this Saavedra has any criminal record."

"Couldn't hurt to run a check."

"How badly was Max hurt?"

"Physically, he's on the mend."

"What do you mean, physically?"

"He didn't like the experience."

"Who would?"

"Max thinks maybe . . . I would. He thinks maybe I court danger."

"Max sounds like a cop's wife."

One more edit and this brief is ready to file. Original and one copy to the court and another to the ball-bouncing Mr. Skyler. It's pretty good, if I do say so myself. But the law, as ever, is less and more than a straight line. All of the New Mexico cases on point support my position: Nobody can get at secrets told in therapy. And the majority of cases from other jurisdictions with client/psychotherapist protection rules are in accord.

The legal reasoning is that trust in one's therapist is at the heart of whatever emotional healing is possible in therapy. If the law were to require therapists to betray such trust when the police asked them to, those in society most in need of help would be the least likely to seek it.

But, on every issue, there are two or three appellate judges in the United States who march to the sound of their own stomach gurgles. A couple of these individuals have unburdened themselves at length on the subject of giving the protective privilege to "mental patients."

It is in such situations, one opines, *that wise judicial discretion must be the torch to lead the way.* Read that as the judge gets to ignore the statute if he doesn't like the result.

I put stamps on the copy to Skyler and head for the mailbox, passing the garage with a sense of awe. In the six days it's taken me to cover the ten sheets of paper in this envelope with legal argument, Angie and her two-man crew have managed to frame and roof a two-car garage and nearly complete the kitchen repair.

Today, they're regrading the driveway. Angie is bouncing around on some kind of electric rock crusher, making one hell of a racket and grinning from ear to ear. I wave to her as I head down toward the road.

The Prather mailbox is one of those rural things big enough to receive a Christmas goose. It is daily stuffed with Prather mail which it is now Patrick's task to sort. I scoop the bundle of letters and leaflets and bills inside into one arm and toss the envelope containing Skyler's copy of my brief into the empty cavern for pickup.

According to Judge Cuthbert's schedule, there are only ten days left. W. P. Skyler now has seven days to review and answer this brief and I have three days after that to reply to his answer. Of course, I can count on Skyler's finding the cases favorable to him and arguing that they're persuasive. But I'm on the right side and I've made the best argument I can make—done everything I can to keep Jimmy's secrets secret and thus to keep Sam safe. Done everything I can—on this front. But the legal skirmish is only one front in what has become a multifaceted war. The other battles are proceeding somewhat more dubiously.

Before turning to the next skirmish, I pause for a few deep breaths. The scent of charred wood is more muted now than on the day I first drove up this driveway, but it's still in the air. How long does it take, I wonder as I walk back up toward the house, to completely erase the traces of tragedy?

I dump the mail on the middle desk in Alan's office annex. Patrick has taken up temporary residence at this desk and has made himself pretty much at home and very much indispensable. It took him no time to decipher his brother's (and my) various organizational systems.

By now every piece of paper from the library stacks, from the vault shelves, from the heaps on the floor, has been placed in a coherent order. Thus classified and grouped on the tables, they tell a fuller, though not much different, story than the one I'd already pieced together. We know more precisely how Alan's scams worked. Patrick has charted every complicated intercompany and intracompany transfer of funds. We have emptied every drawer and closet, including the vault. We've touched and catalogued every paper file in Alan's office and every electronic file on his hard drive. Without Patrick's help, this would have taken many more weeks. He looks up as I enter the room.

"It must be hard for you, seeing your brother's life through this"—I swing my arm in a wide arc over the tidy stacks of paper records—"detritus."

"I've begun to think of what I'm doing here as a kind of penance, Matty. I sometimes think the mark of Cain is really about the guilt of a brother who survives when, had he cared enough, they might both have survived."

"Patrick, I don't exactly read the Bible regularly . . ." *At all, for that matter,* I could add. "But Cain actually killed Abel. The situation here is a little different, don't you think?"

"Alan was my brother. I could have shared my good fortune with him with an open heart. If I had, maybe he'd still be alive. I should have been my brother's keeper, Matty. Anyway," he says, shaking his head, "helping to clean up the mess and, in the process, maybe find out what really happened to him is the least I can do."

Patrick stands and paces randomly. "I guess I'll be moving from here into Denise's rooms, if you have no objection."

"I've already gone through the journals and albums in her office, and I don't think there's so much as a stray pin in her bedroom."

"Well, I'll take a look anyway."

Before I can drool out my gratitude again, the phone rings. I grab it. "Yes?"

"Matty."

"Max?"

There must be something odd in my voice, because Patrick, who was in the process of leaving the room, stops short, turns, and raises an *are-you-all-right* eyebrow. I nod a lie to him and turn my attention back to the telephone.

"Matty, I've been trying to call," Max says. "But I keep playing the conversation we would have out in my mind."

"And?"

"You obviously like the kind of life you're building. You like the danger and excitement . . . I find the whole thing pretty appalling and, frankly, a little stupid."

"What?" I can feel myself bristle. Less than rational *and* stupid.

"Wait, wait. Don't say anything yet. I've been afraid that at the end of our conversation there will be a conclusion I can't live with. So I haven't wanted to begin."

"And yet you called."

There is silence on the line. "I also can't live without you any longer," he says.

I can feel my pulse quicken. "So?" I say noncommittally.

"I have an idea." His voice is tentative. "That is, if you'd be willing to try something?"

When I don't answer immediately, he adds, "I'd rather wait until all the details are worked out before I explain. Could you just trust me for a few days?"

"You think what I'm doing is *stupid*?"

Never let it be said that I hold a grudge.

NINETEEN

———⟡⟡⟡———

ALL THAT MISSING MONEY. CHECKS WRITTEN TO TUMBLE-
weed from Sagebrush, portions of which were rapidly
moved from Tumbleweed's account to Yucca's account. Checks
written out of Yucca almost weekly in amounts from $4,000
to $9,000, always made out to cash and always with change
added perhaps to deflect unwanted attention. The total for
that skim alone is over a quarter million a year.

Nothing in Alan's records provides a clue as to what happened to all that cash. There are missing bank records.

And that isn't all that is missing. According to Dr. Rosenbloom, the doctor and dentist groups were buying back
their old properties from the Resolution Trust Corporation at
thirty cents on the dollar. But there are no contracts in
Prather's records indicating any such buy-backs. There are no
contracts with the RTC at all. I call Frankie.

"You remember the RTC, the federal agency that came
into being to resolve the savings and loan crisis," I say. "Is the
RTC still in business?"

"Beats me," she says.

I call information for Santa Fe. No listing for the RTC. I try

Albuquerque. There is a listing for one Resolute Truss Company. They specialize in heavy-duty undergarments. I ask the information operator for a listing in Washington, D.C., for the Resolution Trust Corporation. I emphasize the final "t" in Trust. She gives me one in Arlington and one in Alexandria.

The Arlington number has been disconnected. The Alexandria number is answered by a machine that gushes, *"Hi, Terry and I are out. Hopefully, we're doing something fabulous or naughty. Hope you are too. Leave a message. Bye."*

Probably not our government at work.

I try another D.C. operator. This time, I ask for the Federal Deposit Insurance Corporation. The FDIC existed before the RTC: They're my best bet for a successor agency if there is no longer an RTC. Sure enough, a lovely southern voice informs me the RTC went out of business in 1993 and, "we've taken over their functions. How can we help?"

I tell her I'm looking for the details of RTC sales of specific notes and mortgages in New Mexico in the early nineties. She groans and says maybe such information would be in Archives. I'm transferred and transferred again and then transferred to an office in Dallas and then transferred back to D.C. again. If Alan Prather wanted evidence of his deals buried, he could hardly have chosen a better grave. I leave my name and number everywhere and each bureaucrat dutifully takes it.

If the legal process should fail to protect Jimmy's secrets, I have exactly nine days to find out what happened to Alan and Denise Prather so that Detective Baca will turn his searchlight away from Jimmy's murky past. The money trail, as Claude Raskin called it, still seems the most likely avenue to pursue.

"Surely," I plead with the clerks at FDIC on the second day, "surely information about the RTC's sales of notes and mortgages must be available somewhere."

Yes, of course. But they'd have to have the loan numbers or at least the name of the institutions that made the original loans and the years they were made. I go back to Prather's files. Bit by bit, I piece together such sparse preliminary information as there is and have another go at it. By the third day, there's nothing to do but wait for the government to return my calls.

I share the great RTC mystery with Baca and with Patrick and with Frankie. Nobody has a clue. While I have him on the phone, Daniel Baca tells me that his record-pull on Saavedra has turned up nothing. He says he called the Saavedra house in Taos. A young male said both his mother and father were out of town. The kid didn't know when they'd be back. I can picture the teenager with the yellow earphones covering for his parents yet again. What does a kid do with training like that?

At three in the afternoon my time, and the last minute of the workday in Washington, D.C., my phone rings.

"Ms. Donahue? Ms. Prouse here, FDIC. You called yesterday?"

"Yes, yes."

"I have pulled up the records you requested. They're on my screen now. Our Dallas office archived all the RTC transactions for the Southwest. The paper records are fairly voluminous. Perhaps I could read to you the summaries I have on the screen and we could go from there.

My God, the ultimate oxymoron, a helpful bureaucrat.

"Please."

"I've pulled up purchasers of RTC-held notes by the fifteen partner names you gave us: Drake, D.D.S.; Krause, M.D.; Rosenbloom, M.D.; Valentine, D.D.S., Wel—"

"Yes, yes," I say again. "And were they in partnerships that purchased notes from the RTC?"

"Indeed, they were, Ms. Donahue. Six partnerships. Six purchases. Almost identical terms. Notes and mortgages bought out of the RTC receivership for approximately ten percent of their face value."

"Ten percent? As in ten cents on the dollar?"

"That's correct."

"Not thirty cents on the dollar?"

"As I said, ten cents . . . every last one of them."

                    .   .   .

This evening, Angie has taken Sam to a Disney movie. Patrick is fixing us a couple of Sapphire martinis, when the phone rings. It's Claude Raskin, returning my call. Patrick places the cold glass in my hand. The bowl of it chills my palm.

"Yes, Claude," I say into the receiver, "Alan told all of you that you were buying the properties back for thirty cents on the dollar from the RTC. But he was actually buying them for only ten cents on the dollar and pocketing the other twenty cents. That's right . . . yes . . . maybe four million and none of it's in the company bank accounts. Of course I will—"

Patrick approaches with an olive on a toothpick. He holds it about a half inch above the gin and asks with his eyes. I nod; he plops the olive in.

"Oh, by the way, Claude," I continue, "Rosenbloom mentioned a dentist, a guy named David Drake, who had a heart attack recently, but I understand he was very bent about the money he lost with Alan Prather. You know anything about . . . oh? When did he die? Did Drake leave a wife . . . children?"

By the time I get off the phone, Patrick has finished his drink. "What was that all about?"

"A dentist with a special hatred for your brother. I thought . . . well, you know. But he died a few months before Alan died, so I guess not. I might go talk to his son anyway."

"Why?"

"Apparently David Drake, Jr., inherited Daddy's dental practice. Maybe he inherited some of his daddy's hatreds too."

"Seems a little farfetched."

"Probably."

"You want my opinion—that's just a useless exercise."

"It's a loose end."

He stares at me for a moment. He shrugs. "Whatever. Think I'll go back to work now."

I watch his back all the while he heads down the hallway to Denise's suite. Then I finish my drink and decide to go for an evening walk. The road is dead quiet. No dirt bikes are racing past the secluded mansions tonight. I trudge up and down the hillside roads.

When I return, I notice a thin blade of light beneath Denise's door. The door swings open under the pressure of my hand. Patrick is slumped in the rocking chair by the window. A stack of books and an open box are on the floor beside his feet. His eyes are closed.

"You awake?" I whisper.

"Come on in."

There are no other chairs here in this cell, so I sit Indian-style on the rug and look up at Patrick. He looks drawn and haggard.

"What's wrong?"

He opens his eyes but doesn't answer.

"It's a strange room, isn't it?" I say. "It would be hard to find two married people with such different tastes. Makes me wonder what they ever had in common."

"Everything, once," he says.

"Really? I guess I just assumed . . ."

"You should have known her. Alan was still in college and one weekend he brought home this fantastic woman to meet the family. She was quite beautiful in those days, quite . . . special. Did you know she'd been a dancer?"

"I had no idea. This is before she studied psychology?"

He nods. "She was touring with a small regional ballet company at the time. She was the most exotic person I'd ever seen. Enthusiastic about everything—food, clothes, people, mostly travel. Later, during Alan's fat years when the money was flowing, they went all over the world together: Africa, India, the Caribbean. She's the one who started collecting. Alan learned his appreciation of esoterica from her. All that stuff in his room? Denise picked most of it out."

I'm stunned. "And this?" I indicate the sparse room. "A reaction to her illness?"

Patrick nods again. "It was her way to cope. Huntington's is caused by a defective gene, you know. If you have the gene, you get the disease eventually. Her father had the gene, but it didn't show up until he was in his late forties. There was no genetic testing in his day. Whatever fears she had for herself, Denise handled them privately. She had a practice here in

Santa Fe by the time her father was really ill. Life was pretty good for her, personally, despite Alan's surfacing money problems. Then she had an unplanned pregnancy. By that time, it was possible to get tested for the gene and to have the fetus tested too. . . . Both results were positive."

"Did Denise tell you that? Did she keep in touch with you?"

"As a matter of fact, she did. Alan never did call or write much, even when he was still speaking to me. Denise was the one." He shakes his head. "She decided to stop the pregnancy. She told me about it as though it were merely a decision not to pass on such a heritage. But apparently, it was more. That's when this"—he gestures—"this monkish life began."

"What about Alan? Did he help her? Did he care?"

Patrick sighs. "Alan had his own problems. I think he was probably so absorbed with his financial troubles that for a long time he just didn't get it."

"You think he stopped loving her?"

"Oh, my, no. He always loved her—in his own way. But he was distracted and she was shutting him out. He'd failed at everything. He couldn't afford any kind of treatment for her. He couldn't even pay a private nurse. She called me often about how depressed they both were. Later, she just stopped calling. And she stopped answering the phone. That's why I wasn't surprised when they . . ." He falters.

"Even so, Patrick, suicide seems such an unlikely choice for someone in her profession. Would your brother have . . . could he have . . . killed Denise for what *he* thought was her own good?"

"I think Alan probably would have done anything for her."

The next morning is a blur of activity. I explain the RTC connection in considerable detail to Frankie, then repeat it all for Detective Baca.

"If I've done the calculation right, Daniel, upward of four million dollars, maybe more, has vanished from the face of the earth."

"How are you getting access to bank records?"

"Every company name I've been able to think of has been run against both open and closed accounts in every New Mexico and nearly every regional bank. No matches. And we don't find the name Alan Prather as a signatory on any other account at any of these banks. My bet? The money went to Switzerland."

"Just because he and Saavedra went skiing there a few times?" Daniel sounds dubious.

"Genevieve Moreno told me her husband went with Alan to Bern because they liked true alpine skiing."

"So?"

"There's lots of good skiing in Switzerland. There's St. Moritz, Zermatt, Verbier, or Champéry. But not Bern."

"And you know this because you're an alpine skier?"

"I got on the Internet, punched in *Skiing in Switzerland*."

"Enterprising."

"It turns out you can find better slopes right around here than around Bern. Say, for instance, Taos, thirty minutes from Saavedra's house."

"Well, then, it's conclusive," the detective says sarcastically.

"Okay, okay. But it is interesting, don't you think? The problem is, even if I could identify an account, Swiss banks are completely unimpressed by orders from a U.S. Bankruptcy Court. Hold on a second, someone's trying to get my attention."

Sam, who's been noticeably absent since the construction excitement started outside days ago, has been in the house all morning. For the past few seconds he's been pulling at my shirttail.

"What?" I say, cupping my hand over the receiver. "Do you need something?"

"He's crying."

"Who's crying?"

"Patrick. Come see."

· · ·

Patrick sits in the same rocking chair as he did last night. In fact, now that I notice, he hasn't changed clothes since last night.

"Patrick?"

He looks up and raises his hand to me. In it is a sheet of paper which he holds at the corner. "Here. Read this."

Not asking why we are taking such precautions, I take the corner between my own thumb and index nail, hold it up, and tilt my head so I can read the words written on the dangling sheet. It is a letter dated over two months ago which begins simply: *Denise* . . .

I've seen enough of this handwriting lately to recognize it instantly, so I'm not surprised when I scan to the bottom of the letter and see another single name: *Alan.*

"Where did you find this?"

"Between the pages of *Final Exit,* the little book by the founder of the Hemlock Society. It was in the pocket of her robe. Go on; read it."

March 3

Denise,

You asked me to think about it and I've thought about it. I'm willing to go through with it if you are. In business, when an enterprise has failed, you close the doors. There is no sin in that and there is no sin in this. But the suggestion that you go alone is unbearable for me. I love you and, despite everything, you still have some feeling for me. It must be both of us or neither of us, my darling.

You say that if we are going to do this, we have to do it before things get any worse. I know I must be the one to choose the time and the method for us. I promise you, the method will be both foolproof and painless. And the time will be soon. Now and forever,

Alan

TWENTY

I CAN'T GET BACK TO THE PHONE FAST ENOUGH. I HIT RE-dial, and while it rings, I tell Sam to go find his mother. This letter has everything to do with their future. It shifts Jimmy's criminal past a step further from scrutiny and his family's future a step closer to safety.

"Santa Fe Police Department, Detective Division."

"Hello, Matty Donahue again . . . is Daniel Baca still there?"

By the time Baca picks up, I'm virtually bouncing in place. "You won't believe what we found."

"Matty?"

"The suicide note."

"You're kidding."

"Well, the next thing to it anyway. But *I* didn't find it. It was Patr—"

Patrick snaps his fingers urgently. When I look at him, he places his index finger against his lips. Uh-oh. This sentence can't end up where it was heading.

"Uhm . . . uh, Daniel . . . I . . . came across a letter from Alan Prather to his wife, uh . . . written a couple of months before the explosions. So, I guess it's not technically a suicide note.

But, it's a pretty amazing document. In it, Alan Prather . . . I guess the right expression would be *alludes* to a double suicide."

"I'll be there in half an hour."

As I replace the receiver in the cradle, I tell Patrick, "The police are coming here. And, thanks for catching me before I said your name. You know, it may not be necessary to hide your presence much longer, but maybe for now—"

"I'd better make myself scarce."

"Yeah."

Patrick has no sooner left by the back door than the front bell rings. Surely Baca can't be here already. I head down the hallway in time to see Sam tugging Angie across the foyer in my direction as ordered. But she yanks him to a brief stop so she can answer the door, and when she opens it, I hear welcome in Sam's voice.

"Hi, Max," Sam says eagerly. "Matty's in the bedroom with Patrick."

Oops. Not altogether the greeting I would have wished.

"In the bedroom?" asks Max. "With who?" asks Max.

It's the first time I've seen Max since Nurse Rachel's back porch. He looks kind of sweetly muddled as he turns to Angie and asks more pointedly, "Who's Patrick?"

I stride purposefully forward and peck him on the cheek. "Sorry, you picked a busy time. There's been a kind of . . . development."

"Who's Patrick?"

"Sambo," I shift my attention, "you think you could catch Patrick? He just went out the back to take a hike up the mountain. He thought you might like to go with him."

"I want to stay here," Sam says mulishly.

"No, Sam. You go with Patrick," Angie orders. She's eyeing me for some lead while Sam digs in, holding on to the bottom of her shorts with clenched fist and regarding both of us with clenched jaw.

I shrug. "It's probably better if you're not here anyway," I tell Angie. "Patrick can fill you in."

Angie scoops up her son and throws him on the hip

opposite her tool belt just as though he weren't, at five, already half her size. She heads toward the back without another word.

Some people do that, just respond immediately and efficiently to a tricky situation solely on the basis of trust. Others insist that you stop, right now, and explain everything.

"Who's Patrick?" Max asks. A case in point.

"Alan Prather's brother. Listen, you remember Daniel Baca, don't you?"

Max studies me a moment, then decides to allow a marginal diversion of attention. "Sure. The detective who sponsors low-rider clubs, right?"

"Baca will be here any minute. He's coming to get that." I've placed the letter on the foyer table and I point at it now. "Read that."

Max ignores the letter.

"Matty, would you care to hear what I've been working out about us?" he asks peckishly.

There's hardly any exasperation in my voice at all when I turn my face from the letter and face him. "Of course I do."

"Relationship counseling."

I hear the restrained eagerness in his voice and try to rise to it, but what comes out of my mouth is dishrag limp.

"Oh," I say.

"What does 'oh' mean?"

"It means . . . yes. I guess. I mean, look, Max, can I think about this for a while?"

Max dips his head in tepid assent.

"Okay, okay," I say. "I can see that was the wrong answer. So . . . yes; relationship counseling," I say as firmly as a politician making a campaign promise. "Yes!"

"I think it's the thing to do, but only if you really want to, Matty."

Oh, Jesus. Only if I really want to. Really want to go back into therapy. Really want to spend an hour a week talking to one of Max's brother-shrinks while the two of them figure out what's wrong with me. How could a girl not *really* want to do that?

"Max, I want there to be an 'us,' " I say truthfully. "If you think relationship counseling will help, I'm game. It's just that, right now . . . I . . ."

"Right now you want me to read that letter." He's suddenly all cooperation.

I nod. "But don't touch it!"

Max looks down at the letter, reads it, then reads it again and whistles.

"Son of a bitch," he says.

When Baca reads Alan Prather's letter, he says pretty much the same thing. His voice suggests that the suicide note is going to cause his captain to lose even more enthusiasm for allocating manpower to a murder investigation.

The following day, when Claude Raskin reads a copy of the letter, he adds "dang" before he says "sumbitch."

But yesterday, when W. P. Skyler read it, he was unmoved to such profanity. The assistant district attorney suggested to Baca that with her lousy reputation Matty Donahue probably forged the letter herself to distract everyone from the session tapes. He told Baca that he wasn't about to be outmaneuvered by some shady lady lawyer.

I kind of like the sound of that. I picture a sign nailed to a pole at 940 Canyon Road: "Shady Lady Lawyer," it reads. And maybe a hinged "open/closed" flap hanging from a branch of the apple tree above my hammock.

The letter changes things profoundly for me and for Jimmy and Angie and for Sam. Certainly now the scenario of a double murder by one of Denise Prather's criminal patients has become much less plausible. Even Daniel Baca seemed ready to consider other possibilities.

Perhaps Skyler really thinks me capable of such duplicity, because he subjects the letter to both handwriting and fingerprint analysis and only reluctantly admits that the handwriting is Alan Prather's; the fingerprints are Alan and Denise's.

In the days that follow the discovery of the letter, pretty much everything gets better. Angie is off the antacids. She gives Jimmy the news that it's just possible the police may close the Prather investigation even before Judge Cuthbert rules on our motion to quash the subpoena. Her voice is bright and chirpy and their marital problems seem to have nearly vaporized. Even without *relationship counseling*, I notice. I can hear only her end of their conversation, of course, but they regularly talk shop and, I gather, she's making plans for Jimmy to come home soon.

"Honest, babe," Angie tells him. "It's going good here. The job's on time and on budget. And, Jimmy, I can get other contracts. I know I can. When this is all over, we can ... yes, both of us; and you can do all the important stuff: estimating, handling the subs, keeping the books. . . . So, who cares about the break-back stuff? You're too smart for all that anyway. We could set up shop in ..."

Amid all this growing enthusiasm, there has been not a peep to her from Jimmy about Chatto and Fat Boy being in Jemez. As I listen to her bubble on about their future, I struggle a little with my own complicity in that silence. A while back I'd wondered whether Jimmy might not just take off, never to be seen again—maybe with his dear cousins—before we ever even get a ruling on the tapes. But this doesn't seem to be in the cards.

As his mother's mood has lightened, so has Sam's. He likes to watch Angie work and is especially observant that it is she who's giving the orders on the job site now.

"She bosses those guys around," he informs me as the four of us sit down to what we laughingly call dinner. We dine nightly on canned goods chosen by Sam. Tonight it's canned yams, Vienna sausages, and SpaghettiOs.

"And they do whatever my mommy says them to do," Sam finishes softly, as though he were imparting a shameful truth.

"Why are you whispering?" I ask him.

"I don't know," he whispers, genuinely puzzled.

Patrick will be leaving us soon. He's done what he could to help organize things and to look for an answer he never believed was here. But the letter from Alan to Denise effectively put an end to any lingering doubt he had about how his brother died.

A few days ago and very much in code, he told me that when he leaves, if he should happen to come across any audiotapes among his things, he'd leave them on a shelf in Alan's office. Just in case Judge Cuthbert denies my motion to suppress the subpoena; just in case the police don't lie down and roll over because of the discovery of the "suicide" letter. In short, just in case production of the session tapes should still be necessary one week from now.

Unfortunately, Patrick's precaution may turn out to be necessary. I've read and reread W. P. Skyler's brief and he has outdone himself. It is well reasoned and logical and meticulously documented with a few on-point court opinions and with more obiter dicta which buttress one small point or another. But most damningly, with a surprisingly masterful blend of emotional argument and something akin to poetry, Skyler has made attractive the claim that the public good is larger than the criminal secrets of any one individual.

Added to this is the fact that the judicial climate in this area may be changing. In the recent past, there have been more than a few high-profile cases that have whittled away at real or imagined privileges. It is clear now, for instance, that a president's governmental lawyer and a presidential bodyguard must testify if called before a grand jury. Skyler would surely have argued that a president's shrink, had there been one, must testify too.

The bottom line is, the prosecution's brief is much, much more persuasive than I'd expected. My odds of losing this motion and being forced to turn over the tapes—which I'd blithely put at forty-sixty—may indeed be closer to fifty-fifty. The image of me retrieving those tapes from a shelf in Alan's office and delivering them up to the law makes me shudder.

I turn my mind from the subject and look fondly at Patrick, who is quietly stirring SpaghettiOs around on his plate.

He feels my eyes on him and looks up.

"Why did you really come here?" I ask him.

He pops a little pellet of sausage into his mouth and bounces his eyebrows up and down a couple of times like Groucho Marx. "I liked the sound of your voice on the phone."

Sam, trying for the eyebrow maneuver, twists and wrinkles his nose.

"No, really," I say to Patrick.

He sees that I'm serious, pushes his plate away, and folds his hands on the table. "The farther away I sailed," Patrick explains, "the more alone I felt. It's not just what I said earlier—that I'm the only family they had. It's also that they were the only family I had. I've had closure on so many things in the past year or so . . . The money . . . I don't need a real job anymore. I don't even have a solid place to live; I live on a boat, for godsake. The more I thought about it, the more my brother's death began to seem like the last paragraph in a long chapter. I can't explain it, really. Maybe I just came back to say good-bye, to put a period at the end of this sentence too. You understand?"

"I guess so."

"That, and I *really* liked the sound of your voice on the phone."

I laugh.

"What are you going to do next?" he asks.

"Beats me." I nod in Angie's direction. "If the hot-shot contractor here doesn't get too busy with multimillion-dollar jobs, I should have myself a rental house and a fancy new office by the end of the month. Whether I have something to do in it is another matter."

"You're in transition too, aren't you? Maybe as much as me," Patrick says. "But I meant right now. How would a couple of days on a sailboat in Melaque Bay strike you? We could fly down tomorrow."

Angie and Sam turn to me. My mouth hangs open a fraction too long. What stuns me more than the offer, itself, is my urge to accept it. I nip the instinct in the bud.

"I have so much to do—"

"Like what?"

"I have to respond to Skyler's brief."

"Sure," Patrick presses, "but how long can that—"

"And . . . no matter what happened to Alan and Denise, there's still a pile of money missing and it's my job to find it."

"Is it, really? You've already done more than—"

"And," I persist, "I'm not done finding out what had the Saavedras so spooked either. And I've made an appointment with David Drake, Jr., who has set up practice in his father's old dental offices. He admits that before his stroke, his father was obsessed with Alan." I find myself talking faster, running out of breath, tacking on one task after another. "And I've got the name of another disgruntled investor who got drunk one night in the La Fonda bar and told the assembled that he was going to blow Alan Prather's ass to the moon."

Patrick shakes his head, "Why?"

"I *intend* to find out once and for all what really happened in that garage."

"Matty," he says sadly, "this isn't your job. I think maybe this is becoming an obsession with you."

"But it's what I think that counts. And what I think is, it ain't over till it's over."

"You do it too," Sam says to me.

"Do what too?"

"Boss guys around." He makes it an accusation. "You and Mommy both. Daddy says boys are the bosses of girls."

Angie and I turn together to stare at the little macho man sitting on his knees with SpaghettiOs all over his pale blue shirt. He stares back, head lowered and shoulders hunched— a baby bull. I study his countenance and think: *Oh, my darling boy, that ship sailed before your father was your age.* And it would be a terrible waste of a young boy's life to wait on the dock for it to return.

"Your daddy's wrong about that," I say simply. "When people need a boss for a certain thing, the best person to be the boss is the person who knows the most about that thing."

Sam looks unconvinced.

TWENTY-ONE

꧁꧂

A COPY OF JUDGE CUTHBERT'S RULING LIES ON THE TABLE
before us. With shit-eating grins on our faces, we sit
looking fondly at the court order. Angie commands: "Read it
again."

"...'and therefore,'" I intone, "'it is now ordered, adjudged,
and decreed that pursuant to ...'"

It's been only three days since my response to Skyler's
brief was filed. Cuthbert's decision has been mercifully swift.
Yesterday, fearing the worst, I'd retrieved the tapes from the
shelf where Patrick left them. I'd divided them into batches
according to the letters and numbers on their spines, which
represent client initials and chronology of sessions. I'd wrapped
each client's tapes separately in brown paper and rewritten
the identifiers. On Jimmy's packet I'd printed *JA12345678*.

Angie says she talked to Jimmy about my decision to com-
ply with whatever the court ordered. Jimmy had responded
sensibly: If that happened, he told her, he'd voluntarily turn
himself in to the police rather than run.

"Get to the good part," Angie now demands.

"Okay, wait, wait; okay, here ... 'and said tape recordings

enjoy the protection of the psychotherapist/client privilege . . .
and that such privilege may be exercised without revealing the
identity of the person claiming the protection . . .'"

Angie emits a little squeal of delight. "Then it's really over?
The cops will never know about Augusto Santiago now, right,
Matty? Jimmy and me and Sam can start a life?"

In answer, I go to Alan's office, retrieve the packet wrapped
in brown paper marked *JA12345678*, drop it into a large
metal wastebasket, and return with the basket in my arms to
the kitchen, where I set it on the middle of the floor before
Angie. The packet looks quite small all alone there at the bottom of the trash basket—trivial really.

There is, of course, the chance that W. P. Skyler might ap-
peal this decision. I wad some loose paper and nestle it
around the packet, find a match, and hold its flame low
against the paper until it lights. Still a distant chance that I
could be disbarred for destroying evidence. The fire sputters
and, for a moment, I think it won't burn, but then, very slowly
the flame swells.

"I don't see why you can't start a new life," I tell Angie. I
look at her face upon which hope, like the fire, is spreading.

In the days following the Judge's Order, a kind of sweet calm
settles around us as the summer days lengthen and, like returning refugees, we begin to reinhabit our former lives.
Angie completes her work on the mansion and she and Sam
move back to their cracker-box house on Declovina Street.
She returns to work on my Canyon Road money-pit. But the
handwriting is already on the wall: My pitiful renovation will
soon be too small a project for Angie to consider. Frankie has
sung her praises to her rich friends and Angie's already been
asked to submit bids on two new jobs. Jimmy has decided to
finish the job in the Jemez mountains before joining his wife
and son.

Baca hasn't given up on his investigation, but he has
turned his attention in other directions and his captain is
making noises about shutting things down altogether.

As for me, with Jimmy's secret safe, the Prather murder investigation no longer holds a threat. So I'm willingly, even eagerly, helping Daniel Baca in any way I can. Most of my help as an unpaid assistant-grunt to a police detective dovetails nicely with my remaining work as well-paid assistant-grunt to a bankruptcy trustee. This is for the benefit of the Prather creditors, but maybe it will help Baca too. The mansion has been put on the market and an on terms offer to purchase has been made. I'm to stay until it has been approved by the Bankruptcy Court.

By the time Angie gets finished on Canyon Road, everything up here will be stored or sold or shredded. I'll be ready—more than ready—to move back home. Max, bless his pointy little head, has set up our first relationship-counseling session for the week after next. The new shrink has advised that it would be best if Max and I stayed apart until then.

In the meantime, my days seem full. Files into boxes, boxes marked for storage or destruction. Frankie has hired appraisers and auctioneers for the art and furniture. Each day more stuff is taken to market: Apache skin dance skirts—gone; the monkey iron—sold. The statue of Short Bull fetched a pretty penny for the creditors. The Paul Bunyan table was carted out today. Even though Alan Prather's bedroom is nearly denuded, I'm still sleeping there soundly each night, showering in his shower and peeing in his john.

Before each workday begins, my ritual is to turn on the bathroom TV to get the morning news as I squeeze the first dab of paste onto my toothbrush. My brain takes some warming up before it can digest the events of the day. So, this morning, as I flip on the TV set and turn to step into the shower, I'm still pleasantly oblivious to the world outside this bathroom.

The cascading water drowns the sound of the breezy network-news show. So I don't know they've switched to the local affiliate until I reach out to grope for the towel and hear the first fragments of disaster.

"... turned himself in ... Abeyta voluntarily ... refused counsel after being read his rights. Abeyta ..."

Water dripping with every step, I clamber out of the shower and turn up the sound on the set. The report is quite clear, but my mind reels from it: I can't absorb what this pretty talking-head is telling me about Jimmy Abeyta.

She and her anchor pal go on to another local story, then to weather and then to morning traffic. I can't breathe. The background set changes back to the network: a kitchen in New York. A Martha Stewart–clone shows us how to peel lichee nuts without marring the flesh.

Eventually, the locals come back. The story is repeated. Jimmy Abeyta has confessed to a long-unsolved drive-by shooting. Old footage is shown of Augusto Santiago's pickup truck riddled with bullet holes . . . more weather . . . more traffic . . . back to the network . . . then *the* story again.

"*Abeyta acted alone,*" reads the Channel 13 newscaster. "*His confession, made voluntarily, out of his own remorse, clears up a mystery which the Santiago family has lived with for more than six years.*" One of the *Los Duranes* residents drinks courage from the crowd and speaks to the camera. "*We just want justice, man. One way or the other, we're gonna have justice.*"

I have to listen to the same report once more before I can turn it off. I slump onto the toilet seat. I try to make sense of it. Last night, Jimmy walked into Santa Fe police headquarters and told them a story that would cost him many of the remaining years of his life.

And the story he told them was a lie.

He said he'd been *alone* in the car that day six years ago, had driven *alone* into the *Los Duranes* compound; *alone*, sprayed bullets into the bed of the pickup; *alone*, killed the old man. No one else was implicated.

All my work! My sacrifice, the weeks of worry, of putting myself in professional jeopardy. All for nothing! These are my first thoughts, and I begin to punctuate them by bouncing my forehead against the wall as I sit on the toilet seat. What the hell, what the hell, what the hell? The bouncing becomes rhythmic pounding as tears stream down my face. *What the hell . . . ?*

Eventually the tears are spent, the pounding slows, self-pity recedes. A few fledgling thoughts for someone other than myself creep in. Then the questions. The answer to the first—why protect Chatto and Fat Boy, when giving them up would've cut years off his own certain prison sentence—is obvious. Jimmy is still protecting his son from his cousins. What isn't at all obvious is why Jimmy would volunteer any story at all when they were home free—all of them.

I make a few calls to officialdom. Jimmy has told the cops he didn't have a lawyer and didn't want one. The clerk on duty at the jail tells me, like a polite appointments secretary, that except for immediate family, "the inmate isn't receiving visitors."

I call Angie. There is no answer. I get into my Toyota and head south to see firsthand what all this is going to do to the only person who really matters.

TWENTY-TWO

———∞∞———

H E'S IN THE BACKYARD, SITTING ON THE DIRT. STUBBY, summer-bare legs encircle a loose mound of dry dust. He's stirring the dust with a stick and he doesn't look up.

I sit down beside him.

"You okay?" I ask the perennial stupid question.

"My dog died."

"What dog?"

"Jack."

"You had a dog named Jack? I didn't know."

As a matter of fact, I know perfectly well that Sam does not and did not have a dog named Jack or a dog named anything else, because we've talked about dogs a lot.

"I want a big one," he had told me months ago.

"I want a big one too," I'd told him. "A boxer, I think."

This had cracked him up—that a dog could be a boxer. There were questions: Do they have boxing gloves? Do they fight in a ring? The whole subject of dog breeds was thus opened and, for the next couple weeks, he'd wanted to know the breed of every dog we saw in books. I'd tried to answer his questions about the loose parentage of the mutts who wandered into the compound. Sam changed his mind daily about what kind of dog he'd have someday. But, by the end of the two weeks, the subject had been shelved in favor of Sam's more recent interest: mastering the art of bubble gum.

"What did Jack look like?" I ask him now. "Was he big? What color was he?"

He chews his lip. "Black," he says irresolutely.

"Ummm. And how did he die?"

"Somebody shot him."

"Shot him?!"

No answer.

"Sam, where is Jack now?"

He shrugs.

"Does anybody know who shot Jack?"

He pokes the stick savagely into the mound. He does it again, and again. . . . Not unlike someone banging their head against a bathroom wall.

A few minutes ago in her kitchen, a red-eyed, newly smoking Angie had lit one cigarette off the butt of another and aimed the fag at the screen door, directing me to where her son sat in the backyard. As I return now, I know she's been watching us through the window.

"He saw Jimmy's picture on TV," she tells me, "before I even knew about it. And people have been calling. One of the neighbors brought a casserole, for christsake; like it was a funeral or something. Oh . . . God! What are we going to do, Matty? What am I going to tell my baby?"

"He says his dog died."

"What?"

"Dog. Sam says he had a black dog named Jack and somebody shot it."

"Jesus. Oh, Jesus, oh, Lord. Jack? Did he really say that?"

"There is a Jack, then? A black dog?"

She stabs another cigarette butt into the sink. "There was.

He died a long time ago. But he wasn't black; he was brown and white. And he wasn't Sam's dog . . . he was Jimmy's. Jack's been dead for years, long before Sam was born. All Sam knows about Jack is the story."

"And . . . the story is?"

"Jimmy killed Jack," she says grimly, hugging herself. "When he was a kid—eleven or twelve, I think. Apparently, the animal used to wander into the street all the time. This pissed off Jimmy's old man, who bitched that Jimmy wasn't taking care of his mutt. So one day, the dog gets hit by a car. I guess it was hurt too bad to fix or too bad to fix without a lot of trouble and money. Anyway, the dog was in bad shape, in a lot of pain, and Jimmy tried to carry it to the vet's or someplace. But his old man caught up with him. He told Jimmy he had to shoot the dog."

"And Jimmy did? Shoot Jack?"

"Yeah."

"And he told Sam about it."

"Jimmy talked about it a lot"—Angie winces, then twists a fist deep into her gut as she watches her son through the window— "to a lot of people. It's like he couldn't let it go. He had different versions, you know, like different lessons to take from it. Like his father was a shit; that was his favorite. Or growing up is tough; or you got to take care of poor dumb things that can't take care of themselves. He talked about shooting that dog a lot. Sam was around, so he would have heard."

"You ever hear Sam talk about that incident before today?"

She shakes her head.

"I didn't even know Sam was paying attention. Why would he?" she implores.

That night I call Max.

"He says somebody shot 'his' dog. What's happening, Max? What's happening in that little boy's brain?"

"I don't know, Matty."

"But it doesn't sound good, does it? He's trying to process what he's heard about his father's killing someone, trying to make sense of it, don't—"

"Matty, I really—"

"—you think?"

"—can't analyze Sam's behavior in this situation without spending some time with him. And you know how I feel about—"

"FUCK IT! Fuck professional distance. You could actually be of some goddamned *use* to somebody!"

The silence on the other end of the line stretches until its length becomes palpable and visible to my mind's eye. Max stands on the platform of an antiquated railway train moving away from my station at great speed until he is a mere dot on the horizon.

"I'm sorry," he says tersely.

"Screw it," I say.

Family visiting hours are in the late afternoon. Angie gets a sitter and rides with me the short distance to the county jail. I am not allowed in. I sit on one of the hard benches in the bright, modern lobby. In the half hour before Angie comes back out, I do what I always do; I watch people.

There are others like me here, people on the fringe of the drama. Family members and friends of visitors. Most are women. Many are grandmothers holding babies on their laps while their teary-eyed daughters sign in to see their jailbird husbands. These waiting women are quite various: skinny and fat, young and old, kempt and wild, angry and sad. But they share a common look about the eyes. It doesn't take me too long to put a name to the look. It is helplessness. I recognize it easily, because I know the feel of that look from the inside.

When Angie comes out, she's wearing the look too. In the car, she stares out the passenger-side window, acknowledging my stream of questions with flat, numb answers.

"He just says he did it."

"But—"

"He says people have to pay the price for what they do."

"But not Fat Boy? Not Chatto? Only Jimmy has to pay the price?"

"He says Chatto and Fat Boy have to do what they have to do and he has to do what he has to do."

"But why now?" I argue pointlessly. "Why did he have us go through all of this if he was just going to turn himself in?"

"He said to tell you he's sorry. This is the way he wants it."

"What about Sam? Is this the way Jimmy wants it for his son? Did you tell him what's been going on with Sam?"

"He says he's doing this for Sam."

"For Sam?"

"He says he can't explain it to me. That I just have to trust him. He says it's going to get worse before it gets better, that he knows it'll be hard for Sam but that in the long run, this will be right for him."

I lose it. I pull the Toyota over to the shoulder of the highway and slam on the brakes.

"Angie, what in God's name are you talking about? What is Jimmy talking about? What's he protecting Sam from? Fat Boy and Chatto? He said he wasn't worried about his craphead gang cousins. They had no reason to threaten anymore. Tell me the *truth,* Angie! What's going on?"

She sniffles and wipes her eyes and starts to talk and can't get any sound out. She digs around in her pockets and comes up with a crumbling antacid tablet. "I swear to God, Matty, I don't know."

The look stays on her face—the defeated, helpless look.

As sunset turns to evening, we sit in silence in the front seat on the shoulder of the road as cars and trucks whoosh by us. After a while, she asks, "Can he make some kind of plea?"

"If he was going to try to deal, he would have had a hell of a lot better chance if he'd had me, or any other lawyer, bring him forward in conjunction with plea discussions, not *after* he's handed the D.A. the whole story. But yes, he can probably still improve his position—make a deal with the D.A. He should. He needs a lawyer."

"He says he doesn't want a lawyer. But, could you . . . maybe just talk to somebody . . . see where things stand?"

"Angie, he's going to have a lawyer whether he wants one or not. The Court will appoint one."

"He swears he won't cooperate. Matty, couldn't you just call somebody? Maybe the district attorney's office. Somebody? Please? You wouldn't have to be his lawyer—just find out where things stand."

Back at the mansion, I take the phone off the hook and go to bed and stay there for almost twelve hours. I wake, eat cold food out of cans, and go back to bed. I decide to drink. The Prather liquor hasn't yet been carted away, and it feels like a sour-mash kind of night. I paw through the Prather CDs, slip in an old Ronstadt, and listen to Linda sing the songs of her father and, incidentally, the songs of old Santa Fe. I turn the stereo volume up loud enough to hear a mile away, pick up the bottle of Jack Daniel's and a glass, and head for the patio. On my way, I grab the portable telephone and sit in the moonlight with it in my lap listening to the songs of love and troubles and drunkenness.

Finally, I turn my mind back to the problem that sent me into hibernation. Angie has no idea how counterproductive it would be for me to call the D.A.'s office just to see how things stand. After another couple of slugs of Black Jack I begin to sing along, "Ay . . . Ay . . . Ay . . . Ay . . ."

Long ago, in another emergency, Daniel Baca gave me his home phone number. When I've consumed enough of the Black Jack to act more foolishly than usual, I dial the phone.

A woman's voice asks me to wait a moment. How odd that I've never asked Detective Baca about his family. A wife? Children?

"Matty?" Daniel sounds sleepy and concerned. "I'm sorry," he says.

In my alcoholic haze, I can't figure out what he's got to be sorry for.

"Ay . . . Ay . . . Ay . . . Ay," sings Ronstadt.

"Jimmy Abeyta was the client you were trying to protect, wasn't he?"

"Well, it didn't take you long to figure that out, did it? At least now you see that I was right all along. He was in deep trouble, but his trouble had nothing to do with Alan and Denise Prather."

For several seconds, Daniel doesn't answer. Later, I will remember this silence on the other end of the line. But at the moment, I'm not tracking well and, fool that I am, I rush in.

"Daniel, I know I shouldn't be calling you at home, but Jimmy's wife was wondering . . . could you give me some idea what the D.A.'s going to do with this? What kind of plea may be possible?"

"Plea? Matty, nothing's possible now."

"I know I'm not Abeyta's lawyer, but—"

"You don't know, then?"

"Know?"

"Abeyta made a second confession."

"A *second* confession? What are you talking about?"

"It was on the ten o'clock news. I thought that's why you were calling. Abeyta confessed to murdering Denise and Alan Prather."

I taste the sour mash rising in my throat.

"He gave full details," Baca continues. "Told how he got access, how he rigged the car, how he put the Prathers into it, how he got away. He described the dirt bike he used. He described watching the fire from a ravine five miles away. He said it was like watching hell. He even watched the fire trucks move up the road—too late. He told our guys he stashed the bike in the employee's parking lot behind the Inn at Loretto."

"Daniel, no . . ."

"And that's exactly where they found it, Matty. It's been there all this time with a canvas cover over it."

TWENTY-THREE

—◆◆◆—

H<small>E'S SITTING IN THE FRONT YARD THIS TIME. THE WEEDS</small> have been neither mowed nor watered since his father left, so the dying foliage that surrounds him is a foot tall. Sam seems to be absorbed by the swarm of grasshoppers leaping around and between his splayed legs. He doesn't look up as I approach. I'd like to spare him my growing sense of dread, so I try to call some breezy greeting. But as I get close enough to see what he's doing, I swallow the words.

Half buried in the weeds, an upside-down glass jar traps two grasshoppers. In front of the boy is a bright yellow Tonka truck and heaped in the bed of the toy are dismembered insect torsos. In Sam's left hand, between thumb and index finger, is the body of yet another victim. In Sam's right hand, between thumb and index finger, is the grasshopper's leg.

"WHAT ARE YOU DOING?!"

He gives me a brief sidelong inspection, showing no sign of fear or shame.

"Killing bugs."

"Sam, stop it!"

This time he looks me straight in the eye as he pulls the last remaining leg off the grasshopper and tosses the body on the pile.

In the house, things are not much better. Angie is on a ladder in the center of the living room, taking screws out of the ceiling hook that had been installed for Jimmy's exercises. Descending, she tosses the hook into the packing box on the floor. The hook falls on top of a tangle of straps and piles of Jimmy's jeans and Jimmy's shirts and Jimmy's shoes and Jimmy's music tapes.

"Do you know what Sam is doing out there?" I hear the rebuke in my voice.

She takes a swig of Maalox directly from a giant economy-size bottle, lights a cigarette, and inspects the room like an auditor. She seems to be making sure she's deleted every single item that doesn't calculate.

At the wall near the sofa, she stares briefly at a twelve-by-sixteen professional color photograph in a gold frame: a younger Angie with beatific, crooked smile; long, copper hair curled into sweet-sixteen corkscrews; white lace dress; long white gloves. Jimmy wears a lilac tuxedo with black collar and cuffs. Riding in the crook of his father's arm, Sam, at about two, wears a matching baby tux. The satin pillow he carries has two wedding rings on it.

Angie blows a mouthful of smoke at the image. Then she takes the photo down and tosses it on top of the rest of the junk in the packing box.

Her eyes light on "Samsonville Station." The train set is much as it was the last time I saw it—that morning with Jimmy lying prostrate next to it on the floor—running through miniature cities and countryside, through a papier-mâché mountain mounted on an AstroTurf-covered sheet of plywood. It was perfectly obvious then, as it is now, that this lovingly constructed complication of tracks and bridges and toothpick signs has been the fulcrum around which father and son adjusted and balanced their relationship.

She smokes her cigarette all the way down to the filter,

swallows more Maalox, and begins the destruction. At first, she merely picks tentatively at the glued-down buildings with her thumbnail.

"Angie, for godsake. Is that really necessary?"

With more certainty, she begins to uncouple trains. She pulls up sections of track and, Godzilla-like, throws whole blocks of the miniature city into the trash box.

"Angie!"

"MOMMY!"

Sam stands in the doorway, stricken. His little face is stricken. He moves his eyes from the destruction of the train set on the floor to his mother's face.

"I told you to stay out of here till I call you." Her voice is harsh and unyielding, but he doesn't move.

"Do you hear me?"

He wipes the hovering tears away with the back of his arm.

"Go play with your friends. Go. Go. Go."

When he doesn't move she shrieks, "JUST GET THE HELL OUT OF HERE . . . NOW!"

He's gone.

The echo of the slammed door dies behind him. She sits on the floor, buries her face in her raised knees. She stays like that, rocking back and forth, until she begins to whimper. Then, ever so gently, she collapses sideways into the fetal position.

"God, God . . . oh my God," she croons . . . "Oh God. What have we done?"

I kneel beside her. "You know," I venture, "if Jimmy really did what he says he did . . ."

She doesn't move her head from the floor, but she asks, "What do you mean, if?"

"Hasn't it occurred to you that Jimmy might be lying?"

She sighs, gets to her feet, sits on the sofa with her elbows resting on her knees. She lights yet another cigarette. Her left leg jiggles like a jackhammer. She looks drained and wired at the same time. "What's occurred to me is that for the first time in his life, that bastard's probably telling the whole truth."

"Maybe," I say.

"Screw 'maybe.' I told you I couldn't know if Jimmy'd told me everything. Well, now I know. He didn't. He'd already killed once. Why wouldn't he do it again to protect himself?"

"He might confess to protect Sam. To protect you too, for that matter."

"I don't really give a shit anymore," she says, rising and moving toward the front door. She opens it and uses her Maalox bottle like a theater usher's flashlight to show me the way out.

Over Angie's shoulder, I see a heavyset woman in purple pants and flip-flops marching across the front yard. Each of her hands, like a giant paw, grips the arm of a little boy. The boy on her right is blond and dirty and has blood smeared across his face. The boy on her left is Sam.

The woman barks at me, "Mrs. Abeyta?"

"No," I say, and indicate Angie, who turns in time to have Sam more or less thrown at her midsection. Sam tries to get around his mother's legs and disappear into the house, but she grabs him by the shirt as she looks warily at the woman.

"Uh, yes? You're Mrs. . . . . ah"—Angie's eyes flick from the woman to the bloodied child— "Benny's mother? Benny, what happened?"

"Sam smashed me—" begins the child.

"Your little shit could have killed Benny! He had *my* Benny down on the driveway, pounding his head against the concrete."

The woman reaches out to grab Sam, but Angie blocks the move. The woman's eyes narrow. "Your brat would have caused brain damage if I hadn't pulled him off," she declares.

"Sam?" Angie is looking down at her son as if seeing a stranger. Sam stares at the fat woman's purple knees.

"Like father like son," the woman says.

"What?"

"Look, everyone knows what kind of people you are. I don't want your little monster near my son again."

After Angie slams the door, I watch purple pants drag her off-spring across the street by his elbow. I can hear Angie shriek at

Sam on the other side of the thin door. I stand on the concrete stoop like a lost person for nearly five minutes before I regain the presence to start digging in my pocket for my car keys.

Behind the wheel, my hand trembles slightly as I turn the key in the ignition—maybe the effect of last night's sour mash—or maybe of glimpsing Sam's future. At the corner, deciding which way to turn paralyzes me for another few minutes until, without consciously knowing why, I head south.

South is the direction of Santa Fe police headquarters. I don't even know if I want to see Police Detective Baca or if I want to see Daniel, my *almost* friend who thinks I'm a "thoroughly honorable person," the one whose voice on the phone last night carried his concern. *"I'm sorry Matty, I thought you knew."*

But it is Police Detective Baca who has the capacity and, with a nudge, possibly the will to alter this nightmare. Jimmy's confession is false. Has to be false. It's crazy to believe Jimmy murdered Denise Prather. If he had, wouldn't he have taken the session tapes away with him the very night he did it? Can't anybody with a brain see that? Once Detective Baca realizes the killer left the tapes behind, he'll see how ridiculous Jimmy's confession is. The cops get fake confessions all the time. My friend will help me figure out why Jimmy Abeyta made one.

I pull into the lot and shut off the engine. Somebody must have threatened Jimmy . . . or bribed him . . . or . . . and whoever did that must be the real killer. Car door open, I get stuck in my own seat belt and trip over my own feet and drop my purse on the ground and order myself to get a grip.

Inside the station house, I'm directed down a hallway full of uniformed men and women talking and walking and weighed down with metal. At the reception desk for the Detective Division, a young woman, plump and sleek as a seal, stands up. She looks over the top of a maze of cubicles.

"Nooo, sorry, ma'am. He's not . . . oh, wait! Hey, Sheila, have you seen Detective Baca? This lady—"

Sheila doesn't stop, but yanks a thumb down the corridor the way she came. "Conference Two. They just wrapped it up."

Taking my cue from Sheila, I hie myself down the hall. Daniel Baca has more than a few reasons to give me a full hearing. Daniel is a bootstraps-up child of the barrios himself. These days, he sponsors a low-rider club for barrio kids. If anybody should know about . . . ah . . . here it is: CONFERENCE ROOM TWO. I turn the knob.

His pinstripe back is facing me. He's casually slumped deep into his chair, head back, arm loose in the air, hand open ready for the catch—

Thwack.

The little rubber ball comes to rest in his palm. W. P. Skyler slowly swivels his neck at the sound of the opening door. When he sees me, he smiles.

"Ahhh," he purrs. "Look who's here."

Daniel is standing. He was in the process of placing a manila folder on top of the pile of manila folders in front of the assistant district attorney. He gives W.P. a sour look and me a pained smile.

"Matty," Baca says, "we were just finishing up. I'll be right with you if you'd care to wait in the—"

"Not at all, not at all," Skyler insists like a society maven who wouldn't hear of making a guest feel unwelcome. "Ms. Donahue, we were just talking about your boy. Really, really, have a seat."

Skyler taps the pile of folders with his ball as his eyes follow me into the seat across from him.

"Detective, I think Ms. Donahue has an interest—hell, a *right*—to know what's up. Don't you?"

Daniel says gently, "Matty, I've turned the Prather case files over to the D.A. I understand his office is going to present to the grand jury next Thursday."

"You still representing the guy?" Skyler asks me.

"I, uh . . ."

". . . because I got word he was refusing counsel."

"I am not representing Jimmy Abeyta."

"No, huh?" Skyler hesitates only a moment. "Well, what the hell? It's a matter of public record. If anybody's entitled to know what's in these"—he taps the files—"it'd have to be Ms. Donahue here. You want to run it down for her, Baca?"

His whole body as stiff as his knife-creased jeans, Daniel Baca says, "Matty, Jimmy Abeyta gave us chapter and verse."

"Tell me."

"When Augusto Santiago died a few months back, it was of complications from getting shot seven years ago. Dr. Prather heard about Santiago's death and called Abeyta. She said she knew how awful this must be for him. Wanted to know, did he want to come talk to her about it? Turns out he did want to.

"When he got up to Irongate, according to Abeyta, Prather was practically on her deathbed. But they talked a little anyway, and this time her advice is to purge himself of guilt. She tells him it would be a great weight off his shoulders. She says she knows this because she's preparing to meet God soon herself."

Skyler is so relaxed, he's practically tossing his ball in his sleep. "Predictably," Skyler says to me, "this advice scares the living shit out of your client."

I sink lower into my chair. My chest hurts.

"So, anyway," Daniel picks up the story, "Abeyta figured, because of Denise Prather's medical condition, people would buy her suicide and the cops would never come looking for a killer."

Baca pauses and studies the pained expression on my face before he goes on. "But Abeyta didn't know anything about Alan Prather. Didn't even know there was a husband."

"What?" I blurt out. "You're telling me Jimmy just killed Alan Prather for good measure?"

Whish-thwack.

"Something like that," Baca answers. "Apparently, the husband surprised him—just appeared suddenly after he's already got the wife in the car. Abeyta says he didn't have any choice. He ends up hitting Alan Prather with the wrench he's using to clamp in the hose. Then he props the husband into the car too.

"But Abeyta gets second thoughts. What if the husband comes to before the exhaust kills them both? And even if the husband dies, the police might see where the wrench had hit him."

Whish-thwack!

"Abeyta had been a grease jockey once," Baca continues. "He showed us how he put a pinprick hole in the fuel line and another in the gas tank. Our in-house guy says it's dead-on accurate."

"Jimmy would have taken the tapes," I say stubbornly.

"He didn't have time," Skyler retorts. "He'd rigged an explosion that could have blown up half a mountain. It would have, too, but for the reinforcement in the garage walls. Your boy was in a panic. He ran. But, being his lawyer, I guess you already knew all that, didn't you?"

I say nothing. Having extracted as much blood as he's going to get in this round, Skyler takes his leave.

When he's out of the room, Daniel says, "I'm sorry it worked out this way, Matty."

"It didn't happen," I say.

"Okay," he says, humoring me.

"Listen to me! It couldn't have happened that way. If he'd gone there to protect his secret, Jimmy would have stolen the tapes, no matter how panicked he was. And Jimmy drives a GTO, not a motorcycle. If Denise was the only one he was going to kill, he would've put her in the driver's seat, not in the passenger's seat. Jimmy's back has been injured. He can barely move himself, much less cart other people around and crawl under cars. He couldn't have figured everything out, couldn't have arranged everything so quickly."

"You done? Is that all? Because if you are, it's not enough."

"No, I'm not done."

"What else?"

"He wouldn't have done that to Sam."

"To who?"

"You have children?" I demand.

"Two. A girl and a boy."

"Jimmy Abeyta has a son."

"Most criminals have kids, Matty."

"It's a scary thing, isn't it? Being responsible for a child? So many forks in the road. So many ways for a child to turn. A kid can be skipping along, headed for some sweet, golden future . . . the road is suddenly blocked . . . there's a detour. He can't find his way back."

"It happens all the time. Every scumbag we pick up was once somebody's cute little kid."

"Jimmy's cute little kid's name is Sam."

"They all got names, Matty."

"Look, Jimmy could have walked in here and confessed to the Santiago killing anytime. Why didn't he? There were so many mitigating circumstances in that shooting, the sentence could have been pled way down. It makes no sense to kill to protect that story. But if he was caught for Denise Prather's murder, he could never hope to get out of prison. It makes no goddamned sense. He wouldn't have risked leaving his wife and child alone."

"But he's done just that, hasn't he, Matty?"

"Daniel, just suppose for a minute that I'm right. If Jimmy didn't do this, somebody must have bribed him or threatened him to say he did."

"You have any candidates?"

"Maybe."

"Any evidence?"

I'm silent.

Baca shrugs. "There's no way I can keep a case open when we have a point-by-point confession to two crimes. The D.A.'s office is preparing the Criminal Complaint at this very moment. There are no other suspects. Matty, the i's are dotted, the t's are crossed. It's over."

I'm like a beheaded chicken who can't stop running around in circles. "But, Daniel," I argue, "I've been looking. I've got leads. What if I find something? Evidence? What if . . ." My voice falters.

As Daniel steps through the door into the hallway, he turns to me and says tiredly, "Look. Whatever you were doing, go on doing it. Maybe it'll help you. And if you turn up anything,

I'll be glad to take a look at it. Okay? Seriously, what is it you were going to do today?"

"I was going to go to the dentist."

Daniel looks confused.

"There was this pissed-off dentist, one of Prather's investors; he's dead. I have an appointment to see the dentist's son."

"So go! It'll probably help you to see this through. I mean it. Really, you go on. Go to the dentist."

Then he shuts the door. For the second time today, I am lost in strange territory behind a closed door.

TWENTY-FOUR

---ˢˢˢ---

Dr. DAVID DRAKE, JR., D.D.S., IS ONE OF THOSE POLITE, earnest young balding men who instantly remind you of a grown-up Opie Taylor. His nurse has put me in one of the bead-curtained examining rooms with a stack of magazines. Drake pops his head in every few minutes while he waits for his paying clients' X rays to develop or molds to harden. Muzak fills the air.

"Dad wasn't the only one who hated Alan Prather, you know," he says during his third appearance.

"But I gather, with your father, the hatred was particularly deep."

"I guess that's true. They'd been friends for a long time. Dad was not only Alan Prather's dentist and his golf partner, he really admired the guy; he trusted him. Of course he felt betrayed."

"Was your father's heart attack . . . ?"

"Connected to his obsession with Prather? Who knows? But he died before Prather did and, if what you're asking is whether Dad passed on his grudge to me, the answer is no. I have a life of my own. In fact, although I've been working here for two years, I never even met Alan Prather face-to-face. Can you excuse me for a few minutes?"

He pops out again and I wait. I look around the little cubicle. On the ceiling are enlarged color prints of flowers and mountains and sunsets. On the wall, photos: of the young doctor and his family, three cherubic little girls and a pretty wife; of the young doctor with the smiling gang at the office; of the young doctor with a group of children in front of a church.

I could be feeling depressed about how unlikely this guy seems as a murderer except that new information has just been imparted to me that is threatening to cheer me up. I take this little respite to process it. When Dr. Drake pops his head back in, I say, "You said your father was Alan Prather's personal dentist?"

"That's right. Although I don't imagine Prather would have come in to have his teeth worked on during the last few months of either of their lives. They weren't speaking, you know."

"But Prather didn't ever transfer to another dentist? Didn't have his dental records shipped to someone else?"

"No."

"So, they were still here? The records? Alan Prather's dental records were still here when you inherited the practice?"

"Sure."

Before I can ask another question, he excuses himself again. By the time he returns, my voice is nearly shaking in anticipation of his answer. How could I, how could everybody, have been so blind?

"So," I say carefully, "when the police got Prather's dental records to compare them to the burned body, they got those records from you ... from right here in your office?"

"That's right."

"But you'd just inherited the practice. You'd never actually looked into Alan Prather's mouth yourself? So, you wouldn't have been able to look at the X rays or the charts you passed on and say for sure that they belonged to Alan Prather? Did you even examine the records before you turned them over to the police?"

"They had Prather's name on them," Drake says defensively. "The police asked for them. We sent them."

Back at the echoing, nearly empty mansion, the telephone is on the floor. I sit next to it with my back against the wall and start dialing: Daniel Baca, Patrick Prather, Angie, Frankie. Even Max.

"Daniel, I didn't even think of it, did you? That Prather could have switched dental records. He'd once been the building manager of the dental complex. He had keys, access."

"Matty, this is pretty farfetched, don't you th—"

"All Alan Prather had to do was get the X rays of whoever he planned to kill and substitute them for his own."

Silence.

"Don't you see?" I plead. "Now it finally begins to make sense. Prather skims; he hides the money, at least six million; he's prepared to kill his wife, maybe even because he actually loves her and can't bear to see her suffer. And he's apparently prepared to kill someone else too. Remember what Claude Raskin has said from the beginning? Alan Prather is on some beach somewhere sipping Cuervo Gold."

"And yet your friend just confessed to murdering him."

"Okay, I haven't got everything figured out yet. But you can't ignore this possibility."

"Bring me something."

"What more do you need, for godsake?"

"The money. If what you're suggesting is true, Prather would have gone to the money. He would have emptied out the account by now. The *Swiss* account, if you're right about that too. So, if the money's gone, if you can find the account, and if the money's been withdrawn *since* the explosion, you've got me. I'll fight my captain and I'll fight W. P. Skyler too. If you find that account and find it empty, I'd fight everybody to open the case up again. But, Matty, short of that—"

Find the account. Find it empty.

"Do you know there are more than forty banks in Bern alone? And none of them will even return my calls."

"It's the best I can do."

My next call is to the Sea Door Marina. I leave a message for Patrick with as much hope as if I were placing a slip of paper in a bottle and tossing it on the waves. Frankie is out. No one answers Angie's phone.

Finally, I dial Max's number. I need to talk to him about all of this. And if he's not willing to talk about this, I want to hear his voice anyway.

"Good," he says, "you remembered what day it is."

"Day?"

"Our appointment, Matty."

Dr. Louise Fried says to me, "Now, Matty, you try it."

"Okay," I say. "Max says he's scared half the time and—"

"Not *'Max says.'* Don't distance yourself, Matty."

"Okay, Max *'is'* scared hal—"

"Matty, you're trying to put yourself in Max's place. Try to remember to use the 'I' form when you mirror Max's words. And, if you feel comfortable with it, try to mimic his posture and body language at the same time. The more we can become the other person, the more easily we can access channels of empathy."

"Uh-huh."

"Want to try it again?"

I've been sitting across from the two of them for more than fifteen minutes. During this time my own posture, should anyone want to access channels of empathy, has gone pretty much the way of the juvenile delinquent who habitually sits in the back row of any public high school classroom. I'm somewhat more limited than the delinquent because the office of Louise Fried, Ph.D. in clinical psychology, has no desks to tilt backward, and the walls upon which one might lean instead display pretty color prints in bulky frames. So I make do by slumping forward in her comfy chair, hugging a pillow between my chest and my interlocking arms of steel.

"Want to try again?" she repeats, and holds her hand out for the pillow.

"Sure," I say, relinquishing my security pillow with bogus nonchalance. *What? This old thing?* I take a furtive gulp of air and prepare to play by the rules. Max considerately holds his position so I can imitate it.

Here goes . . . Let's see. Okay. Shoulders forward toward my partner; elbows on knees; fingers lightly laced as Max's fingers are lightly laced so that at any moment they can spread wide to invite the other in; head up and eyes focused on my partner. Eyes focused on Max who is focusing on me who is focusing on him who is—

"I'm scared half the time . . ." I begin to echo the lines Max had uttered a moment ago. "I'm afraid Matty's going to get herself killed . . . I'm afraid I'm going to lose her."

"Good, good. This time, did you feel Max's fear?"

"The channels of empathy were accessed," I parrot, acting more like my imaginary delinquent than I would have wished. "I mean, yes. Yes, I understand what Max is saying. I really do, but—"

"Tell it to *him*."

"Max, I understand—"

"No—"

"Really, I—"

"You don't. You don't really want to understand." Max says it flatly. "If you understood, you wouldn't take chances with your life like this."

"That's what I said about Jimmy and Sam."

"Oh, shit," says Max.

"Who are Jimmy and Sam?" asks Louise Fried.

"Maybe you're right," I tell Max. "If I risk my neck, I take the risk for both of us."

"Jimmy and Sam are exactly who?" persists Fried.

"I could lose you, Matty."

"I could lose you," I echo.

Silence.

"There," says Dr. Louise Fried. "That was much better, Matty. How did that feel?"

TWENTY-FIVE

———◊◊◊———

FIND THE ACCOUNT. FIND IT EMPTY.

    I spent fruitless hours yesterday, reinspecting what remained of Alan's papers for some—any—evidence of foreign bank accounts or new domestic accounts. Nothing.

Today the files went to a shredding company and Frankie sent the salvage truck for Prather's file cabinets and desks. There are indentations here and there in the carpet from the missing furniture. The vault is empty, the walls are bare. A couple of antiques are tagged and scheduled to be removed for auction.

The few things that more or less "belong" to me are in a disorderly heap on the floor of Alan's office. There, in a cardboard box, are the items I'd asked Angie to gather before I left for Taos: phone bills, calendars, Rolodexes. Denise's little black phone book is on top. It's nearly two A.M. when I carry this stuff out of Alan's office and shut that door for the final time. In Alan's bedroom, I take a last look at the items in the box, trying to see each anew and as though it meant something.

There are hundreds of phone numbers from all over the country on Alan's Rolodexes: partners, lenders, suppliers,

friends; but there are no cards for Swiss banks. In fact, there
are no international numbers here at all. I can't decide if this
is odd or not. The man went skiing in Switzerland. Wouldn't
he make hotel or airline reservations? I quickly scan for a
travel agent. There is none. I decide it probably is odd.

By comparison, Denise's black book is almost bare: Patrick's
number, some friends, various doctors and associations, and
many names I don't recognize. Most of the numbers are in-
state. One has the area code of Kansas. The name listed with
that number is Pleasant Lakes Nursing Home. What the hell?
I sit on the floor and call. I'm told by a sleepy nurse on night
duty that Denise's mother hasn't been able to speak for over
a year.

"She simply forgot how to make words," the nurse tells me.

One number in Denise's book catches my attention because it begins with "01," the first digits of international
phone numbers. The name listed beside it is St. Be. Once
again, what the hell?

"*Oui?* St. Bernadette."

"Hello, do you speak English?"

"*Moment!*"

Another voice. "May I help you?"

"I'm calling from the United States."

"Yes?"

"Where are you?"

"I beg your pardon?"

"Sorry. I have your number but I don't know where you
are. What country? What city? Is this a hospital?"

"Oh. Yes, I see. You have reached the St. Bernadette Hotel,
Bern, Switzerland."

I quite literally drop the phone, then grab it by the cord.
When I collect my wits, I ask what time it is there—ten A.M.—
and what street the hotel is on—The Belpstrasse, Number 48—
and do they keep records of regular guests who might have
come often over several years, a sort of a VIP list—yes—and is
there a record of a Mr. Alan Prather on that list?

There is not.

A Mr. Eugene Saavedra?

No.

Anyone at all from Santa Fe, New Mexico?

Again, no.

Would he go back another year? Another?

The desk clerk is more polite and cooperative than one could dare ask, but in the end, it seems the call has been for nothing. I hang up.

Five hours later, I bolt upright from a fitful sleep. I fumble for the black book, find the number for St. Bernadette.

"I'm really, really sorry to bother you again," I mewl into the phone when the English-speaking soul of civility is back on the line. "And this is probably a silly question, but . . . is there by chance a bank on your street . . . uh, Belpstrasse?"

"No."

"Oh . . . well, please forgive me."

"Not at all, Madame."

I've already taken the phone from my ear when I hear "If it is only a matter of finding a bank, perhaps Madame would be interested in the Bundesbanc? It is just around the corner from here. It is a small bank but quite excellent. Are you planning to visit Bern in the near future?"

"You know, sir, I may be planning on just that."

I call Claude Raskin, my best shot at getting instant airfare to Europe to recover loot. Small matter that I'm hoping for a different result—*find the account; find it empty.*

A secretary informs me Claude has gone fishing. I call Frankie. She opines that while the Bankruptcy Court could write a letter to the Bundesbanc asking for cooperation, the Bundesbanc would probably use that letter for toilet paper. And the Court sure wouldn't approve funds for such a trip even if we wanted to wait weeks to get a hearing. The notion of flying halfway around the world on my own nickel to follow such a thin trail of crumbs seems absurd.

And yet, Denise Prather did have a telephone number for a hotel in Bern, around the corner from a bank. There's probably a bank around the corner from every hotel in Bern. But Denise had *this* hotel's number. Why? Probably a dozen innocent explanations. None occurs to me.

I call the airlines. A flight leaves Albuquerque for New York at nine-thirty in the morning. I can make a connecting flight for Switzerland at four-thirty East Coast time. With so little notice, there are no deals, each seat will be full price. And in Bern there will be the cost of a hotel room, and cabs to pay for with my own meager funds. . . .

The telephone rings.

"Matilda?"

"Patrick! Thank God!"

"I got your message. I take it you missed me."

"I need your help."

"Anything." His voice gets immediately serious. "What do you need?"

"Money."

It's after three P.M. as I hurry along the moving ramps at JFK toward the international concourse. As I approach the gate, I scan the rows of plastic chairs. People at airports are wonderfully neither alone nor together: a businessman flicks a speck from the knee of his trousers and, over the top of his book, warily eyes the young mother, awash in children, sitting across from him; a student sleeps across four chairs, his head on his backpack, oblivious of his foot edging toward the woman reading aloud to her husband from *Europe on $20 a Day*.

Which reminds me of the twenty-six dollars cash and two maxed-out credit cards I have in my purse. Even though it might have been awkward for Patrick to ignore my brassy request for funds, it was generous of him to pick up the tab for this fool's errand.

"I'll make the arrangements," he'd said. "Your tickets will be ready at the counter." I dump my backpack on one of the molded plastic chairs and plunk myself down next to it to wait for my Swissair connection to Bern. I'm asleep in less than five minutes and I don't awaken until I hear the voice.

"You know," the voice teases, "anybody could just walk away with that backpack."

I open my eyes. The light behind his head blinds me for a second.

"Patrick?"

"Thought you could use some company," he says, sitting in the backpack's seat.

"You're coming along? You're coming all the way to Switzerland?"

"Well, I figured—just in case you have the correct bank identified, you're going to have better luck if you have Alan's executor and heir with you when you start making demands."

I knuckle the sleep out of my eyes and smile. "You know what I'm hoping we'll find, don't you? I mean, if anybody gives us any information."

"Sure, you told me on the phone. An empty bag—an account from which all the funds have been withdrawn. Which might mean that my brother is still alive somewhere. Well, I don't believe it. But I do understand why you have to pursue this. And if you have to pursue it, I guess I have to pursue it too."

It isn't until I find myself seated, surprisingly, in first class with a glass of champagne in one hand and a hot moist towel in the other ("For your forehead," the stewardess explains, "it's quite soothing") that I take a long look at my traveling companion.

"It seems I'm always thanking you," I say, tipping the glass to him. "Thank you."

"I know you must be worried about Sam. How's he doing?"

"I don't know. I've called and nobody answers. I am worried. But right now I think the best thing I can do for them is to be on this plane."

The Bundesbanc is smaller than I'd envisioned and more modern. Where I'd imagined old European opulence—carved pillars and frescoes, marble floors and hushed tones—I find, instead, featureless lines, gray walls, and all the charm of an Otis elevator. Along the corridor, we pass modest offices furnished with aggressively plain desks and gray metal cabinets. The light has a peculiar greenish tint. From behind the desk of the closet-sized office to which Patrick and I are escorted, a thin, neat, mid-forties man in a good but not excellent gray suit rises.

"Herr Weiker, your American visitors," announces our escort.

"Ah, yes." Mr. Weiker gestures to the chairs squeezed between his desk and the outer wall. "Welcome, please. I understand from your wire, Ms. Donahue, that you believe we may be holding funds belonging to a deceased bankruptcy debtor?" He regards me speculatively.

"Alan Prather."

"And you"—he turns to Patrick—"you are the brother of the deceased? I confess, I hadn't expected the two of you to arrive together. When there is both a family interest and a creditor interest, we are more familiar with a somewhat . . . how shall I put it? . . . a more antagonistic atmosphere. Nonetheless, the bank is not at liberty to release information . . ."

Patrick has brought with him both Alan's Last Will and Testament and Denise's companion document. Both name him the executor of their estates. I lay out the death certificates and the bankruptcy petition and relevant court documents as well as the letter from the bankruptcy judge which Frankie had faxed to the St. Bernadette Hotel that morning.

Herr Weiker reads and nods. "These documents would be adequate," he informs us, "if there were an account here in this name. In the case of numbered accounts, however, no information can be accessed by us without either the account number itself or the personal code."

"Personal code?"

"A word or number or series of letters and numbers decided upon by the customer himself rather than by the bank."

"Like a PIN number?"

"If you like."

Herr Weiker has been here before. He shakes his head sympathetically and rubs his hands together. *So extremely sorry we just can't see our way clear to turn loose of your money.* He's rising in his seat now—about to show us the door. Patrick reaches for the small box of gray notepaper on the desk and writes something. He nudges the sheet of paper toward Herr Weiker. Weiker sits back down. He examines the note, reviews the file again.

He grimaces. He picks up the phone and confers. He taps his pen repeatedly. He says, "Mmmm." Eventually, he leaves the office to "consult upstairs."

"What did you write?" I ask Patrick.

"Our mother's social security number. Alan used to use it all the time to get access to her assets. I figured maybe . . ."

When Herr Weiker returns, he is smiling thinly. "Your papers seem to be in order. I've been authorized to acknowledge the existence of an account in the name of Alan Prather."

The first shoe to drop.

"And?" I press. *Find it empty.*

"I'm extremely sorry, but in order for us to release specific information or funds on that account, we will need for each of you to execute waivers of liability."

"Yes, of course," Patrick says.

"Bring them on!" I add.

But the waivers taking the bank off the hook for any mistake it might be about to make have not been drawn yet. That will take much of the day. The legal department will have to approve, don't you see? Herr Weiker is unmoved by my impatient plea for speed.

Perhaps we would care to take in the sights of Bern. "There is an excellent place to lunch just around the corner, on Schwarztorstrasse. I often eat there myself." Everything one needs in Bern, it seems, is just around the corner from a bank.

Lunch just around the corner is served slowly in gradually more sumptuous installments. Swiss efficiency appears to take a backseat to Swiss gastronomy. My agitation grows through cucumbers in dill sauce and white asparagus and prosciutto and the first half-bottle of wine. Sensing it, Patrick reaches across the narrow table and, with a finger, raises my chin until he can look into my eyes.

"I'm anxious to have the answer too, Matty. But we'll have

it very soon now. And just at this moment, you are in a fine restaurant in fairly good company. We have one day to spend in a pleasant European city."

I smile wanly. "This isn't what I came here to do."

"It's not my place to advise you, Matty, but you said once you understood the need to take intermissions in life. Circumstances have created this . . . place between acts. Maybe we could enjoy it."

There comes a time early in every relationship where A says to B, "Tell me about yourself." Patrick never said those words when we were in Santa Fe, and their absence subtly signaled that a relationship wasn't in the cards. But today, somewhere between schnitzel and pastry, Patrick Prather asks the who-is-Matty-Donahue question.

I reflect that it's been a long time since I've heard it and a longer time since I've wanted to answer it.

"I think I'd like another glass of wine."

My story comes out in bits and pieces—the death of my fiancé and his son. My role in their deaths. My guilt. My year of desolate hibernation. The predictable suspension from the bar that came from ignoring clients until their cases had been hopelessly screwed up.

"You were in love with this man?"

"He died three weeks before we were to be married."

"And his own son killed him?"

"And then turned the gun on himself. Tommy was schizophrenic. He didn't take his medication. He wasn't hospitalized."

"But that can't have been your fault."

"I'm the one who got him out of the hospital. My legal argument was impeccable. My judgment was in the toilet."

The sun comes suddenly and brilliantly out from behind a cloud and streams through the window. It is low enough in the sky to skip lightly across the white linen tablecloth and sparkle through the throng of stemware that has taken up residence on our little table—a new glass for each new wine. I swirl one of the glasses and watch the light dance.

"That chapter of your life is over," Patrick says.

·   ·   ·

Now that all the keys have been turned in all the locks, Herr Weiker is cordial and full of goodwill when we return.

"Sit, sit, sit."

After we've each signed our name no fewer than fourteen times, Herr Weiker scoots a single folded sheet of gray paper toward us.

"I think you'll find all is in order." He's begun to enjoy the small drama.

It's even more of a drama to me than Herr Weiker imagines. If the number on this sheet of paper is zero—if this account was wiped out sometime after the explosion—Alan Prather is almost certainly alive somewhere. *Find it empty* and Alan Prather himself is the murderer. *Find it empty* and Sam's prospects get a shade or two better.

I open the paper before me.

"Well?"

To the extent the small gray man is capable of such expression, Herr Weiker beams.

"Well?" he repeats. "As you see . . ."

The page is blank but for a single number. The amount is in Swiss francs.

". . . In dollars," he explains, "it comes to precisely seven million six hundred thousand four hundred twenty-three dollars and thirty-three cents."

"I see."

"How would you like to take it?"

TWENTY-SIX

───❧❧❧───

T
HE SEVEN MILLION WILL BE WIRE-TRANSFERRED TO
Frankie's trust account at the Santa Fe National Bank
within a half hour after the bank opens tomorrow morning.
Frankie says she's personally going to be standing outside the
bank door by eight A.M..

"I just want to physically see the deposit slip." She laughs.
"I can still hardly believe what you've done. The creditors are
going to canonize you. Raskin is half in love with you already
anyway. Honest to God, Matty, this is the biggest recovery of
assets I've ever seen in a bankruptcy case. Aren't you thrilled?
Matty? Matty? Are you there?"

I shift the phone to the other ear and stare out the window
into the rain that has settled into a steady gray drizzle. The St.
Bernadette Hotel is a clean, drab, businessmen's hotel. Last
night's sleep here was fitful and hopeful. Tonight, at this sorry
dead-end, I'll be numb enough to sleep the sleep of the dead.
"No, Frankie. No, I'm not thrilled."

"When does your flight arrive in Albuquerque? I'll meet
you."

"I can't get out of here until noon tomorrow, and my car's

at the airport anyway," I say tiredly. "I'll be fine on my own. By the way, have you heard from Angie? I've been trying to reach her."

"Not only haven't I heard from her, she was supposed to survey the site at her new job yesterday. But she never showed up. Never even called. Now I'm embarrassed that I recommended her."

"That isn't like Angie. I'm beginning to worry about her."

"Speaking of worried, your friend Max has been calling. Apparently, you missed some kind of appointment. He said he's worried. I told him you and Patrick Prather were in Europe. Hope that was okay."

Patrick and I have taken adjoining rooms and, through the thin walls, I can hear him singing in the shower. This time, for Patrick, the proof is positive: All the embezzled money is still in the account where Alan put it. Ergo, once and for all, Alan is dead. And Patrick is apparently so happy to have that door slammed for good that he's been careening from one Broadway show tune to another.

But when he comes to my room later, he tones down his glee for my sake. He pours me a scotch from the minibar and shakes his head.

"Come on, Matty. Sitting in this room isn't going to help anybody. We've still got a little daylight left. What say we see the sights?"

I rest my head against the cool window of the trolley and watch the close-packed, orderly buildings go by through a curtain of drizzle.

Patrick touches my shoulder. "I know you hoped to find the account empty, Matty. But maybe it's time to consider the possibility that Jimmy Abeyta really did what he says he did."

I don't answer. Patrick suggests we get out and walk for a while in the rain. As the trolley pulls near the entrance to the ancient Bear Pit, he tugs at my sleeve and I give in to him. We walk to the wall that overlooks a great hole in the ground. As I stand in the rain, gazing down into the pit, Patrick stands behind me. When I shiver from the cold, he wraps both arms around me.

"Hundreds of years ago, Matty, when Duke Berthold founded this city, he decided to name it for the first animal he killed on a hunt. The animal was a bear and so the city was Bern. The bears are the symbols of the city; on the city seal and the city flag."

"So why keep real ones in a concrete pit?"

"Bottom line? I guess the purpose is the amusement of humans."

I turn away. We walk a long time in silence. We stop to get a drink. We talk about things, about the history of Bern and about the human condition. He orders another bottle of wine. We agree that people are profoundly wonderful and gravely flawed. My mind keeps returning to Jimmy and Sam.

Patrick tells me he was married once but it didn't work out. I tell him I don't know if things will work out between Max and me. I tell him I don't even know what "work out" means. He brings what's left of the third bottle of wine back to the hotel with us. I say no to one last glass.

"No. I'm going to take a shower to sober up."

When I come out of the bathroom, I'm wet and weary but not sober. Patrick is sitting on my bed with my pillow on his lap.

"They don't change the sheets every night in European hotels," he says, lifting my pillow to his face.

"No?"

"It smells like you," he says.

A crimson band streaks across the darkening sky as United Flight 452 begins its descent. From this angle, nothing disturbs the flat, clean line of the western horizon. The bloody ribbon of sunset looks as it might if humans had never inhabited the planet.

I keep my forehead pressed against the airplane window until the sky has become tame with pink echoes. I wait in my seat, patient as an invalid, while the stewardess welcomes us to Albuquerque and wishes us a safe journey to our final destination. Depressed and bone-tired, with my backpack looped loosely over one shoulder, I exit the plane and slouch down the gangway toward the gate.

By contrast, my fellow passengers seem eager and energized, hurrying along to meet families or lovers or futures. Safe journey to my final destination indeed; I think this may be about it for me. Ah, my old friend self-pity; I see you're still in tow.

Apparently, there was some kind of celebrity or maybe a returning favorite son on our plane, because I can hear a small brass band ahead striking up "For He's a Jolly Good Fellow." When I round the corner and get a full gander at the gate area, there are big "Welcome Home" signs. Whoopee, I think dismally. The sound becomes louder as I approach. The greeters begin to cheer and clap. I look around idly to see who the star may be. Other passengers are looking around too, wondering, like me, who we've been traveling with. The mayor? Some local basketball hero?

Then the musical selection changes to "Waltzing Matilda," a song that has always made me wince. Despite the rah-rah display, this is no crowd of sophomores. These are middle-aged men in ... for christsake ... business suits. Twenty-five or so middle-aged men in business suits ... singing, "And you'll come a-waltzing Matilda with me."

Champagne corks are popping.

"Welcome home, Matty," says one of the men.

"Congratulations, Matty," says another.

"Give her some air here," says Claude Raskin. "We got a lifetime to thank this little lady."

Outside the airport, our small zoo of celebrants organizes itself along the curb. Someone takes my car keys, someone else hands me a wet glass of champagne. The limousine pulls up first and, despite protests from the security patrol, doesn't pull away from the curb until a short, honking and hooting caravan, including my Toyota, has formed behind us.

"Did you ever see the like?" asks Claude Raskin to the limo's occupants.

Claude pokes his head and shoulders out the sunroof and

beckons to the gang behind. More honking. The big gleaming
car moves smoothly into traffic. The guy next to me is placing
a dainty napkin on my lap and thrusting a tray of caviar,
chopped onion, and toast points at me.

"Beluga," he says.

"Nothing but the best for the hero of the hour," says a familiar voice.

I look up. "Dr. Rosenbloom?"

Rosenbloom introduces the limo's other occupants. As we
pull onto the interstate, champagne is pouring fast but no
faster than the questions:

"How did you find the bank?"

"Had Slick had this account all along?"

*"Is there really, really going to be enough to pay all of us off in
full?"*

"How will the IRS treat the interest earned in Switzerland?"

"Where are we going?" I ask at last.

"Back to Santa Fe," says Claude. "We got the best banquet
room at the La Fonda Hotel for this here wing-ding."

"Oh, Claude, no." The idea of celebrating this nail in
Jimmy's coffin is ludicrous.

"Like the doc here says, nothin's too good. You saved our
bacon, young lady. You sure did."

"I couldn't have done it without the help of Alan's
brother."

"Hell, we'd even break bread with the snake's kin. Where
is he?"

"He flew back to Seattle from New York." Remembering
what almost happened between Patrick and me last night,
and remembering that it didn't, I add, "I doubt if he'll be
coming back to Santa Fe again."

"His loss. We'll just have to heap our thank-you-kindlys
on you. Honest to God, Matty, we can never make this up to
you. But we're sure as heck going to try!"

Unable to control himself, he stands unsteadily and ya-
hoos out the roof window. Honkers behind us respond. I
smile and try to look pleased. I try, too, to keep my mind on
what they are saying: cattle contracts for me to look over, real

estate deals, oil leases. There is apparently no end of the big-fee legal work that will be coming my way from these guys.

Claude has been doing some checking up on me and he tells the others, "Matty here used to have herself a hell of a law practice. She was a real force to be reckoned with before her ... troubles."

The guy beside me kisses me exuberantly on the cheek. Troubles? What troubles? More bubbles are poured and more are spilled and more off-key rounds of "Waltzing Matilda" are sung. Feeling like a wallflower at my own debutante ball, I sink deeper into the seat as we near Santa Fe city limits.

"What's the matter, sweetheart?" demands Claude. "You look lower'n a lizard's belly."

"Is there a telephone in this thing?"

He produces one instantly and hushes the serenaders as I dial. As with my earlier calls from Europe to this number, the rings go unanswered. When the mobile operator cuts me off, I immediately dial again. Some primitive sense of urgency is upon me now that I'm getting so close to Sam. *Where are they?*

All these days and I don't know what's been happening to him. I should never have left. What did I accomplish anyway? I just supplied more proof that Alan Prather was, indeed, dead. Far from exonerating Sam's father, I've thrown another lump of sod into his grave. I dial again.

As we turn off the highway onto Cerrillos Road, Santa Fe's long north-south drag, the phone is picked up.

"Hello," I say. "Angie?

No answer ... quick, short breaths.

"Sam? Is that you? This is Matty. Hello?"

"Huh ... huh ... huh ..."

"Sam?"

"Mommy's got ... blood in her mouth."

TWENTY-SEVEN

————◦◦◦————

S AM IS STANDING BAREFOOT WITH HIS BACK PRESSED against the bathroom door. His shirt is on inside out and he has peed all over himself. Angie's head rests on the rim of the toilet. A trickle of blood stains the seat and more blood is in the bowl. Quite a lot is on the floor next to a Maalox bottle.

"The ulcer?" I ask her.

She presses a fist into her gut and rocks.

"Can you move?"

She nods.

I rush back to the front door. With annoyance, I see that the revelers are spilling noisily out of their cars into the quiet residential street. Claude has taken a position on the tiny stoop, where he is wringing his hands. "I called nine one one," he blurts out. "They want to know what the situation is before they send a car. What should I tell them?"

"There's a sick woman here, Claude. I think I can get her to the hospital in my car before an ambulance can get here."

"Let's put her in the limo." He's slurring his words.

A horn honks from the caravan, then another. A door slams and a contingent of drunks weaves its way toward us.

"Can you get rid of them?" I snarl.

"We just want to help, Matty."

"Claude, give me my car keys. The best help you can give me right now is to clear everyone out. Can you do that?"

Back in the bathroom, I squat to help Angie to her feet. Sam hasn't moved.

"Sam, find a bag! Put in some pajamas and clean clothes for yourself. Go on, go on!"

Slowly, he moves away from his mother. She pushes herself up and I lift.

"Did you call a doctor?" I ask.

Angie groans.

"It's okay, never mind. I'm taking you to the hospital. Can you walk?"

She nods and we make our way to the car. When she's settled into the seat, she opens her mouth to say something. The only thing that comes out is pink foam.

I dash back into the house. Sam's not in the kitchen or dining room or living room or bathroom. In the back of his mother's bedroom closet, he sits in his soiled clothes. In his lap is a blanket and his mother's big purse.

"Come on. Quick. We have to take Mommy to the hospital." He hugs his blanket to him.

"You have to come! Mommy's already in the car. Goddamn it, Sam, *hurry*!"

Tears begin to trickle down his face. But he still doesn't move. More softly, I say, "We need to tell the doctor how long Mommy's been sick, Sam. Could you help us figure that out?"

He shakes his head.

"Because that'll help the doctor know what medicine to give her."

"Mommy's going to die." After a second, he looks up at me and adds, "Isn't she?"

"I don't know."

His face screws up and when I reach for him, he screams. I tug at him and he twists away. Around him on the closet floor I can see the remnants of recent meals: spilled cereal, a jar of jelly, a slice of bologna.

"Oh, my God, Sam—"

I sweep him and the blanket and the purse into my arms. He smacks me in the face and pulls my hair and makes little baby, panting cries. I carry him that way to the car and pry his fingers from my hair and push him down into the backseat, where he curls into a ball as tight as a grub. I drive fast into the night.

"If I die—" Angie says softly.

"You're not going to die."

"Will you take care of him?"

"You're not going to die."

"There's enough money now. For his college and—"

"Angie—"

"Eloy finally paid. You know ... Jimmy's accident. Two deposits ... in my account. Enough ... to support—"

"Be quiet!"

"But, Sam ... needs ... could ..."

More bloody foam from her lips.

"... you ... ?"

I race into the drive at St. Vincent's Hospital. In the emergency room, someone decides that one of Angie's ulcers has perforated. She's leaking stomach acid into her abdominal cavity and they can't stabilize her. A surgeon is called; the long wait begins.

Hours later, I leave a marginally cleaned up Sam asleep on the couch in the visitors' area. I follow a nurse down the hall and into the semidark room. Angie is sleeping off the anaesthesia.

"The doctor talked to you?" the nurse whispers to me.

"He said the operation went well."

She nods. "Mrs. Abeyta is going to be fine. But she needs rest. It may sound crazy, but it's probably a good thing surgery was necessary. This way insurance will pay for five or six days here in the hospital. Are you family?"

"Friend," I answer.

"Well, anything her friends and family can do, to reduce her anxiety. She needs to be kept stress-free."

Now, there's a likely prospect.

After the nurse departs, I study Angie's sleeping face for a long time. Eventually, I head back to where Sam is sleeping on the couch.

But Sam's not sleeping on the couch. Sam's gone.

BE CALM! There's going to be a simple, safe explanation. My brain orders my adrenaline back into whatever gland is pumping it out by the quart. Too late. So much for brains. Heart racing, I prowl the corridors: men's bathroom, women's bathroom, nurses' station.

"Have you seen . . . ?"

". . . No?"

"He's about so high . . ."

". . . With a man, you say? No, I don't think that could have been . . ."

But I follow a pointing finger, and as I round the corner to the vending machines, there they are. Sam is in his arms, legs straddling the man's hip and the blanket clutched to his chest. His face is close to the man's face and they're looking intently at each other. Both are paying close attention to their conversation.

"Max?"

He turns.

"Hi, Matty. Sam and I got hungry." He points to a vending machine. "We've got it narrowed down between Fritos and Snickers. You want something?"

"How did you know we were here?"

"Frankie," Max says. "I'd been bugging her to give me some news of you because I didn't know who else to bug. So, when Raskin called her tonight, she called me and I called him. He said there was some talk of bleeding . . . a medical situation of some kind. But he told me you insisted they go on without you."

"It seemed the wrong place to bring a party."

"When you weren't at Angie's, I called the hospital. How is she?"

"Angie's going to be all right."

Sam's eyes grow big and searching.

I nod. "Really, Sam. The doctor says Mommy's going to be just fine. But she has to stay here and rest until she's well enough to come home."

Sam's arms tighten around Max's neck.

It's time to figure out our next move. Literally. Even though the Prather mansion at Irongate is now totally secure, there are no longer any beds or groceries there. And who knows what shape my place on Canyon Road is in? I can't see taking Sam back to his own house, where he's apparently been taking his meals in his mother's bedroom closet. We decide on Max's house for tonight.

We are all business, Max and I. Like a long-married couple making necessary arrangements until an emergency has passed. For now, at least, we keep a lid on our personal conflict. Max says he'll pick up some things for Sam tomorrow morning. He takes the keys for Irongate so he can get the rest of my junk from there. Tomorrow is soon enough for other things.

Sam doesn't want to let go of Max, so I drive. When we get to Max's house, Sam still doesn't want to let go—so the two of them sleep in Max's bed and I sleep on the couch.

It's nearly noon when I wake up still feeling the effects of jet lag and disappointment. Where do I go after the dead-end in Bern? I stretch and look around. Max has geraniums growing in clay pots on a deep window ledge. Outside, there are more pots, more flowers, and a small fountain on a dappled patio. A bird perches on the fountain rim. Chopin is on a stereo somewhere. The scent of freshly baked bread fills the air.

This oasis is all so . . . Max. Even his sudden appearance at the hospital last night. Despite everything, Max cared and worried and intuited. He put his own apprehension aside and just showed up.

I can hear the two of them talking and I snake my head around the arm of the couch until I spy them through the archway. Max is at the stove. Sam is standing on a chair next to him so they're about the same height. It looks like Sam's been dressed in fresh clothing.

Max's deep voice, a pause, then Sam's. Slowly, I realize that there is a lilt at the end of each of Sam's sentences. More slowly, I recognize the lilt pattern: questions. Sam is asking questions again. If I know Max, he's teaching the kid to cook.

Every instinct tells me to stay put. Whatever magic is happening between those two is best left undisturbed.

I sit back, rest my head against the cushion, close my eyes, and put the question again. Where do you go after you reach a dead-end? I guess you back up. Start over. Rearrange the bits and pieces. See if there are any new pieces. If you still want to help that boy in the kitchen, you try again.

My conscious mind hasn't been exactly working wonders. Maybe it's time to turn things over to the subconscious. If you let it, the human mind can work like a kaleidoscope. Little items you've gathered from here and there will come together to form a pattern. But twist them a fraction or change your perspective and they seem to form another. Bits number one and two: Alan Prather writes a letter to his wife promising to kill them both—Jimmy Abeyta swears he killed the Prathers. Bits three and four: Alan Prather's body was so completely destroyed, it could be identified only by dental records—Prather's dentist can't guarantee the records he turned over were Alan's. Five and six: Alan Prather spent years socking away money in a secret account—he never went to get it. Seven and eight: Gene Saavedra was obviously afraid of something—Saavedra's wife told Baca a patient had threatened Denise. And it seems there's a new bit: sudden money in Angie's account—Eloy has finally come through, she said last night. Guilt? Generosity? Or hush money?

The pieces swirl and threaten to form a single coherent pattern, only to lose themselves to chaos again.

"How about some breakfast?"

Max lowers a tray to the coffee table by my side. On it are thick slices of fresh bread and a slab of real butter and a tub of cherry preserves and a cup of coffee and juice and ... I'm a little choked up, so I just nod.

"Where's Sam?" I ask.

"Sam wants to stay in the kitchen for a while."

I raise my eyebrows.

"Let him find his way," Max says.

"He doesn't want to be with me?" I do a lousy job of keeping the hurt out of my voice.

"I think," says Max kindly, "that Sam is terrified. He's trying to hold on to his center without relying on anyone. The people he usually trusts to take care of him seem suddenly unreliable. It's very tough stuff for a five-year-old boy to distrust everyone he loves."

"But you?"

"I'm safe. He knows me, but I'm not in his inner circle. He can afford to take a small chance with me."

I peer into the kitchen. Sam is just sitting on the chair now, staring at the wall. His hands are folded in his lap.

"Oh, Max . . ."

"I think he'll get better."

"But you're not certain."

"Matty, nothing's certain."

TWENTY-EIGHT

—◦◦◦—

AFTER BRUSHING MY TEETH WITH MY FINGER DIPPED IN
Max's Colgate, I yawn my way back down the hall, only
to find the house empty. Of people, that is, not of things. In
fact, there are plenty more things stacked and dumped by
Max's front door than when I took myself to the bathroom.
Taped prominently to a cardboard box stacked atop another
cardboard box is a note from Max:

> You said you needed this stuff from Irongate. So we picked
> it up while you were sleeping. Sam and I might stop in to
> see Angie if he's ready—or we might go shopping. We can
> talk about everything later. I love you.

I'm actually grateful they're gone because it gives me time
to think. I pace Max's floor while I do it. All right, I say to myself, all right. So one money trail may have terminated in a pot
of gold and a dead-end. But now there would appear to be a
new money trail. How much, I wonder, did the newly generous Uncle Eloy put into Angie's account?

Where is Angie's purse? I'd brought it along with me last

night. After a brief search, I locate it and paw through it until I find Angie's checkbook. I riffle through the pages of the register until I find the recent deposit entries Angie has made. I do a double take— My mind resists accommodating the numbers I see on the page before me.

The two large sums in the deposit column total five hundred thousand dollars. Too much to be conscience money from Eloy Abeyta for Jimmy's old injury? The timing too coincidental? About the right amount, maybe, at about the right time—to be a payment for Jimmy's confession. Fat Boy and Chatto sure had reason enough to want to keep Denise Prather quiet. Maybe they did kill her after all. But why would the uncle sacrifice one innocent nephew for the other two guilty ones. If it wasn't Eloy who made these deposits, who?

Whoever this generous benefactor was, he would have to have had Angie's account number. But if Jimmy were cooperating, he would have provided that number. And if a person made these deposits by mail . . . say by cashier's checks, there would be no way to trace them. But who other than Eloy would have had both this kind of money and knowledge of Jimmy's past?

After going around in a few more circles, nothing makes sense. So I give it a rest for a while and turn to the boxes from Irongate. In the top box are my clothes. In the box underneath are pens and markers and the debris of my now-stagnant murder investigation. On the table are heaps of mail that had apparently accumulated in the Prathers' cavernous mailbox. Propped against an armchair are the white boards I'd lugged up there to think on. Now that all the money has been reclaimed, this half-erased money map of red circles and blue arrows is as useless as faded school assignments found on the blackboard in the middle of August.

I swiftly dispatch the accumulated mail. A cluttered mound of advertising flyers and billing envelopes and occupant junk goes into the trash. An orderly stack of bankruptcy-related material is subdivided for further attention. I'm left, then, with four bulky envelopes that might actually be interesting.

I've been pessimistically optimistic about my chances of

receiving these envelopes since the day I talked to Ms. Prouse of the Federal Deposit Insurance Corporation. I'd asked her to send me documentation of the RTC's sales of the foreclosed properties to Prather-controlled companies. From our phone conversation, I already know the agency sold some of that property very cheaply to Prather. What I don't know is why.

Why would an agency of the United States government give this kind of preferential treatment to these particular private citizens? Were the properties truly so worthless or problematic that ten cents on the dollar was the best price the government could get? Apparently not, since the doctors in Prather's thrall were chomping at the bit to pay thirty cents for them. What, then? Who'd made such stupid decisions for us taxpayers anyway?

On the phone Ms. Prouse had explained, somewhat defensively, that in those days, the early nineties, all of the RTC compliance officers were making difficult decisions—in trying circumstances—as rapidly as possible.

"They were certainly well qualified, Ms. Donahue. Those jobs weren't given to just anybody off the streets, I assure you. The compliance officers were respected bankers and financial officers drawn from the private sector. And," she'd added, "they were paid quite well."

Could she identify the specific compliance officers who'd approved these particular purchases?

"Not without a lot more checking," she'd said wearily.

I'd badgered and whined and she'd mumbled about how much time it would take and I'd said I'd be willing to wait and I knew what a pain in the neck I was being and . . . please.

Ms. Prouse had reluctantly taken the Irongate address and said she'd see what she could do but that not to expect much because she couldn't work miracles. But Ms. Prouse was wrong. The contents of the envelopes before me are, indeed, miraculous. A person recently returned from a dead-end trip could hardly ask for a more promising new avenue.

From each envelope, I pull thick, meticulous documentation of every purchase I'd inquired about. There are: property appraisals, foreclosure consents, purchase offers, federal guidelines, and file-closure certifications signed by a compliance officer. For every one of these deals, the signature of the compliance officer is the same.

This compliance officer had been a mortgage banker of decent repute and a New Mexico resident familiar with commercial property values—an eminently reasonable choice for the RTC. His name, signed in a flourishing scroll at the bottom of each certification on the table before me is: *Eugene Saavedra*.

"My, my, my."

I'd like to talk this out. When will Max be back? I pace. I dial Frankie's number. It's Saturday. Her office is closed. I pace. I call St. Vincent's. A nurse tells me Angie had visitors for a few minutes but she's sleeping now. I try Patrick's number. When we said good-bye at JFK yesterday, I hadn't expected to be calling him again so soon.

"Couldn't bear a day without me, huh, Matilda? I'm flattered."

"I wanted to talk to somebody familiar with Alan's business practices."

"Less flattered."

"It turns out it was Gene Saavedra who was the RTC officer who approved your brother's funny business."

"How did you come upon this little tidbit?"

"And that's not all. Somebody has deposited a half million dollars into Angie's account."

"Matty, where the hell are you getting all this information from?"

"It doesn't matter. But you see what this could mean, don't you, Patrick? Saavedra had obviously been paid off to give his old friend a sweet deal. But then your brother's bankruptcy filings meant somebody would be going through Alan's financial records. Saavedra was in grave danger of having his fraud uncovered. And, as you know, there were no records of RTC transactions in Alan's files. Somebody must have taken them."

"Matty, hold on. Last week you were certain Alan was still

alive. Now this. When we found money in the Swiss account, I thought that was the end of all this crap."

"Crap? Did you hear me? *A half a million dollars!*"

"So, now you think Saavedra bribed Jimmy Abeyta to confess to murder?"

Max comes in with an armload of bags. He smiles at me and busies himself putting things away and pretends to ignore my conversation.

"Somebody did," I say to Patrick. "Of course I can't be sure it was Saavedra."

"And just how do you imagine Saavedra would have even known about Abeyta in the first place?"

"I don't know."

"And why would Saavedra want to kill Denise?"

"I don't know. I suppose it could have been Eloy who paid Jimmy off. I don't have all the answers yet."

"Look, Matty, Jimmy Abeyta confessed to killing my brother. That's the only answer there's ever going to be."

"You're wrong, Patrick. There are answers. I don't know yet whether they're in Jemez Springs or Taos but, either way, it's time for another little trip."

Max's head snaps up. He doesn't look happy.

Patrick explodes. "That's so goddamned stupid! This thing is *over*!" Then a long silence. "Forgive me, Matty"—I can almost hear him wrestling with his anger—"but I think you need to give your fevered brain a rest. Why don't you come out to Seattle, spend some time on the boat with me?"

When I don't answer, he presses. "Come on, Matty, it would be fun for you. We still have some unfinished business, as I recall."

With my eyes on Max, I say, "My unfinished business is here, Patrick."

Max is studying me as I set the phone down three minutes later.

"Where's Sam?" I ask him.

"Outside. We stopped to see his mother and he was very quiet. He hasn't said much since, but he's thinking things over." Max indicates the telephone. "So now you're going back to Taos and to Jemez Springs? To what?" His voice is shaking. "To confront possible murderers? Is that it? Is this"—he contemplates the ceiling—"really what you want to do with your life?"

"It's not my life, Max. This is just an isolated event in my life. A series of events, maybe, but—"

"You don't know how much I want to believe that. Help me."

His plea hangs in the air. What can I honestly promise him about my future, our future? I say the only thing I know is true. "I don't want to lose you, Max."

He closes his eyes. "You know, I thought maybe I'd already lost you. You went to Europe with another man. Now I come home and find you on the phone with him."

In spite of everything, a smile begins to spread across my face. "You're jealous?"

"I am."

"It's nice to know you're human."

"Mmmmm."

"But I guess that doesn't solve anything between us, does it?"

"No, it doesn't," he says sadly.

TWENTY-NINE

I WALK TO THE WINDOW AND WATCH SAM. HIS FEET DANGLE about a foot above the ground. His hands are folded neatly in his lap and his chin rests on his chest. Except for one foot swinging monotonously up and down, he is profoundly still.

"What I truly want to do," I tell Max, "is to take Sam away from all of this. Look at him out there. I want to see him writing his name in a rainbow of colors again. I think he's at some kind of crossroads. He could go . . . could end up like . . . Fat Boy . . . Chatto."

"Yes."

"He won't even talk to me. Why is he rejecting me?"

"For the moment, Sam seems to be rejecting females in general. He wouldn't talk to his mother this morning either. I think he may feel his choices might be limited to becoming a criminal or becoming a sissy. He says women try to boss him around."

"He told you that?"

"And he wants to know more about his father. He asked me what jail was like and if we could go visit his daddy."

"Christ."

"For what it's worth, I think his small attachment to me is healthy. It means he's looking for other male role models. It wouldn't hurt to let the two of us have some time together."

"I don't get it, Max. I thought you weren't willing to get involved; now, all of a sudden, you're wading in with both feet. Tell me this isn't all about being jealous of Patrick."

"The prospect of losing you hurt more than I could have imagined. But that isn't what this is about. You're in the middle of a crisis. I'm in love with you. I'm here. I know how to help. I've got no choice for now. We can deal with us when this mess is over."

"You're a saint. You know that?"

"I do."

"I'm sorry this is so hard on you." I look out at Sam again. "I know I can't spirit him away from his life. But, Max, if I'm right about Jimmy, I owe it to Sam to try to prove it."

Max is silent.

"Max, before we have to decide anything, give me time to finish this one case. Can you do that? I have new information—it's promising. Really, I—"

He grimaces at my enthusiasm but cuts me about one inch of slack. "You know, during our visit this morning, Angie talked some about that money. She said when it showed up in her account, she went out to the jail to visit Jimmy. Jimmy told her that Eloy wanted to make it right after all these years. He should have had insurance when Jimmy fell off that scaffold. That he'd always meant to pay for Jimmy's injuries."

"How tidy."

"Hello, Mr. Abeyta, this is Matty Donahue. Do you remember me?"

"Yes, of course. You are my nephew's *abogada*."

"Well, no, sir, I'm not Jimmy's lawyer anymore. Since Jimmy turned himself in, he won't even speak to me on the telephone. I understand he's representing himself now. Of course, you know about his confession, don't you?"

"*Sí, sí.* It is a great moral weight lifted from my nephew's shoulders. How can I help you, Ms. Donahue?"

"I'm sure that the money from you will help lighten his load."

Uncle Eloy doesn't miss a beat. "Yes," he agrees, "it is what I could do to help Jimmy's family. I should have paid that money for Jimmy's injury long ago. I should never have been without insurance. I have felt great shame about my negligence."

This stops me. Other options fade in light of Eloy's open acknowledgment of payment. But some impulse urges me toward one of those reckless leaps into a dry pool.

"It's a lot of money," I persist. "Very generous."

"It should have been even more. I would have given my life to make it up to Jimmy."

"Still, a hundred thousand dollars . . ."

The pause on the other end of line makes my heart quicken. ". . . Uh . . . yes, *sí. Es mucho dinero . . .*"

I don't push it. I change the subject. "Angie is in the hospital, Mr. Abeyta. She has a perforated ulcer."

"*Dios mío!* Does Jimmy know? Will she be all right? Where is Samuel?"

"I think she's going to be okay but she needs lots of rest. I have Sam for the time being. Since he won't take my calls, I thought perhaps you could let Jimmy know."

"Yes, *sí, sí.* But young Samuel must come to me."

My blood runs cold.

"I would have to object to that, Mr. Abeyta."

"I am Samuel's family, Señorita Donahue. I can come to pick him up instantly. Give me your address."

"I'll come to you, Mr. Abeyta, in Jemez Springs. I have to make a trip to Taos today anyway. It's no trouble for me to stop in Jemez Springs. I'll meet you in a public place—Los Ojos—in two hours. We can talk things over there."

"A bar is no place for a child, Miss."

"Los Ojos in two hours, Mr. Abeyta. And please come alone."

·   ·   ·

Hung from the rough-timbered walls of Los Ojos Bar are dusty animal heads, brittle skins, and rusty rifles. The interior is so dark that I have to stop inside the door to let my eyes adjust. The bar itself off to my left is straight out of an old western—each of the barstools is a huge ax-hewn Ponderosa log. At the rear of the murky interior, smoky cones of light funnel down over pool tables.

A game is in progress, and the guy with the cue is bent low, sighting his shot. His black hair is shorn close except for a small curly tail at the nape of his neck. The shooter's nose is mushed in the middle, giving him a malevolent Porky Pig look. Around the edges of the island of light, cowboys, bikers, and old hippies sip from longnecks and watch the play. To the rear, a lump of lard with long, black hair balances his butt across two chairs.

I stop well short of the pool tables to scan the bar and the high-backed wooden booths to my right. There he is, in the second booth: trim, muscular, and ramrod-straight. Eloy's collar is buttoned up to his acne-scarred chin, and his shirt-sleeves are pulled all the way down and buttoned at his thick wrists. His work-roughened hands are folded neatly on the table in front of him—much like his great-nephew's recent pose, I notice.

I slip into the booth so that I'm facing Eloy and can still keep an eye on the pool players in back. The waitress takes our order for two Coronas. Eloy waits until she has retreated before he speaks to me.

"Where is Samuel, Ms. Donahue. You were to have him with you."

"It's like you said, Mr. Abeyta; a bar isn't a good place to bring a child. But I see"—I let my eyes drift to the pool tables— "that you didn't come alone. The one with the cue—that would be Chatto?"

"If my nephews make you uncomfortable, Miss, I will ask them to leave."

"To the contrary, I like them where I can see them."

"Where is Samuel? Samuel should not be left with strangers at such a time as this."

"Angie's going to be spending some time in the hospital, Mr. Abeyta. She needs to have Sam near enough to visit. Sam needs that too."

Eloy twists his craggy carpenter's hands and gauges me through hooded eyes. Finally, his lips purse and he nods almost imperceptibly.

"The ulcers, they are very bad?"

"Very."

"Angela may not be able to work for some time. I will take care of them—take care of Jimmy's family."

"The money you gave them will do that, don't you think?"

He examines me but says nothing.

I say, "Five hundred thousand dollars . . . a lot of money."

"You said one hundred—"

"I lied to you, Mr. Abeyta."

"Why?" Outrage vies with curiosity. "Why would you do such a thing?!"

"To see if you knew the difference. To see if you'd pretend you did. And you did pretend, didn't you? So let me turn your question around. Why would *you* do such a thing?"

"I did. I . . ." He vacillates. "I did give Jimmy some money."

"You know, sir, I believe you probably did. For a while there, I thought maybe you really had paid off one nephew to protect the other two. But then you'd have known exactly how much had been deposited."

Eloy Abeyta looks away.

"You don't even know now, do you?"

A separate dining room is visible through an archway. Despite Eloy's assertion that a bar is no place for a child, whole families are sitting in the dining room talking and laughing and eating Famous-Jemez-burgers and homemade cherry pie.

Sam's great-uncle watches the children wistfully.

"Did Jimmy ask you to do this?" I ask Eloy. "To cover his lie?"

Eloy continues to stare silently at the families in the dining room.

"I think whoever paid Jimmy off is a murderer. If you know, please tell me. It's still not too late to help his family."

Eloy eyes me levelly. "Jimmy may be a better judge of how to help his family than you are, Miss."

"No, sir. I don't believe he is. I believe Jimmy's been terrified. Terrified that one day he'd be caught for killing Santiago. Terrified that, in spite of you, Chatto and Fat Boy might harm Sam. And Jimmy'd stopped believing that he was necessary to Sam and Angie. He'd let them down. And no matter what Angie said about their working together, she was proving, every day, that she could make her way in the world without him.

"I think that's the shape Jimmy was in emotionally. Then, all of a sudden, money—a fortune was added to that mix. And Jimmy decided to sacrifice his life. An instinct you'd probably understand, no?"

"If that were true, who are you to say my nephew is wrong?"

"Sam needs his father more than he needs a half million dollars. Please, Mr. Abeyta, I know you know something about this. Tell me what it is!"

"After she leaves the hospital, Angela will come up here with us. Samuel will be with his family."

"With you and Chatto and Fat Boy? I would die before I let Sam go into such a home."

For the first time, Eloy looks genuinely troubled. "You are wrong. My boys thought they were shooting at an empty pickup truck. It was long ago. A crime of half-man, half-boy. You yourself have forgiven Jimmy for this. Why not my other boys? Ernesto and Chatto have repented. They do penance, they—"

"No, sir." I say it sharply. "Your nephews are stone killers." I sense tension and sudden movement from the pool tables, but I continue speaking directly to Eloy. "Or they would be if either one of them were halfway competent. The day after you and I first met, Chatto and Fat Boy tried to kill me and my friend."

"DO NOT SAY THOSE WORDS TO ME. THOSE WORDS ARE LIES!"

At the sound of Eloy's furious voice, two men move across

the room toward us. Eloy glares across the table at me as I proceed to tell him what I've suspected all along.

"That day in the trailer, Mr. Abeyta, I made a wild threat against your nephews. You must have told those two I'd threatened to turn them over to the police. Didn't you? The next morning they must have followed us to the hot springs."

"LIES! If you believed such a thing, you would have gone to the police, there would have been charges—"

"I couldn't prove it, and—"

"Exactly. You couldn't prove anything. You make reckless charges."

"—and I would've had to say why I suspected your nephews. And that would've implicated them in the Santiago shooting. And *that* would've betrayed Jimmy and endangered Sam's life. I could no more lead the police to these two"—I hook my thumb at the two men—"than I could put a gun to Sam's head."

The one with the flattened nose stands at our table. His cousin lumbers a few paces behind.

"You did tell them about the threat I'd made. Didn't you, Eloy?"

Silence.

I look up into the two young faces, then back at the horror creeping into the weathered face across from me.

"So they had a very good motive to kill me."

"She's a fucking liar, *Tío*." The voice is tight with fury.

"There was a witness, sir," I continue evenly. "Unfortunately, he couldn't describe the car. And he didn't get a good look at either of the men that morning. He couldn't see the driver at all."

"See, *Tío*, this is just some *gringa puta* shit. She don't know nothing."

"The witness did say one thing about the man who ran down the hill and jumped into the car though. He said the man had a kind of mashed-in nose."

The first nephew takes a step backward.

"*Chatto.*" I roll the name around on my tongue as I stare at its owner. Chatto pivots away. He stiff-arms his cousin until the fat one begins to move too. We watch them make their way to the door and, when they've gone out it, I turn back to Eloy.

"The Spanish dictionary," I continue, says *chatto* means 'snout.' I'll bet your nephew's had that nickname since he was little."

"You are not going to the police with your suspicions?"

"I've told you why I can't."

The face across from me is as sad as any face I've seen on another human being. "This is maybe a trick? You don't know those boys."

"Mr. Abeyta, whatever you choose to believe about your other nephews, don't let it blind you to what's best for Jimmy and Sam. Do you know who gave Jimmy the half million dollars? You must know something. You knew enough to lie for him."

Eloy grips the end of the table and slowly pulls himself out of the booth. I watch him until he's out the door. When the waitress brings our beers, I drink both of them down slowly and try to think where to go from here. Eventually, I order a Famous-Jemez-burger myself and then pie and a cup of coffee. It's late by the time I leave the bar. Families and even pool players are long gone.

It's been raining and the steeply pitched parking lot is nearly empty. Lights are aimed at a giant mural of hard-drinking cowboys painted on the side of the building. But the rain battens the light down and holds it close to the wall. I slog through the mud and broken asphalt up to my Toyota and slip my key into the door lock.

The key isn't necessary. My car is unlocked.

The hands around my neck pull me forward and down into the car. Fingers dig into my throat and strangle my scream. I'm dragged headfirst across the driver's seat until my face is in a lap that smells like Levis and unwashed crotch.

"Drag her ass in here! Now hold her still!" The voice is Chatto's.

From over the backseat comes heavy grunting and fat

hands grabbing at my legs—pulling them forward until my back is near to breaking.

"Shit, man! This fucking little car." The other voice.

I twist and contract and help my captors so they won't accidentally break me into pieces.

"Get her keys! We got to get out of here fast."

I feel my shoe slip off. My ribs grind against the gear-shift lever.

"Hurry," Chatto orders.

The car door slams hard on my ankle and I scream from the pain of it.

"Shut her up!"

. . . I think I've probably been unconscious for only a few seconds, because I'm still in my own car but upright now in the passenger seat. Chatto is in the driver's seat with my key in the ignition. Fat Boy is still behind us. His arms pin me hard against the seat.

"Where are we taking her, *carnal*?"

"Where nobody will ever look," Chatto says as he turns the engine over.

"Ella es muerte."

With all the strength I can summon, I swing my clasped hands blindly backward toward Fat Boy's cheek. I connect and immediately lean forward and pull at the door handle until I hear it pop. At the same time, I kick out at Chatto until his hand falls away from the key.

But the seconds gained are expensive. Chatto uses his freed hand to savagely twist my injured ankle. I feel my body go slack as Fat Boy tightens his grip around my throat.

THIRTY

—◦◦◦—

A CLICK! A CREAK! THE DOOR SWINGS OPEN—WET AIR whips through the car. Instantly, Chatto's fingers release their grip on my leg. His head and shoulders are yanked away—toward the open door. The slab of arm around my neck loosens as Fat Boy shifts to help his cousin.

"*Tío!* Shit, man!"

Free to move again, I reach my right hand down to the lever at the side of my seat and pull for all I'm worth. The seat shoots backward and the crunch of the seat pinning Fat Boy's legs is satisfying. I turn in time to see his arms flail like a windmill. He'd lowered the rear seat-backs in order to accommodated his girth, so now there is nothing to stop him from falling backward except his pinned legs. He flops sideways like a beached whale and I scramble out of the car and around to the other side, where Eloy Abeyta is pulling his second nephew headfirst out and down into the mud.

"Fucking son of a bitch, let me go, *viejo!*" Chatto's torso is twisting in the muck.

However much the odds have changed in the past seconds, they aren't likely to stay this way without help. Eloy may be wiry and he may be strong, but he's not young. I desperately scan the rainswept parking lot. Eloy must have parked somewhere; his nephews must have parked somewhere . . . but the nearest cars are way down there on the street. I need a weapon: a rock, a stick . . . anything. Upholstery tears and metal crunches as the whale in my backseat tears the living hell out of my car. There isn't much time.

The top of the hill is closer than the bottom. I head that way. I slip and my ankle explodes in pain. I fall, crawl through the ooze, get my footing again, and slip again. I advance like a snail through the pounding downpour and the pain until I reach the top of the lot. There, parked behind the bar, is a pickup truck loaded with construction materials. I use it to steady myself and make my way around the side to the door handle.

Shit!

Not this time. Can't be so lucky twice. I flatten myself against the locked door and inch back to the truck bed. I scrabble to free a two-by-four as long as me from the stack and start lugging it behind me as I slide and fall my way back down to my car. Eloy is on the ground now, and Chatto is on top of him with a forearm braced against the old man's throat. In his other hand a knife is held high.

Another second will be too late. I stand unsteadily and use my last scrap of strength to lift the board and swing— knowing that the swing will take me with it. I won't be able to keep my balance and so, if I miss my target, this old man and I are done for.

The solid crack is like the sound of a bat hitting a home run in Wrigley Field. Chatto's head doesn't exactly go flying into the bleachers, but the knife slides from his hand, and he slumps. I'm sprawled on the ground and Eloy struggles for the two-by-four, grabs it, and scrambles to his feet, holding the board in his hands like a broadsword. He begins swinging it slowly back and forth. Fat Boy, who is finally freed, stops in his tracks.

"Tío . . . !"

WHACK!

"*Por favor, Tío.*" Fat Boy crosses his arms in front of his face. "*Tío, no!*"

WHACK!

Eloy's shirt is soaked and mudstained. The old man braces himself and swings again ... and again.

Over the rain, I can hear Eloy Abeyta's sobs as he pummels his hideous and beloved nephews. Both of them are on the ground now, beyond doing anyone harm for a long time to come. Yet Eloy won't stop. The swinging is steady and unrelenting. They will die here unless something is done.

Even if I could stop him, do I want to? Letting these two ruined souls die here in the muck on this rainy night doesn't immediately strike me as a bad thing.

But I pull myself up. Chatto's smashed face is so bloody that the red-black flow is visible even in the darkness even through the mud. Fat Boy's breath is coming in ragged gurgles. Eloy will be a murderer soon.

"You've got to stop!"

His head turns toward me reluctantly, the board in his hands raised for another crack.

"You can still help Jimmy," I say, keeping my voice steady. I point at his brothers' sons on the ground. "Even they can help Jimmy if they're alive to testify ... Eloy, if you don't stop this now, you will never see Sam again."

Eloy rides with me to the shabby little police station. My statement to Officer Leyba takes a long time. During it all, Eloy sits silently by my side in a metal folding chair, seeming not to listen or care.

Leyba had been leaving the station as we drove up, putting the key in the lock and calling it a night. Two hours later, the room is alive with activity as the JSPD works out the logistics of what is, for Jemez Springs, a crime wave.

Should they use the village ambulance without chains or irons to transport dangerous prisoners? Apparently, even the rear doors don't lock. It is a problem. The one named Jake is wearing a pajama shirt. Jake has been manning the phones—

well, the phone anyway. He calls Taos and Albuquerque and Santa Fe and, long after midnight, finally gets someone in Santa Fe to agree to dispatch an ambulance with special security.

Now the lot of them have left for Los Ojos Bar to supervise or help or interfere with the transfer of prisoners. Officer Leyba is shaking his head at me. He pulls at his nonexistent beard.

"We haven't had but one violent assault up here in the past year. And here you are—a victim twice in one month. You must admit, it's not your regular thing." Leyba's voice purrs amiable wariness. I've explained everything to him: how Chatto and Fat Boy attacked me; how Eloy saved my life; everything.

Eloy says nothing, merely nods in confirmation when asked a direct question. His posture is rigid, his hands are folded, his eyes stare blindly at a blank wall. From time to time tears roll down his face.

I tell Leyba that I'm sure Chatto and Fat Boy are the ones responsible for my last assault. There's no longer a reason to keep this information to myself. Eloy hears but doesn't protest. The officer wants to know the full names of the cousins and I supply *Ernesto* from memory. But I confess I don't know Chatto's real name.

Leyba points to the ringing phone on Jake's desk. "I need to take that." After he talks for a few seconds, he excuses himself and leaves. One by one, everyone has drifted off to bed or to the bar. Eloy and I are alone in the room again for a long time. The rain has stopped.

"Jesús."

"What?"

"Chatto's name," says Eloy. "My brother's wife named him Jesús."

"Oh."

"Now they are all dead or in prison: Jimmy and Ernesto and Jesús and Miguel and Raymond . . ."

"Not all," I say, ". . . not you."

"We are a star-crossed family."

"Not Sam."

"Not yet."

"Genes aren't destiny."

"*Sí*, I used to think the same." His tears have cut deltas through the dried mud on his face. "But no more. I have tried with these boys. I brought them to God's door and they pretended"—he gives a bitter little laugh—"pretended to pray and ask forgiveness. *Dios mío*, it was a lie, all of it. They were bad boys and they became bad men. Born to it."

"No."

He looks me in the eye. "If not, then it is I who failed them."

"Eloy, I don't know when it becomes too late to save a human being. I do know the damage done early to a child is deep; it etches like acid into the soft new soul. But some people survive even the deepest wounds."

He shows no sign of hearing.

"Your brothers and you and your nephews were wounded early. All of you. Yet, somehow you managed to heal. And Jimmy still has some chance to come out of this whole."

He says nothing.

"And if he does, Sam will have a very good chance."

Nothing.

We sit in more silence. Leyba returns a few more times during the night. I fall asleep in my chair and wake fitfully. At dawn, I open my eyes and Eloy is sitting as he was when I closed them—ramrod-straight and staring.

"Did you know that Sam has begun to sit just like that?" I ask him.

Eloy shows the barest trace of a smile.

Jake, still in pajama top, opens the door with one hand. A box with steaming coffee and doughnuts is in the other.

"Captain says to apologize for leaving you here so long. We got everything we need now. You can go if you want. Thought you might like some refreshment first. You can use the bathroom to clean up." He looks at our grime and scolds, "I figured you would have already done that by now."

There is something about Jake in his PJ's taking issue with

our personal hygiene that breaks me up. I giggle, then laugh, and pretty soon I'm laughing so hard, I'm whimpering.

"Here, here, now," says Jake.

Eloy comes to me and rests his hand on my shoulders, and instantly, my laughing jag turns into a crying jag and Jake says "here, here" while Eloy pats my shoulder.

He stands there on the pavement as I push my mushy front seat back sloppily into its moorings. When I settle myself, I look out the window at him. He's still filthy. He looks a couple of decades older than when I first saw him framed by the trailer door so few weeks ago.

"Well," I say.

Eloy nods.

"Good-bye, then," I say.

"There was a man," he says.

"What?"

"A man came to see Jimmy one night and three or four days later he turned himself in. The two of them talked in the trailer for many hours. The morning after, Jimmy told me he was going to come into some money and he would need my help to explain it away.

" 'Could you just tell them you gave it to me, *Tío*?' he asked me. He told me this masquerade would protect him if anyone ever asked questions about the money. Probably no one would ever ask, but if they did, would I just tell this one little lie?"

"Did anyone ask?"

"Only you, Señorita."

"Thank you, Eloy. Thank you for telling me. It'll help. I hope it will anyway."

"I try to do the right thing."

"Me too."

THIRTY-ONE

As I drive again through the Jemez Mountains in the dawning light, Max is on my mind. We last made love here on just such a morning—moments before we nearly died. This morning, with my body once again bruised and aching, it's hard not to hear his voice in my brain.

"Other than rational."

I roll the phrase around on my tongue. I actually think I have a rational, even a logical, core. But I must admit, little black cloves of insanity are studded thickly over the surface of my life.

The moment the sun clears the top of the black peaks to my right, Sunday-school-prayer-card shafts of light radiate across the highway, and a soft golden glow moves slowly down the cliff face on my left. I open my window to the smell of cool, damp pine. To me, all of creation seems at least as irrational as it is rational. Seems to have more to do with integrating and disintegrating and reintegrating patterns than with linear processes.

And when you think of it, Max isn't really so taken with rationality himself. How rational, for instance, is it for him to be baby-sitting—and bonding—with Sam? How rational for him to love me?

As a particularly golden day begins, I drop my hand under the seat for the car phone. Pulled from its berth during last night's mayhem. I locate a spiral of cord, fish it out, and plug it into the cigarette lighter. I'm suddenly eager to hear his voice, impatient to share my life.

"Umph, yeah?"

"Good morning, sweetheart."

"What time ... is it?"

"About six, I think. My watch got broken last night. I've been thinking about you. Guess maybe I should have waited until later, huh?"

"Where are you?"

"In the car. In the Jemez mountains—" I begin the story of the night before, but as soon as I get to the dicey part—

"No, Matty, don't!"

"Huh?"

"I can't hear it now. Listening to how you got beaten up in the middle of the night will only make me crazy all over again. I already want to yell at you. I want to tell you to get your ass out of harm's way right now. Come home and stay here!"

Silence.

"Goddamn it! You just can't *tell* me about this stuff. You understand?"

"Sure."

"Look, Matty, I said I wouldn't push you until this latest thing was over, so I won't. But, please ... don't push *me* right now either. Okay?"

"Sure."

"How about this? You can tell me every detail ... later ... when it's over. And then we can talk seriously about where we go from here."

"Sure."

"I'm sorry."

"How's Sam? How are you two guys doing together?"

Max gives a soft, relieved laugh. "We're on an adventure.

I'm teaching Sam how to cuss. His favorite word so far is 'crap.' "

"And this is a good thing, Doctor?"

"It's what's working at the moment. He's been expressing himself pretty thoroughly with his new vocabulary. My chairs are 'too damn high,' and how the 'hell' do I expect him to 'eat this crap?' "

"Swell."

"I took him over to your house yesterday. Thought I'd have a go at cleaning your place up before you came home. Sam spent most of the day in your hammock."

"Oh . . . Max. Is he going to be all right?"

"If things don't get worse . . . if he gets enough support . . ."

My second call is to Daniel Baca's home number. If Eloy wasn't Jimmy's benefactor, it's time to look at the other possibility. The detective's voice is as crisp and efficient as if it were ten A.M. I get a mental picture of him sitting in his ironed jeans and sport coat, eating scrambled eggs and green chili without spilling a crumb.

"I'm glad you called," he says. "I've already spoken to Leyba."

"What? Surely you haven't even been to the station yet this morning."

"I was on last night when the Jemez Springs department was looking for hospital security for Ernesto and Jesús Abeyta. Leyba thought I might like to be personally informed about your second little skirmish in his jurisdiction. Have you heard the latest?"

"Tell me."

"The cousins made a half-assed confession about everything."

"Big whoopee. They were caught on the scene."

"No, no! I mean everything!"

"You mean the attack at the hot springs?"

"Right. So far, Jesús Abeyta says he only climbed the rocks above the springs so he could see you naked. The slide was accidental. And the other one says he don't know nothing because he just drove the car. I know it's bullshit, excuse my language, but as soon as we get the doc's okay for more questioning, we'll get the whole story. Don't worry. With that, plus last night, those boys are going away for a long time."

"I'm glad for that, at least."

"It sounds like you had a hell of a night, Matty. How did you and one old man manage to do so much damage? And what were you doing up there anyway?"

Ahh . . . the invitation to share. Unfortunately, it's coming from the wrong person. And I have no enthusiasm for telling Daniel that I've reached yet another dead-end.

"Daniel, the reason for my call . . . I have evidence that Jimmy Abeyta made a false confession. His uncle says a man, a stranger, deposited money into Jimmy's wife's account just days before Jimmy confessed to the Prather murders."

"*What?*"

"But the uncle says he won't repeat that to anyone. If anybody asks, he'll claim he gave the money to Jimmy himself."

"Can you get me some proof the deposit *wasn't* made by the uncle?"

"No. But I've learned that Gene Saavedra had motive to kill Alan, which would mean he had motive to bribe Jimmy and—"

"Stop it! Just what do you expect me to do with this speculation, Matty?"

I've reached the Y in the road and I brake to a stop. The man asks a good question. What *can* I expect him to do? From this Y, I can turn right, toward Santa Fe and home, or I can turn left and head up the canyon toward Taos. *Nothing* is what I can expect. Detective Daniel Baca is no more free to act on my hunch than I am to ignore it.

I turn the steering wheel to the left and move my toe from the brake to the accelerator.

THIRTY-TWO

———❧❧❧———

FROM THE RAGGED LOOK OF THE SOUTH MEADOW, I'D guess the kid with the yellow earphones hasn't been here for a while. And no sign of life in the front garden either . . . or on the walkway. But as I open the car door, I hear the beat of the once-ubiquitous "Macarena." As I approach the front door, the sound is nearly deafening. I knock . . . no answer . . . knock again . . . nudge the door forward . . .

". . . Hello? Ms. Moreno?"

An army invading through the front door wouldn't be heard over this music. I step painfully down the hallway, favoring my ankle, and calling as I go.

". . . Ms. Moreno? . . . Hello? . . . Gencie?"

I might as well be whispering. The pounding beat is thunderous as I enter the living room. My heart is pumping fast, and God knows what I was expecting to find. But it sure wasn't the sight before me now.

Gencie's plump, wobbly knees are encased in black spandex tights; on top, she's wearing a baggy gray sweatshirt with the neck and arms cut out. She's facing away from me, breathing hard and moving rapidly up on and down off an exercise step about one stride behind the *macarena* beat. Her arms jiggle and wave and hug her shoulders and slap her thighs. On the big-screen television at the end of the room, eight similarly clad women make the same moves with considerably more grace. The average age of the gang on TV looks to be around nineteen.

There is no sign of husband or son. I watch mesmerized as Gencie's fleshy thighs quiver; I can't bring myself to interrupt. The living room furniture has been pushed to the edges of the room; the rug has been rolled and dumped over the couch arm. Three cheap mirrors are precariously balanced on chairs in a kind of poor-girl's imitation of a ballet-studio wall. In a far corner, a minicam is set up on a tripod; in the middle of the floor a treadmill, and next to that a stationary bike. On a table next to the door is a stack of videotapes. I pick up the tapes. Jane Fonda . . . Richard Simmons . . . Raquel Welch . . . Crunch and Grunge.

Gencie spies me in her mirrors and instantly lurches off her exercise step. She punches a button on the VCR, points at me, and yells.

"WHAT HAPPENED TO YOU?"

Since I could well have asked the same question of her, it takes me a second to understand what she means. I move to the mirror and take a gander.

"Oooo, ouch!"

Dry red earth clings to my hair in Rasta-man lumps. Smears of the stuff decorate my face and clothes. Guess I should have taken Jake up on his offer to wash.

"Sorry—I didn't realize I looked so bad."

"Ms. Donahue, what are you doing here? How did you get in?"

"Is your husband here?"

"No." She dabs at her face and neck with a pink towel. "Gene's gone for good."

"Ah . . . well. I think you're the one I need to talk to anyway. Is this a good time?"

"It's an okay time." She eyes me uncertainly. "What do you want?"

Answers. I want answers. But I'm looking over her shoulder at my reflection. I look almost as tired and tattered as I feel.

"Do you suppose I could have a bath?" I ask.

She looks startled, then reaches her fingers out toward my face and touches me lightly.... "Blood," she says.

"Could be, I guess."

"You poor girl! Come on, follow me."

I follow her to a bathroom that is floor-to-ceiling Mexican tiles behind open shelves of fluffy towels. The room smells of lemon soap.

"I'm afraid you'll have to make do with a shower, dear. Here, give me those clothes and we'll see what we can do with them."

"Thank you, Mrs. Saavedra."

"Gencie. It's Gencie Moreno, remember."

"Sorry. Thank you, Ms. Moreno."

"You'll be wanting a bed too, from the look of you."

"I have some questions. I came here to ask . . ."

"Rest first. Questions after."

When I awaken at dusk in yet another strange bed, I think that it won't be long until I sleep in my own again. One way or another, this odyssey is near to ending. Even now, loose ends are being bundled up in tidy little packets: The Prather creditors are satisfied that their money has been recovered and will soon be distributed; Chatto and Fat Boy will serve time for both of their assaults. But, without some major break, Jimmy will likely spend the rest of his days in prison, where his son can visit him on visitors' days until one of them is dead.

This bedroom is tranquil. Shafts of sunlight illuminate dust motes, and I watch the golden flecks swirl and dance. How could Saavedra even have known that Jimmy Abeyta existed? How could the man who lived here have known so much about Jimmy's past crimes and present needs that he could tug exactly the right strings to move Jimmy around the stage?

I find my laundered clothes, which Gencie has left folded at the foot of my bed while I slept. I pull the jeans on slow and easy over my swollen ankle. How much will Gencie tell me about her absconded husband? If he really has absconded.

As I move down the hall, I try to think how to approach her psychologically, but when I near the kitchen, I can hear her talking to someone and, instantly, I feel an adrenaline rush. Who's in there with her? I approach slowly . . . hear only the one voice . . . peek in. She's talking all right, but she's all by herself. "This is me," she's saying to the corner of the room. One or the other of us is wacko.

"This is how I am right now," she continues. "As you see, I'm not like Jane and I'm not like Raquel. But, maybe, I'm like some of you. You be the judge." She holds her arms wide, inviting the unseen audience to behold her ample flab.

"With these videos, you can watch my progress day by day. See for yourself whether my problems and answers match anything in your own life. Okay, let's get started. The dinner I'm preparing tonight will be . . ."

She moves out of my line of sight and I edge farther into the room. She's moved the tripod here into her kitchen and she's aimed the camera at a pile of carrots on a cutting board.

"This," she says, smiling over her shoulder to the camera, "is . . . oh, Ms. Donahue. Just a minute while I turn this off . . . Sorry, I didn't know you were up. I just started taping. I can do it all over again after we eat. It won't be as authentic but—"

"No, no, please, don't let me get in your way. I'll just go into the other room or . . . maybe I could sit in here . . . out of camera range until you finish your . . . uh . . ."

"Segment. I'm going to be doing five segments every day. One or two at mealtimes, either preparing or eating slowly, you know, taking time to savor each bite, like they tell you. Then one segment every other day—shopping for fresh ingredients. Everything everybody always says to do. Well, I'm going to do it—nothing fancy—just low-fat, fresh, nutritious food, plenty of exercise, and all the tricks: Write down what you eat, chew slowly, you know."

"You're making your own diet-and-exercise video? For sale?"

"The video segments will follow my progress from the first day, which was day before yesterday. My goal is seventy-five pounds. But the real test is inches. Inches and strength."

"There are quite a few of those kind of tapes around," I say dubiously.

"But you see who's in them, don't you? Skinny people. Young people. People who don't look at all like the women at home watching them. Maybe some of the diet gurus were fat once, but we didn't see them then. We just have to take their word for it. "But me! I'm just like every fat woman who ever lived. Worse off than a lot of them. I'm overweight and out of shape and not young and my husband just dumped me and my son didn't want to be left behind, so here I am alone, with about enough money to last a year. No job skills . . . well, you see how it is. *Nobody's* going to feel inferior to me. If I can do this, anybody can do this. Right?"

"Uh . . . well, it's . . . ambitious. How did you come up with the idea?"

"You know, I watched *Oprah* all the way through her first diet and then the failure and then the second and I thought maybe I could do that too. But, you know, she's rich and famous and has her own chef and her own personal trainer. I wanted to do a kind of every-woman version. There for a couple of years I talked all the time about doing it. Gene always said it was stupid and I'd fail and I couldn't afford any help and I didn't even know how to use a camera and even if I ended up making some kind of tape or other, if I tried to sell it, it would just end up humiliating me. I know he meant that it would humiliate *him*. Anyway, I just kind of lost heart."

I take a stool at the counter and watch her cut the carrots, thinking how routine her past failure was and how singular— not to say peculiar—her new solution.

"Happens to lots of people," I say, "big ideas, not much follow-through."

"Exactly. After Gene left me, I started to throw all his junk away. I found that camera in his office. You know, in all the time he had that damn camera, he never even took one picture of our family. I messed around with the camera all that day. When I got the hang of it, I turned it on and sat in front of it and just talked. 'Well,' I said to it, 'there you are. What are you going to do with yourself?' Talking to the camera was as easy as talking to myself, which I do all the time anyway. I decided to go back to my old idea."

"To turn your problem into a business."

"Gene took almost all our money, so I had to find some kind of way to make a living. I only ever had the one idea for a business of my own. I couldn't stop thinking about it. I'd wake up every hour at night thinking where to put the exercise equipment, how to market the videos—"

"It's an awesome undertaking, Gencie." I try to keep my misgivings from spilling out all over her enthusiasm. As a lawyer for people who keep business records in the trunk of their car, I'm all too familiar with the mortality rate of start-up businesses. Eighty-five percent of all of them fail within two years.

"I can start all over again. People like me can start over again. Don't you think so?"

Who am I to rain on her parade? "I know a little about starting over again," I say. "I'm on my third or fourth try myself."

"I could tell that about you when I first met you. And you're making a go of it, aren't you?"

I study her earnest frown. This life-business of failing and getting second chances and taking those chances or not taking them and getting third chances . . . the unresolvable question of how many chances a person gets in one lifetime makes its familiar journey through my brain. Is it ever too late? Isn't Gencie's question but another form of Eloy's struggle for his nephews or mine for Jimmy, or for Sam, or for myself?

"What's for dinner?" I ask.

Turns out, what's for dinner is tofu and carrots and brown rice and fresh plums. The camera is turned back on now, aimed at Gencie's plate. She keeps up a running commentary as we eat. As we wash up the plates, after the *segment*, she tells me about her husband's departure.

"He said you were probably not the last one who was going to be interested in his business with Alan. He told me I could come with him if I wanted to, but it was pretty clear he'd just as soon I didn't."

"I'm sorry."

"I take a little walk around the property every evening," she says. "Want to come along?"

The moon is full and low on the horizon. She walks and I limp down the rutted driveway and back again before I say what's been on my mind.

"Gencie, I don't think Denise Prather ever told you that one of her patients had threatened her."

"Oh."

"From what I've seen of you, lying doesn't come easy."

"Huh-uh . . ."

We make two more silent laps in the moonlight before I try again. "What did Denise really say?"

Big, deep sigh. "Matty, she was so bad off when I got there I had to do something right away. So I called nine one one, and they said call Social Services, and so I called Social Services and they said they'd send somebody. I tried to clean her up and get some water into her, make her more comfortable. She kept falling asleep. She'd wake up all of a sudden and try to talk, then fall away again. I was fixing her covers and the Social Service people were already at the door when she said it . . . I guess you'd want her exact words."

"Please."

" 'He's going to kill us.' "

"That's it?"

" 'He's going to kill us.' That's all she said."

"Did you ask her who she meant? Who was going to kill? Who was going to be killed?"

"By then the Social Services ladies were there in the room with us. I was upset and I just blurted out to the ladies what Denise had said. One of them asked her what was she talking about, and Denise opened her mouth a couple of times. But she gave up without saying more. The ladies acted like they didn't believe she'd even said anything. They treated me like I was some silly twit. I didn't say anything more after that either."

"But you thought you knew."

"I just naturally assumed she meant her and Alan. Somebody was going to kill her and Alan."

"And you thought you knew who that *somebody* was too, didn't you?"

She nods in the moonlight, but she doesn't offer the name.

"Why did you think it was your own husband who had threatened them?"

"Because ... Gene was the one who'd sent me to that house that day. I was to get some financial records that Alan was supposed to have all boxed up and ready for him. Alan wasn't there when I arrived, but there was this box on the front porch with Gene's name on it. It was like both of them were trying to avoid each other. Gene had been going crazy since Alan filed his bankruptcies."

"I'm sure he had been," I say. "Gene approved sales of foreclosed properties to Alan for only a third of what they were really worth. That was what he wanted to keep hidden, wasn't it?"

"Gene was obsessed about getting those records out of Alan's hands. I'd heard him screaming to Alan on the phone about it.

"Then, one morning, Gene tells me to go to Santa Fe to get the records. I told him, why don't you go yourself? But he said he didn't trust himself in the same house with Alan. He told me just shut up and go! I did what Gene said, like always."

None of this surprises me. But it still leaves a lot of unanswered questions. We've made our way back to the house and into the living room. I flop against the rolled rug on the couch and watch her do slow, awkward stretching exercises in front of her three mirrors.

"Why make up that lie about Denise's patient, Gencie? Why try to get someone else in trouble?"

"Later, after Denise and Alan died in the explosion, Detective Baca called me. You know, because of my call to nine one one and my name was with the Social Service ladies. Even if they did think I was a twit, they must have told the detective what I'd blurted out, because he asked me who I thought Denise meant when she'd said, 'He's going to kill us.' "

"And so you lied to protect Gene?"

"Well, I knew Gene hadn't really killed those people. I didn't even know for positive if he'd been the one who made the threat. So I sure wasn't going to implicate him."

"Why not just say you didn't know who Denise meant? Why make up a threat from a patient?"

"Gene was still beside himself with worry that somebody might still find out about the RTC thing. What if I was the one to point the police to Gene. He would have left me for sure even if he didn't go to jail. I just wanted to turn suspicion away from Gene."

"But you put an innocent person in jeopardy!"

"But it didn't seem like what I said could hurt anybody. How would anybody know which patient Denise meant? If a patient hadn't really threatened her, nothing would ever come of it. But, maybe it *was* a patient she was talking about that day. I knew a little about Denise's practice from our talks at the country club in the old days. You know, her being alone with criminals—listening to their secrets and such. It just always seemed so dangerous to me. I knew Gene hadn't killed anybody, but they were dead, so somebody had. And so I naturally thought about those patients of hers, the criminals. So, when the detective asked me, I just said it. That's all."

"Wait a minute," I say, pressing harder.

Please don't let this be yet another dead-end.

"Wait. If you believe it may have been Gene who threatened Alan and Denise Prather, why are you so certain Gene didn't kill them?"

She looks at her mirrors, watching me.

"Because," she says, "they were killed on the first Saturday in April."

"So?"

"Gene and I make love . . . used to make love . . . on the first Saturday of every month. He always slept in my room on those nights and I used to stay awake after. I liked to watch him when he was asleep. That's when I could pretend, you know, that things were different."

"Gene was with you the whole night? The explosion was very late—near midnight. Are you sure?"

"Matty, on the night of Saturday, April fourth, even as late as midnight, I was watching my husband snore."

THIRTY-THREE

—❧—

"This tastes like crap." He shoves the plate away with the back of his hand.

"Good. At least now you're talking." I nudge the plate back. "But it doesn't either taste like crap. Chocolate cake is your favorite, and I spent all morning making the damn thing."

His arms are folded stiffly across his chest.

"Come on, Sambo, please . . ."

"Don't. Call. Me. Sambo."

This is an improvement. When Max first brought him over, Sam would neither speak to nor look at me. My own depression at reaching a third dead-end felt impenetrable. Max said Sam and I needed time by ourselves to get reacquainted. So he left us alone last night without a word of warning or advice.

Sam sat like a stone throughout the evening, averting his head at my unenthusiastic suggestions of games or stories. At bedtime, I tried to help him get undressed: He socked me and ran for my closet. I tossed a pillow and blanket in at him and turned on my bedside TV to give him company. He didn't come out of the closet all night. What's to become of this child now? By the first grade, he'll be known as a killer's son. This morning, he'd peed on himself again.

So this chat about how crappy my chocolate cake is and what I can or can't call him seems a step in the right direction. I decide to put my own dismal failures on a shelf and give myself this day with the kid.

"I was thinking"—I'm shamelessly pulling out all the stops—"there's a sign down the road about puppies for sale. Boxers, I think they are."

He flicks his eyes at and away from me.

"I mean, I know you lost your dog recently."

"No. I didn't."

"Oh, I thought . . . I thought . . . you said somebody shot your dog."

"I *never* had a dog." His tone dares me to contradict him.

I limp around, tidying the kitchen, leaving the chocolate cake within his reach. He doesn't take the bait. I sit at the table doing elaborate versions of "Here's the church, and here's the steeple." He ignores me. I bring the duffel bag Max has left for Sam into the kitchen and unzip it.

"Max says you guys went shopping. Mind if I take a look?"

Sam isn't in an answering mood.

I pull out a brand-new pair of shorts and a shirt and a package of underwear.

"Okay if I take the tags off?" He is deaf and blind. I leave his new clothes folded on the table along with a washcloth and a new bar of soap.

My living room is really just the other end of my kitchen, but moving six feet away allows us to pretend we are apart. I plop into an old, familiar chair and the instant I do so, I'm aware all over again of how much I've missed this place, my place. Max has been a wonder here at the Canyon Road house too. While I was up the mountain playing his least favorite game of private eye, he has outdone himself. Not only has he played baby-sitter and child psychologist for two days, he's been housekeeper too. Angie had completed the construction itself, but the mess of sawdust and paint splatters and dirt would have been awful to come home to. Max hired someone to clean walls and wash floors and polish windows and move the furniture back into place.

This morning, he had flowers delivered.

My new "office" and the rental house are still empty, but my little loft apartment is a wonderfully improved version of its former self. A bathroom, big enough for an elf, has been added to the utility closet downstairs. The ceiling of the kitchen/living room on the ground floor has been raised to the height of the loft ceiling. Sunlight from above pours across into the bedroom and down onto the adobe walls and brick floors of the lower floor. At this moment it bathes my new floral arrangement.

"Did you help Max pick out these flowers?"

No answer.

"They're pretty . . . don't you think so?"

Silence.

"Anyway," I persist blithely, "I'm going to get dressed now and go down the street to look at those boxer puppies. If you want to go with me, put those clothes on."

By force of will I keep my eyes off him. As I climb the stairs, I call back, "You can use the new bathroom to clean up if you decide to come."

I shower and dress slowly, giving Himself down there time to stew in his juices and make up his mind. When I do finally make my way down the stairs, I have to contain myself. There he sits at the end of the couch, face scrubbed, hair wetted down, new shirt stuffed into new shorts. The shorts are on backwards, but what the hell. He doesn't look at me, so I don't look at him as I pass on my way to the door.

"Come on, then."

And he doesn't speak as we troop single file down the narrow street. Many of the galleries have their doors open, and statues and paintings on easels spill out into courtyards and edge onto the sidewalks. I pause from time to time to look at a piece. Sam contemplates his own feet. We cross Garcia Street, find the alley entrance where I'd seen the "Boxer Puppies" sign and follow the alley until we find another sign with an arrow pointing toward the back.

Sam and I are escorted to a redwood picnic table on a brick pad in the breeder's backyard. "The bitch is Athena out of Stieger von Clieff," declares the breeder. Alexandra McBride is a stick-thin woman in western denims and cowboy boots. "I'm sure you're familiar with the line."

Sam is a stone on the redwood bench beside me. The puppies are invisible, mewling yelps somewhere out there in the foliage of the backyard.

"I'm sorry," I say, "I'm afraid I'm not really very knowledgeable about breeds."

"Not to worry. You're fortunate to have found a reputable breeder. These are quite valuable dogs, but one must know what one is doing."

"Uh-huh."

Sam slips off the bench.

"Boxers have a history that goes all the way back to Alexander the Great . . ." McBride paces as she imparts this knowledge. "The obligatory specifications of the breed standard are outlined in the studbook . . ."

Sam steps off the patio and out into the yard, moving toward the sounds.

". . . and the muzzle must be one third the length of the head from the occiput to the . . ." McBride wags her finger. Sam has stopped on one of the paths in her yard. He's stooping down . . . kneeling on the gravel.

"The color must be fawn or brindle with sufficient white to enhance the dog's appearance, but the white must never exceed one third of the dog's coat. Here, look at these pictures of color patterns . . ." It is clear that Mrs. McBride has miles to go before she volunteers an actual peek at her litter.

"I guess we'd just like to see if one of the pups strikes Sam's fancy. Could we just take a look?"

"Oh," she says, "I wouldn't advise letting a *child* make this decision."

"Why not?"

"I gather you've never priced AKA-certified boxer puppies?"

"Noooo."

"My dogs' bloodlines are impeccable."

"How much?"

"Under two thousand, if the markings aren't perfect. But most in this litter are—"

"DOLLARS?!"

McBride shakes her head. "I see," she says contemptuously.

"I didn't realize...."

"Perhaps it would be better to call your son back ... before he gets attached to one."

Shit.

I follow the path to where Sam kneels. Inside the flat basket in front of him are four wriggling puppies, perfect examples of the fawn-and-brindle pictures the breeder had shown me.

On Sam's lap is a fifth dog. With the exception of a jet-black nose and eyes, this dog is entirely white. Sam is bent low, holding his ear to the puppy's muzzle.

I hear McBride's boots on the gravel behind us.

"Oh, dear. I'm so sorry. My daughter was to have gotten rid of that one yesterday. Tessy is such a baby, she can't bear to put the white ones down. I've told her and told her, it's best for the dog as well as for the breed."

"Put the white ones down? I don't understand."

McBride looks genuinely pained. "Half of all white boxers are born deaf. Some are blind too. This one probably isn't blind, since his eyes are black instead of pink, but, nevertheless . . . I'm so sorry. We aren't permitted to sell the white ones."

She collects the misfit from Sam's lap and smiles at me dismissively. "Sorry."

"But this is great," I gush. "I couldn't have afforded a two-thousand-dollar dog anyway."

"Sorry."

"And we don't care about pedigree or any of that stuff."

Sam's following this conversation with avid interest. Gone is the stoic withdrawal, replaced by something like eagerness—or fear.

"No," says the breeder.

"But you said you couldn't sell it—"

"That's right."

"Couldn't you give it away, then? We could give the dog a good home. But, if you'd rather, I'd be happy to pay you whatever you think it's worth."

Sam's eyes stay on the dog squirming in the woman's arms. He reaches for the puppy, but McBride clutches it closer to her chest.

"Please, try to understand. I can't sell this puppy at any price and I can't give it away either. It may seem cruel to you, but I assure you it's for the best. If white dogs were allowed into the population, they'd overtake the breed. Albinism, deafness, blindness, early death: These characteristics would show up more and more until the breed would be destroyed. This pup should have been removed on the first day and put to sleep."

I can feel Sam trembling by my side. I can't look at him. It's like sensing the last straw slowly drift toward the burden already piled too high on the camel's back.

Claude Raskin's legal problems alone could pay two thousand dollars in a week. Maybe it wouldn't be such a bad thing to take a few paying clients.

"If you'll take payments," I tell McBride, "I'll pay the whole two thousand."

"I'm really very sorry. I take full responsibility for this. My daughter should never have left this dog in with the others."

"Three thousand?"

"Please, miss. I understand how much you want to make your little boy happy, but . . ."

"You said this dog isn't blind."

"No, but . . ."

I clap my hands together sharply and the puppy's head jerks in my direction.

"And not deaf."

"Not this particular one perhaps. But, you see, it's the future of the breed we have to be concerned about."

"What if I have the dog neutered?"

"Oh, dear. People are always getting attached to one of these doomed puppies. They say they'll have them fixed and sometimes they do. But sometimes they don't."

Sam has left my side now and is walking slowly down the path away from me. I call to him; he doesn't stop.

"I'll pay you three thousand dollars *and* I'll give you written proof of the neutering."

"Four."

"Sam, come back here! We just bought a dog."

Sam insists upon holding the puppy in his arms all the way home.

"Can I call Mommy?"

"Sure."

"Can I call Daddy?" Sam knows the answer to this question.

"Don't think so. Daddy can't take calls in jail. But Mommy can tell him all about your puppy."

We are obliged to stop every few feet to pull the twisting, squirming hunk of licking, black-nosed pup securely back up into Sam's arms.

"Can I call Max?"

"Sure."

"Can I call Patrick?"

"Why not?" What's a long distance phone call to a woman who can afford a four-thousand-dollar dog?

I place the calls. Angie sounds weak but on the mend. After she talks to Sam for a while, she asks for me again.

"He's his old self, Matty. Better, even. How do I thank you for this?"

Patrick's machine doesn't answer, so I make a second long distance call to the Sea Door Marina. The guy there tells me Patrick's boat is still at anchor, but Mr. Prather's been gone for a while.

"I just talked to him three days ago."

"Yeah, I'd say that's about when he left."

Sam insists on dialing Max's number by himself. The two talk about the puppy while Sam lies on his stomach on the floor and the dog scrambles over his back and head and under his chin and in and out through the phone cord. Together, Sam and Max decide on the name, *Mucho*. Sam lets Mucho talk too.

Twenty minutes later, Sam wants Max's phone number again to tell him new stuff about Mucho. I show him the automatic redial button on the phone and head for the couch. I prop pillows behind my head so I can just lie there and watch them. Mucho slobbers all over the receiver, then wets on my newly polished floors. Sam cleans it up with a bath towel and says "bad dog" like he was saying "sweetheart."

My breath catches at this scene and I'm overcome with melancholy. Sam's life isn't going to be like this moment. Jimmy will be executed or imprisoned for life. And the sins of his father will mark Sam's life always. I continue to drink in the child and wait for the cold spot in my chest to warm. But it doesn't warm.

Despite everything, I no more believe Jimmy Abeyta killed the Prathers than I ever did. What right do I have to give up now? So I guessed wrong about the Swiss account. So I guessed wrong about Eloy. Guessed wrong about Saavedra. Every time you fail, you have the same three choices: wallow in the failure, walk away from it, or try again. It's pretty clear to me that if I don't care what happens to my house, Sam and Mucho can do without my attention for hours to come. I lay my head back and try to find the pattern.

Okay, one more time: Somebody gave Jimmy a lot of money to say what he did. It wasn't Eloy. And, since Gene Saavedra was having an after-sex snooze at the moment the Prathers were murdered, it almost certainly wasn't Saavedra who bribed Jimmy. Who, then? Who knew enough about Jimmy to know what buttons to push?

"Matty, can I call Max?"

"Use the redial button. You remember how?"

It had to be somebody who knew about the shooting in Los Duranes barrio seven years ago. Somebody who knew Jimmy and his cousins shot Augusto Santiago as he lay drunk in the back of his pickup truck.

"Matty, Max's phone sounds like beep-beep-beep. Can me and Mucho go upstairs and play on your bed?"

"Okay, but put a towel under him."

The motorbike found behind the Inn at Loretto was registered to Alan Prather. Presumably, the bike was at the mansion before the murders, because the killer roared down the hill on it immediately before the explosion. Since the only other vehicle at the mansion was the Prathers' own Cadillac, how did the killer get to Irongate in the first place?

"Matty!"

I can hear the springs on my bed squeak and recognize the sound of bouncing. Sam's voice sounds excited—just this side of frenzied. Pretty soon here, I'm going to have to exercise a little authority.

"I can see out of your window, Matty"—*bounce-squeak*—"somebody's coming"—*bounce-squeak*—"guess"—*bounce*—"who."

On the day Jimmy was bribed, six people knew about the bullets fired into Santiago's truck—six people who knew enough to bribe Jimmy. Two were the cousins who helped fire those bullets. The third was Eloy. The fourth was Angie, the fifth was me. The sixth was ... oh my God.

Sam is thumping down the stairs as fast as he can with Mucho in one arm. The other hand grabs the banister as he comes.

"I saw him from the window getting out of his car. I'm going to show Patrick my puppy."

Oh shit.

Patrick has been gone from Seattle for three days—ever since I told him I was driving up to Jemez Springs to talk to Eloy. Patrick, who has always shown up at the most opportune moments, has just shown up again. No sooner does he get a piece of information than he's at Irongate, or at the Swissair passenger gate in New York ... or on my doorstep.

"Sam, quick!"

As Sam reaches the bottom stair, I grab boy and canine in both my arms and hustle us to the tiny new bathroom. I more or less shove them in and drop them on the floor.

"Shhhh . . . shhhhh!" I say desperately.

There is a knock on the front door. The bell rings.

"Stop it!" Sam protests. "I want to—"

I clap my hand over his mouth.

"Please, listen to me, Sam! I think Patrick is why your daddy's in jail. Don't make a sound. No matter what! I'm going to get him out of here as fast as I can."

I move my hand away a fraction of an inch.

He doesn't open his mouth, but his eyes are open wide, staring at me. I let my hand fall away.

"Trust me!"

THIRTY-FOUR

—◦◦◦—

"MATTY?"

Patrick's through the open door, moving into the room. I slam the bathroom door and arrange my features.

"Patrick! Surprise! How did you find me here?"

He spreads his arms and I walk into them like a good chum.

"No biggie," he says. "When you called me, you said you hadn't gone back to Irongate. So I just looked you up in the phone book."

He gives me a big, friendly grin to allay my qualms. But does he really suspect I have qualms? Though Patrick's providential arrival seems sinister at this moment, I doubt my developing image of him as much as I dread it.

When a scraping and yipping at the bathroom draw his attention, he shifts slightly and I stiffen.

"Uhh . . . I have a new puppy," I explain hastily, "his bed is in there. Don't bother—"

"Ah, I'd love to see it." He takes a step forward.

To keep him from Sam, I pirouette, turn the knob, kneel, and reach in so fast, you'd think I was born for the ballet stage. Mucho shoots toward me. Ecstatically, Sam grabs at the dog's plump midsection with both hands. Mucho squeals and yelps; Sam holds on stubbornly.

Behind me, Patrick says, "Can I help?"

I wrench the puppy roughly from Sam's startled hands and hiss, "Please, Sam, trust me!"

Before he can protest, I shut the door, turn, and hold up the squirming puppy for inspection. Patrick nods and pets the dog. Miraculously, there's no more noise from the bathroom. If I'm lucky, this silence may last as much as thirty seconds. If Patrick has done what I think he's done, I've got to get him out of this house now!

"Well," I say just a shade too loudly, "whatever brought you back this time, I'm glad you're here. I was just on my way out to make one last inspection at Irongate before I turn in my keys. Want to ride along?"

"I'd be happy to."

And we almost make it out the door. Mucho is back on the floor, scrabbling his toenails wildly against the brick to keep himself upright. Patrick is directly behind me. Two more seconds and we'll be outside.

But luck isn't with me. A thudding sound arises from the bathroom—now thrashing. Patrick turns on his heel.

"Another puppy," I say.

"You said *a* puppy," he points out.

This is it, I think. One more second and he'll open that door. He'll find Sam and realize I've been hiding the child. Then he'll realize why.

Whatever happens after that, Sam will witness it. And if Patrick intends to harm me, he won't leave witnesses—not even little boys and puppies. He moves toward the bathroom . . . hand on the knob. I have to stop him any way I can. He turns the knob . . . with anything I can think of . . . *think*!

"A man came to see Jimmy Abeyta," I begin, "in Jemez Springs, and . . ."

Patrick's hand slides until only his fingertips graze the knob.

". . . and . . . just after he talked to this man, Jimmy became suddenly rich. What do you make of that?"

Patrick turns, the bathroom noises forgotten for the

moment. The expression on his face is unreadable. I open the front door, and this time I make it all the way outside. I'm several feet away before I turn to see if he is following me.

He is.

"Maybe," he says edgily, "the better question is what do you make of it, Matty?"

"Well"—I head for my car—"I guess I make of it that I was right about somebody bribing Jimmy to confess to the Prather murders."

He stops.

Okay, let's give this sucker something new to worry about. Something that'll get him off the dime and moving out of here before Sam comes out of the house—which figures to be any second now.

"There is evidence." I open the car door. "Up at Irongate. That's what I was on my way to get." My instant invention sounds to my own ears like a childish whopper.

"Evidence of what?" His voice is ninety percent scepticism, ten percent dread. But he moves.

"Here." He holds his hand out for my keys. "You seem to have hurt your leg. I'll drive."

It's my turn to hesitate. But only for a second. As he pulls out of the compound, he glances at me sideways. "What kind of evidence could there be?"

He pulls to a rolling stop at the first corner. A young mother with an infant in her arms stands on a narrow bit of sidewalk less than a foot away. She looks right at me. We hold the eye contact. My panic must show because suddenly she has a questioning look on her face. Is anything wrong? the look asks. I open my mouth. I pantomime the word "help." From my lips to hers. The instant she sees, she screams at the top of her voice, "HELP! HELP! SOMEBODY ... HELP!"

Patrick steps hard on the accelerator. As the car jumps forward, the young mother disappears from my view. We are on our way again.

A few miles farther out, as we pass the St. John's College campus, he says dispassionately, "You were signaling to that woman, weren't you?"

I don't answer.

"You finally figured it out."

"Some of it."

"Well," he says philosophically, "I guess the air is cleared now."

I stare blankly ahead. There can no longer be any pretense that I don't suspect him.

"How about you tell me what you think you know and tell me exactly what you've done about it," he says. "And while you're at it, tell me what this *evidence* is."

I realize the concoction about evidence at Irongate could buy me another hour. An hour seems like a lifetime.

"Okay," I tender, "what I think I know: First, the deposits into Angie's account totaled a half million dollars. Not very many people could come up with that kind of money so quickly. You're one of them."

Patrick stares at the sagebrush at the side of the road and signals neither acquiescence nor argument.

"Second, I know you listened to his session tapes, so you knew all about Jimmy's past. And you knew Sam and Angie personally, so you understood exactly where Jimmy would be most vulnerable."

Still no response from Patrick, no nods or head shakes or tics or sweat or eye contact.

"And you knew about Eloy: knew that Eloy thought he owed Jimmy a lot because of the construction accident, knew Eloy was sentimental about his family and might be persuaded to pay his debt by providing a cover story. And finally, you knew the police would accept Jimmy's confession because that's the direction they were looking anyway."

"Is that it?"

"I guess there's one more thing. Thanks to me, you knew exactly where to find Jimmy."

Patrick turns the car up the familiar winding road. I can see the small muscles at the edge of his jaw working. What will he do with me now?

"And the timing is right," I continue, watching that jaw. "Someone offered Jimmy all this money just a day or so after you left Irongate."

He's driving carefully, even slowly. We pass another car and I think fleetingly about making wild hand-signals. I imagine that Patrick and I must look like a married couple going for a ride on a fine summer afternoon

"There is something I don't understand," I say. "Why aren't you worried about Jimmy? He could change his mind and retract his confession at any time."

No sooner is the question out of my mouth than the answer dawns. "He doesn't know who you are, does he?"

I shut up and we ride in silence for another mile or two. It will not really be a good omen for my future if Patrick answers my questions.

"You're right," Patrick begins. "I drove up there the morning I left Irongate. I arrived in Jemez Springs in the late morning and then I watched for two days. Waited for a time when Jimmy would be completely alone. On the second night, after everyone else had left the job site, Jimmy was working late. When he finally came out of the construction trailer I told him I had a proposition for him, told him to go back into the trailer and sit and listen very carefully. I told him this night was going to be a turning point in his life. I told him he could refuse and I'd just walk away and no harm done."

"And he listened to you? Just like that, without even knowing who you were?"

"It was necessary to show him a gun to focus his attention. But once that unpleasantness was past, we sat together, talking in the dark trailer, for nearly two hours. He understood immediately what my offer could mean for his family, and he was as eager to make the plan work as I was. More, maybe. We became conspirators. There was a . . . kind of intimacy to it.

"It was part of the deal that he wouldn't know who I was or how I knew what I knew. Though I must tell you, Matty," Patrick chuckles, "because of the details I knew about him, Jimmy suspects you of betrayal. That was a bonus for me. Made it less likely he'd trust you in the future."

At the entrance to the Prather driveway, he motions me out to open the gate. He follows closely so I don't make any more foolish moves, and I walk slowly, hoping he will go on talking. As soon as he stops talking, I'm going to have to come up with the "evidence" we're supposedly here for.

But I needn't have worried. When we're back in the car, he resumes his story as placidly as if he were describing a movie to a friend. It begins to dawn on me that Patrick may have motives other than finding "evidence" to bring me to this isolated spot.

"I told Jimmy I knew he'd shot Augusto Santiago. I'd listened to the tapes and knew every detail—more than enough detail to convince the police of his guilt for that crime. I told him it didn't matter that his lawyer won some legal motion, because either he turned himself in for shooting up the pickup truck, or I would turn him in."

"But why? Why have him confess to a crime everybody had forgotten?"

"The verifiable first confession set Abeyta up as a killer. He's not just some nut who confesses to a high-profile crime. He's a gang punk who kills for sport. So who's going to question it when the killer says he'd killed again? Nobody. And once he'd confessed to the crime he did commit, he could never go back to the way things were. He's going to prison for a long time no matter what. He's not comparing life in prison to life on the outside anymore. He's got less to lose—less to weigh against all that money."

"You manipulative bastard."

"And there was the added attraction to him that he could get his cousins off Sam's back by taking the whole rap for the Santiago killing onto himself and letting the cousins off the hook forever."

"Icing on the cake," I say.

"Then I explained the financial arrangements." Patrick smiles at this. "I told him I'd make an initial deposit in good faith directly into Angie's account the next day."

"How could you be sure you wouldn't be caught?"

"The authorities weren't even going to look. I predicted they'd be thrilled to get those murders solved, and I was right, wasn't I? Anyway, all you need to make a deposit untraceable is a cashier's check and a deposit slip. Jimmy provided the latter."

"And after Jimmy had confessed to shooting Santiago ... ?"

"I made another deposit into Angie's account, a larger one. And after that, by agreement, he confessed to the Prather killings. After three hours with me, he knew every detail about that night, from the medicine Denise had been taking and the nightgown she was in to how the blaze looked in the night sky from the seat of a motorbike. Jimmy was an apt pupil."

Patrick parks in front of the mansion. When I step out, the air is fresh and the site is pristine. No stench of burned wood, no mess, no activity. No one in ear-shot. Perfect place for another murder.

"You still haven't told me what's to prevent Jimmy from retracting his confession now that he's been paid?"

"What would a retraction buy him? He's still got a murder charge over his head. If he did renege, the authorities would just take whatever was left of the money away from his family— little Sam would just get fucked all over again. My deal with Jimmy is, I make periodic payments as long as I live; if I stop, he can tell the whole story."

As we near the mansion's door, he puts his hand on my shoulder. When I turn to face him, there is something like hope in his eyes.

"It's a good deal all the way round, Matty." He offers this like the lawyer who has the upper hand at the end of a lengthy negotiation. "Everybody is better off than they were before. Jimmy's own life was pretty much a misery anyway. How much worse is it for him to be in prison really? And Sam can have a bright future."

I shake my head.

"Matty," he argues, "it isn't up to you to undo Jimmy's choice about how to be a father, is it?"

I'm beginning to realize that this man wants my approval. Wants me to agree that what he did wasn't really so bad. Does this mean he doesn't intend to kill me?

"Look, Matty, I only agreed to help Alan and Denise do what they *wanted* to do! Alan had it all figured out. He'd been planning it for months. It was Alan who taught me to rig the engine. He'd found the tools to make the holes just the right circumference and he'd figured the timing. He had it down to the half minute. Alan always was the smart one."

"Then why didn't they just do it by themselves? Why did they need you?"

Patrick hesitates, looks skyward, seems to be conjuring an explanation. And in this pause, a seed of doubt begins to sprout in my brain.

"Denise couldn't help at all, of course. She was deeply sedated most of the time, near the end. Alan wanted to be drugged on that night too, to be sure he'd be able to bring himself to go through with it. So, they were going to need help and I was the only one they could ask. But we were afraid we might leave some telltale sign of my ... contribution. I might end up being criminally liable for assisting their suicide. To protect me, we decided to destroy every shred of evidence by blowing everything to kingdom come. That ... and Alan relished the idea of such an apocalyptic finale anyway."

So this is his rationale. Alan and Denise wanted to die and Patrick was no murderer, only a good brother and friend—his brother's keeper after all. And according to Patrick's value system, he did Jimmy a favor too. This feels like maybe good news to me. Maybe Patrick isn't psychologically capable of killing another human being without a moral rationale.

I unlock the door and shut off the newly installed alarm system. While I'm at it, I flip the switch to open the gate below just in case Sam had enough presence of mind to call for help. Patrick appears to be in no particular hurry. How long have I got? If Sam did manage to hit redial and get Max, what would the boy be able to tell? Would Max, God forbid, come looking alone? Would he even know where to look?

Patrick seems fascinated with the vast emptiness of the mansion. Making sure to keep himself between me and the nearest exit, he prowls the house slowly as though it were an ancient ruin. As he roams, he seems nearly to forget me.

Nearly but not quite. He returns to the front door and nonchalantly switches the alarm system back on. He turns to me. He smiles.

THIRTY-FIVE

◆∽◆◆◆∽◆

"W ELL"—HE RAISES AN EYEBROW—"LET'S SEE THAT
evidence, shall we?"

I'm flat out of tricks.

"Oh, oh. There isn't any evidence is there, Matty?"

He leans against the kitchen counter and considers me. He is at ease. His hand is in his pocket.

Staring at that pocket and trying to gauge what else might be in it, I shrug.

"You didn't come all the way up here for evidence anyway, did you, Patrick?"

He gives a little appreciative hoot. "God, Matty, I really do enjoy you. You should've taken me up on my offers. If you had, you could've been sailing around the world right now. A month in the Mediterranean—sun and sea spray and a Monaco condo to take a shower in. Have you been to Greece? Turkey? There's a tiny seaside restaurant in Portofino you'd love."

"Is that a gun?" I point to his pocket.

"It's not important. Listen to me, Matty, we could still do

it. Have you ever tried scuba diving? The colors, the coral, the—"

He stops in mid-sentence. I can hear the siren too. It's getting louder every second.

"GO!"

He grabs my shoulder and spins me around, then prods until I start to move. The gun is out of his pocket now, barrel poking into my lower back in hard, steady stabs . . . both of us moving fast through the empty, echoing rooms . . . down the hall.

The first siren has been joined by another, the sound is very close. I'm going to be rescued, I think almost serenely. I only need to stay alive for a few more minutes, then someone will rescue me.

We cross Alan's bedroom and Patrick motions me into the office. There's pounding at the front door . . . a burst of noise and then a sharp, splintering sound. Just as I open my mouth to scream, to tell my saviors where I am, the alarm goes off. The house fills with whirs and screeches.

Patrick reaches toward the light switches, and I remember those innocuous-looking switches from my first night in the mansion. At once, I know what he intends.

At the press of his finger, the far wall opens a fraction. He muscles me to the opening wall and pulls the leading edge with one hand. With the other, he sticks the barrel of the gun into my mouth.

The taste is acrid. The steel is cold against the warm, wet velvet of my mouth. Hard metal clacks roughly against my teeth. I open my mouth wider to take the gun, knowing, as I do it, how inane it is to be protecting my teeth at a time like this. The alarm wails. What sounds like a company of marines seems bogged down near the front of the house, apparently trying to turn the damn thing off.

I stand mute while the vault door swings open.

He motions me in. What if I refuse? Will he shoot me here with police—surely police—seconds away? Seeming to read my mind, he shoves the gun barrel deeper into my mouth. I gag and take a step backward. He pushes me into the steel cavity, steps in after me, and pulls the door shut. I remember that it takes the wall outside a full two minutes to close seamlessly.

One, two . . . five . . . ten . . . sixty.

The darkness is blacker than any starless night. The now-empty stacks behind me cut sharply into my back. His gun is out of my mouth now and held between our tightly coupled bodies. Patrick is pressed against me from my face, which is smashed against his chest to my feet which are sandwiched between his. The alarm is suddenly far away. In here, the roaring sound is of ragged breathing . . . mine . . . and inches away . . . his. There is no reason for the army out there to start flipping switches. No one is going to find us here unless I can tell them where we are.

I scream.

Patrick makes no move to stop me.

I scream again . . . and again . . . and again . . . and again . . . and again.

THIRTY-SIX

SOME MOMENTS AFTER THE ACHE IN MY THROAT HAS RE-duced my screams to rasps, I realize the distant alarm is silent too. They . . . them out there . . . they could hear me now, maybe. As though my impulse to call for help runs as rapidly to his brain as to my own, he twists the gun barrel up into the soft hollow at the base of my neck. My urge to call out dies.

The natural trajectory of the bullet would be upward—under my chin, through the roof of my mouth, into my brain, and out the top of my skull.

But he won't take that chance. If I move so much as a frac-tion of an inch, the bullet might ricochet off these steel walls in a cascade of crazy angles. He couldn't even be safe if the bullet passed through my brain first. His best scenario, if he pulls that trigger, is that the noise brings the help that may now be only a room away. His worst scenario is that he blows his own head off.

Boldly, I snake my hand up to his hand and crawl my palm up over the gun butt. He stiffens. I wiggle my index finger an-other inch until it covers his. At this moment either of us could pull the trigger.

"A single bullet could kill us both," I whisper.

"There's a way out," he says softly. "I was serious before, Matty . . . about us."

I can hear his heartbeat through his shirt.

"We had some good moments in Switzerland, didn't we?"

Can he possibly imagine that I'm going to take this offer seriously?

"We could still do it, go away together . . . away from everything. We could make the intermission last for a lifetime."

"Right."

"Why not, Matty? You're fond of me. I know you are; in time, you could love me. I helped people do what they wanted to do with their lives. Is that so wrong that you could never forgive it?"

His unanswered question fills this cramped space. He hasn't guessed yet that I know the deeper truth. How much time is passing? How long will the police keep on looking for me?

"I can't get enough air," I say. "Could we turn a little?"

He shifts and I scoot and, little by little, we make breathing room. What the hell? If nobody can hear us anyway, why not tie up the loose ends here and now?

"You hadn't counted on anybody being in this house," I say, "sorting through things; you didn't expect the murder investigation to be reopened. So you had to come back to Santa Fe to keep your eye on things, maybe plant a little suicide note if necessary, or bribe an innocent man; do whatever it took to shape the outcome."

"Matty, so what? At that point, the die was cast. I had no choice but to cover it up. What would you have had me do?"

With my cheek against his chest and our gun cutting a crescent into my neck, another silence passes in our dungeon closet. We stir from time to time in an odd dance—shifting an elbow out of the other's ribs, a knee out of a groin.

"And then," I begin again, "you showed up at the airport in New York . . . supposedly to help me get the money out of the Swiss account. Why did you do that?"

"It was only a matter of time before you got that money back for the creditors anyway."

"But surely you knew the account and number all along. You're the one person Alan would have told about the Swiss account. Why not turn it over to the bankruptcy trustee right from the start?"

"What's with all these questions anyway? I've already admitted everything to you, Matty." He's no longer even trying to keep his voice down. How long will he keep me in here before he thinks it's safe enough to venture out? Was his offer of romance on the high seas just a way to buy some silent, effortless time? How much more of his story will he tell to buy a few more peaceful minutes?

"You don't have to answer my questions if you don't want to," I say agreeably. "But if you're seriously asking me to go away with you, help me understand. Before all this, Patrick Prather had a life anyone would kill for. Why would you risk all that to do what Alan could have done by himself?"

"All right, all right . . . Alan worried about botching the job. Without someone's help at the end, one or both of them might live on as a vegetable for years. The prospect terrified him. This was the last thing I could do for him."

This explanation for risking life in prison for the sake of filial devotion sounds almost reasonable, and it comes easily to his lips. But I'm nearly sure now that the explanation is a lie.

I don't ask why he took the other risk, the totally unnecessary and far stupider risk, of bribing Jimmy Abeyta to confess to his crime. When he took that risk, he had nothing to gain or lose. Patrick was in no danger at all of being connected with his brother's murder or suicide. There was no need to shift blame to someone else, because no one was blaming Patrick . . . or was ever likely to. And the bribe itself could have brought attention to him, could have ultimately led police to suspect him of fratricide. It was a huge risk. Yet, this man—who had little to fear if he did nothing and much to fear if he bribed an innocent man to confess to murder—this man chose to do the latter.

The two of us are so physically close in here that each movement is like the nuzzle of lovers. He has shifted the gun, but there isn't enough room for him to lower it, so it rests gently on my shoulder. Oxygen is growing meager.

"It won't be much longer," he says. "You okay?"

"Mmmm."

"Matty," he whispers into my ear, "I know this is a pretty crazy place to make an offer like this but ... well, what do you think?"

My mind goes back to the days before Patrick left Irongate, when he must have made the decision to take the risk.

Patrick had just handed me a martini and was listening to my telephone conversation with Claude Raskin. That day I'd discovered the RTC connection and I was eager to pursue it. Patrick was unperturbed.

"The cops are eventually going to go away at least for the night," he says. "They'll have moved out of the house already by now, and onto the grounds. All you have to do is stay quiet a little while longer. Okay?"

I nod my head against his shoulder.

"Yes?" he whispers.

"Yes," I whisper back ambiguously, and we retreat once more into our own thoughts:

Only a few hours after that martini, Patrick coincidentally found the "suicide note" which promised to change everything.

We're fast replacing oxygen with carbon dioxide. Is somebody still out there? There's no longer enough air in here to waste in talking. He has begun to make quick sucking sounds.

"We've got ... to ... get ... air ..." he says.

The last night before Patrick left for Jemez Springs, the grown-ups were drinking wine, SpaghettiOs were smeared all over Sam's face, Angie was full of bright plans for the future with Jimmy. All of us were talking about where we would go from that moment: Patrick was supposedly headed back to Seattle, where he would soon set sail again. He was surprised to learn that the "suicide note" hadn't put an end to my investigation. I told him over dinner that night that I still intended to tie up loose ends. Specifically, I told him I was going to the office of Dr. David Drake, Jr.

Sometimes, you have to connect dots over many decades

to understand how, for instance, a man could bring himself to marry this person or to harm that one. But occasionally, human behavior is more about a sudden danger and a lucky open door. Patrick's trip to Jemez Springs has the feel of an opportunistic tangent. He found out, that night, that the suicide note hadn't put me off the scent. Something more dramatic—more final—would be necessary.

"They're gone," I hazard. "How do we get out of here?"

"Behind ... my ... back. Button ... below shoulder."

We shift and I wiggle and strain to reach behind him. He lifts his arm cooperatively, I press my fingers against the steel walls and move them a few inches in either direction. . . . Nothing.

"Lower ... hurry!"

The steel has been warmed by our body heat. My finger pads are slightly damp. Another fraction of an inch down ...

"Can you bend a little?" I ask, and he makes himself slightly shorter so my fingers can probe two more inches. . . .

And there it is. I can feel it. There is nothing to do now but push the button and we'll be out.

But, perhaps, the odds can be evened a bit first ...

"I can almost feel it," I lie. "Just a little more."

He hunches another notch, his gun goes a fraction slacker. I've tried one risky move today; this one needs to work better than the last. My finger is squarely on the button now.

To even up the odds between men and women in close combat, our jokester creator chose to give women one ridiculous advantage.

"Can you give me," I ask, "just a fraction of an inch more?"

I brace myself. My finger pushes the steel button until I feel the door give. All at once, I shove my knee high and hard—deep into his scrotum.

As the door opens, he falls backward onto the floor outside. For a second, breathing fresh, sweet air is the most important thing on earth to me. To him, clutching his balls while he curls into the fetal position seems to have a higher priority.

He tries to get up, but he's racked with dry heaves. He's still holding his gun but only by two fingers. Using the heavy door to catapult myself forward, I leap and stomp on his wrist with all my weight. The vault door swings nearly closed behind me. He squirms and grabs at my ankle; I trip. On the floor, I scramble for the gun. The second I feel the butt, I grab with both hands, and find the trigger. I spin away and fire.

The sound is at once sharp and thunderous, and glass at the other end of the room shatters.

But even with all this noise, no one comes. I look at him still writhing on the floor. If he's right, if the police went off to search the grounds, it may take many minutes before the men outside get to us. If they were even near enough to hear the gunshot. If they're still on the grounds at all.

While we wait, my hands tremble. He's coming back to himself . . . his breathing is less labored. He gets up on one knee. Keeping the gun between my two hands, I walk my hips backward along the floor until my back is against the jamb of the vault. He's breathing normally again, looking at me levelly . . . squinting slightly in appraisal. My hands are shaking. Up to this moment, I've never deliberately killed anything higher on the food chain than a trout.

He can see my indecision, and it tells him everything he needs to know. He smiles. He pushes himself all the way up into a standing position and brushes off his trousers as though he were leaving a picnic.

"I'm going to go now, Matty . . . going to walk out of here while the cops are still searching the hills. Maybe I'll be lucky after all. This isn't the end I'd hoped for . . . but I'll make do."

"Stay where you are!"

His smile widens. "Ordinary women don't shoot people unless their children or their kittens or their jewels are threatened."

"You arrogant shit."

"You've got the gun, Matty. But whatever grandiose notions you may have about righting the wrongs of the world, you are, at bottom, a consummately ordinary woman."

I raise the gun. He turns his back. He is supremely confident. He is also right.

As he walks away, I lower the gun.

Then I edge its muzzle through the inch-wide opening

into the vault chamber and I pull the trigger. He freezes for an instant, then bolts. The roar of the bullet ricocheting off steel walls and steel floor and steel ceiling is astonishing. I fire another shot ... and another ... four in all, and the deafening reverberation goes on forever. The stink of cordite fills the air.

A uniformed officer is first to reach me. He holds a gun at Prather's spine and nudges him forward into the room. Two more officers enter on their heels. The first of the new arrivals holds up his palms to me, his eyes riveted on the gun in my hand. The second is holding a gun of his own in both hands. It is aimed directly at my chest.

"Ms. Donahue? Matty Donahue?"

I nod and get to my feet, shaking and insanely disinclined to give up my weapon. The officer with the upraised palms steps warily toward me, careful to keep out of my direct line of fire. I watch as he lowers one arm and places his hand over mine. His skin touching my skin is quite warm. His hand feels strong, but it trembles.

It is that slight tremble that all at once puts me back in touch with everything. I turn my palm up willingly, and he gently takes the gun from me.

"Matty?" A new voice.

"Daniel?"

I turn to see a worried look on Detective Baca's face. But it is nothing compared to the look on the face of the man behind him.

"Max!"

Detective Baca assesses the situation swiftly. The prisoner has been slammed, face first, against the wall. Both of his hands are held high and flat against the plaster; his feet are wide apart. The frisking officer says that the man against the wall is not carrying a weapon, and Daniel Baca nods. The officer cuffs the man and allows him to slowly turn around. When we can all see the man's face clearly, Max stares at it in a kind of awful fascination.

"I guess this would be Patrick Prather," Max says.

I go to him and touch his arm.

"No," I say, "this man isn't Patrick."

THIRTY-SEVEN

———∞∞∞———

"H E"—I POINT TO THE MAN IN HANDCUFFS—"RIGGED the Prather explosion. And he paid Jimmy Abeyta to take the blame."

"You're telling me," says Daniel, "that Patrick Prather killed his own brother?"

"No, Daniel . . . I'm saying that *Alan* Prather killed *his* own brother."

The prisoner's eyes dart around the room like a cornered rodent. Eventually, those eyes come to rest on mine. Funny, how you can see things once you're sure they're there. Alan's brown-tinted lenses are so obvious now. I can almost see the blue iris rims. He probably did the hair and beard by himself—brown dye and a permanent wave—a couple of hours at most. The shots of gray in the beard were a nice touch. Even with his eyes and hair altered, I might have recognized this face from all the pictures of Alan Prather on television, if it hadn't been for the beard. Now I can make out Alan's sharp jawline, the sculptured cheekbones.

"He was so careful," I say. "Careful never to be seen by anyone who'd known him as Alan Prather. He slipped back into

Santa Fe, came directly here to the mansion, and never left it as long as he was in town. The only people in Santa Fe to see his new face after the murders were strangers: Sam and Angie and me."

The officer nearest Alan Prather begins to inspect his prisoner's face.

"My guess is that anybody who'd been around Alan in the month or so before the end would've noticed his weight gain and facial hair. But there wasn't anybody around, remember? He'd fired secretaries, maids, caretakers, everybody."

"I'll be a son of a bitch."

For once, Baca doesn't ask me to excuse his language.

"Right from the beginning," I say, "Claude tried to tell us all that Alan was capable of. He guessed Alan had killed his wife and some other '*poor, nameless fucker and turned them into crispy critters*,' remember?"

"I do," says Baca.

"But even Claude never guessed the second crispy critter was Alan's own brother. And Claude, predictably, lost interest when the creditors magically got their money back. That's what Alan expected me to do too—lose interest when the Swiss money was found. In fact, that's why he was so helpful to me in Switzerland. I'd momentarily picked up his scent, so he tossed a few million bones to distract me. The loss wasn't significant to him—after all, he had Patrick's wealth."

My ankle is killing me. This little exposition has taken its toll, and I begin to slump. Max moves to my side.

"Sam?" I ask him.

"He's okay."

Daniel Baca motions to Alan Prather and says to the officer, "Read him his rights. Let's get him out of here."

The officer dutifully recites the Miranda and begins to draw Alan away.

"Please wait," I call. "Detective, I'm pretty sure I know most of this man's story, but I haven't got all the details. If you could hold off taking him away for a little while, I think he'll tell us everything."

Daniel nods to the officer who has a lock on Alan Prather's arm, and the officer steps to the side.

"Why would I do that?" It's the first time Alan Prather has spoken since he was cuffed.

"Because," I say with more than a little satisfaction, "you're supposed to be dead. Even if you had the dream team, there is no way on God's earth you walk away from this."

"Fuck you."

"So, why not indulge yourself? Tell us how smart you were. You were going to take Patrick's life, weren't you? Not just kill him . . . but *become* him."

A sneer spreads across his mouth.

"I figure, as property manager, you'd have had no trouble getting into the medical building. You'd even have had keys to individual offices. And Dr. Drake, Sr., had recently died. His practice had been taken over by his son. So it was no big thing for you to substitute someone else's dental charts for your own. But you'd have to do a little forgery, and you'd have to get your hands on Patrick's dental charts somehow. Enlighten us about the particulars."

Alan Prather has nothing to say about dental charts.

"A couple of other things I wonder about: How did you fool the folks at the marina in Seattle?

"You'd have been good at forging your brother's signature, I'm sure. But there would've been people handling those assets who would have known Patrick personally: brokers, bankers, money managers."

Patrick still isn't answering.

But from behind me, Max makes a suggestion: "Mail and phone and fax and e-mail. It's possible these days to carry on an entire business, much less a wealthy retirement, without ever being in the room with the people who service you."

I take a second to register that Max is volunteering suggestions in a murder investigation. It has the feel of a sea change. I twist around to get a better look at him. He instantly understands the question in my glance and shrugs.

"Alan here," I say slowly, still eyeing Max, "probably picked his brother up at the Albuquerque airport and brought him directly here. That would account, Daniel, for there being no car here other than the Cadillac. So, if he was careful, and his luck held, nobody would ever know Patrick had come to Santa Fe."

"And then," Max jumps in again, "he could have used Patrick's return ticket for himself."

"Right . . ." I agree, staring at Max. "Alan dumped the motorbike at the Inn at Loretto because there's an hourly shuttle to the Albuquerque airport from there. He'd have been in Seattle in time to pick up Patrick's messages and Patrick's identity before anyone knew Patrick had left home."

Daniel Baca puts the next question directly to Alan. "How did you get your brother on the plane from Seattle to Albuquerque in the first place?"

I answer for Alan. "I think he probably just told Patrick he needed his help. He would have said it was an emergency, I imagine. And Patrick would have come, too, wouldn't he? Would have come to give his little brother more advice . . . and probably to assuage his own guilt. That part of your charade was true, wasn't it, Alan? Patrick felt guilty about you. Guilty for being your parents' favorite, the golden child, for getting richer and richer while his big brother's life was turning to dust. And while Patrick was drowning in guilt, you were choking on jealousy."

I turn to Daniel. "You see, at the very moment Patrick Prather was reaping life's sweet rewards, Alan Prather's life had become unbearable. Patrick had sold the company he built for hundreds of millions. He'd bought a yacht and was about to set sail for a future of undeserved bounty. Alan, on the other hand, was being sued by former partners for fraud. Alan was in danger of being charged criminally. Alan was filing multiple bankruptcy petitions. Alan was watching his wife die. And that was the hardest part, wasn't it, Alan? Because you actually loved her."

"Denise was the only good thing in my life," Alan responds.

"I imagine that when you made your first plan, when you

began stashing money away in the Swiss account, you thought you and Denise would have some good time left, didn't you?"

"I did."

"But then she got worse. There wasn't going to be any good time for Denise. So you decided to wait until she died of natural causes. After she was gone, you'd empty the Swiss account and start your new life. I suppose you probably felt guilty about that, but it's what you were going to do, wasn't it?"

"I always loved her. Even at the end."

"I believe you, Alan," I say softly. "And I believe . . . when you began to make your second plan . . . you told yourself you were doing it for love. Denise was getting worse daily. She wanted to die. She wanted your help. You told yourself killing her was for the best, didn't you?"

Alan Prather stares at me.

"You understand a lot."

"When you described her wasting away—the inability to swallow, to '*wipe her own ass*,' isn't that what you said? I should have realized—the brother-in-law, who lived thousands of miles away, wouldn't be likely to know such intimate details. You knew things about Denise's daily struggle only a daily caretaker would know. Only a husband.

"But I didn't get it then. I couldn't conceive of a man who could kill for love and kill for hate in the same act. Tell me, was the suicide note you came up with real? Was there ever a time when you intended to kill yourself along with Denise?"

This is his chance to spin the story his way. Or his chance to tell the truth. Prather looks at the room full of cops.

"The son of a bitch started giving me a hard time all over again. How I should have done this and I should have done that. How Mom was right to give all the money to him because he had enough discipline to handle wealth. I would have just fucked up an inheritance, like I fucked up everything else.

"How he's going to help me out of the mess I've made. But I've got to toe the line from here on in. I was Patrick's older brother, for christsake! Now, '*he's*' going to put '*me*' on an allowance, the goddamned fucking generous asshole."

"My beloved brother," he laughs, "insisted I go to Seattle for two weeks. This was so he could lecture me for fourteen solid days before he doled out my first month's allowance. Well, I took his arrogant, condescending shit. But I used the time well. As Patrick, I went to the office of his new dentist, told the receptionist I was moving again and wanted to pick up the dental charts they'd just received. The girl just smiled and asked me to sign a release. I walked away with Patrick's file and all those little X rays displayed in cardboard holders. All you have to do is to flip out the films and put them in my cardboard holder at Drake's office. Then I made the deal with a new marina so when I got back I could move the boat a couple of miles down the sound. Patrick was new to Seattle. He had no family and not many friends. Few people called and fewer still left messages. I ignored them. Nobody called more than once."

In the car, I say to Max, "Where is Sam?" Did he call you? How did you know where to look? Is he okay?"

"Could you move over here a little bit?" Max asks. I scoot across the seat and Max puts his arm over my shoulder as he drives. "That's better. I was beginning to worry I might never get to feel you near me again."

"Sam?"

He kisses my forehead. "Let's see, question one: Sam is at your house with Daniel Baca's wife and two kids. Two: Yes, apparently Sam hit the redial button again. When I answered he gave a pretty coherent picture of what had happened. He said Matty told him to trust her and so he did."

"He really said that?"

"He heard you tell Patrick you were going to Irongate. I'd just arrived at your place when Baca called. He said some hysterical woman called the station with your license number. She thought she'd just witnessed a woman being kidnapped. Baca said somebody was on their way over. The somebody turned out to be his own wife with their kids in tow. Three: I think Sam's probably fine. But the Baca kids brought their own dog along, so I wouldn't hold out too much hope for your furniture."

We drive in silence and I sink into the simple comfort of his body so near. As we turn onto Canyon Road, I reluctantly shake off the sweet, soft feeling to turn, at last, to the sharp, hard subject which has been waiting for us.

"The case is over," I say.

He squeezes my shoulder.

"You said you'd give me till this case was over before we had to make choices."

"Uh-huh," he says.

"I guess time's up."

He pulls over to the side of the road, shuts off the engine. "Matty, I've made a decision. I can't help but see how alive you are when you're involved in this stuff. Even tonight, I watched you . . . listened to you. You were exhausted and in pain." He touches my cheek. "But in the midst of all that, you were . . . excited. You were goddamned astonishing."

"Am I wrong, Max, or were you just the least bit interested in putting the pieces together, back there, yourself? Is this a change of heart?"

"More a belated capitulation to reality. I still hate what you seem to relish doing."

"But?"

"I'm going to be in your future, Matty. If solving crimes is in your future too, then I better start making room for solving crimes."

"You can do that?"

"I can try."

EPILOGUE

<hr />

1. Jimmy Abeyta pled to voluntary manslaughter in the death of Augusto Santiago. He was sentenced to eight years and has already been transferred to the New Mexico State Prison. With good time, he'll serve four.

2. Patrick Prather died without heirs, and so his entire fortune escheats to the treasury of the State of Washington. In the normal course of things, we can expect that the Washington's state's attorney's office will claim the half million Alan Prather deposited into Angie Abeyta's bank account.

3. Alan Prather has been charged with two counts of first-degree murder, one count each of kidnapping and bribery, three counts of obstruction of justice, eight counts of fraud, and individual counts of twenty-two other specified crimes. W. P. Skyler is prosecuting the case. The media reports that he'll be asking for the death penalty.

4. Angie's ulcer surgery was successful.

5. Eloy Abeyta has invited Angie and Sam to come to live with him in Jemez Springs. The offer includes a full-time job for Angie as well as the hint that she and Jimmy may someday take over Eloy's construction business.

6. I've pressed Angie hard to refuse Eloy's offer and stay in Santa Fe instead. I've shamelessly pleaded with her to move into my newly renovated house. I've offered a ridiculously low rent on what was supposed to be the source of my retirement. Angie understands that my motive is to see Sam daily.

7. Angie has taken Eloy up on his offer.

8. Max and I have committed to ten more "relationship counseling" sessions. Last week, we had to pretend to be each other for the whole hour—bobbing up and down in the channels of empathy as though they were the healing waters of the Ganges. But, yesterday, when I signed up for sky-diving classes, Max had to go lie down for a while.

9. Claude and the boys were as good as their word, for a time. With the first of their legal retainers and a sort of tame zeal on my part, I put down payments on office furniture and hired a part-time secretary. But, it turns out, the boys are used to meeting with their legal talent in more formal surroundings. So, notwithstanding the spiffy new desk and computer and copier and file cabinets, this hangout on my glassed-in back porch troubles some of them. Most look dubious and one never came back after the first look. On the other hand, a couple of them say they're getting the best legal service they ever had.

   I don't mind the attention to dry detail that this kind of legal work demands, but I like it liberally juiced with adrenaline spurts. This conflict could probably be accommodated. But the one thing that probably can never be is my addiction to long afternoon naps out in the hammock.

ABOUT THE AUTHOR

PAT FRIEDER is a lawyer and former teacher who lives with her husband in Albuquerque, New Mexico. Like Matty Donahue, Pat grew up in Santa Fe. Also like Donahue, she has practiced law in both Santa Fe and Albuquerque. During part of this time she served as an Assistant Attorney General for Criminal Appeals for the State of New Mexico. Her first novel, *Signature Murder,* won the first place award in the mystery novel category at the prestigious Southwest Writer's Workshop Fiction Competition.

BANTAM MYSTERY COLLECTION

____57204-0 **KILLER PANCAKE** Davidson • • • • • • • • • • • • • • • $6.50

____56860-4 **THE GRASS WIDOW** Holbrook • • • • • • • • • • • $5.50

____57235-0 **MURDER AT MONTICELLO** Brown • • • • • • • • • $6.99

____57300-4 **STUD RITES** Conant • • • • • • • • • • • • • • • • $5.99

____29684-1 **FEMMES FATAL** Cannell • • • • • • • • • • • • • $5.50

____56448-X **AND ONE TO DIE ON** Haddam • • • • • • • • • $5.99

____57192-3 **BREAKHEART HILL** Cook • • • • • • • • • • • • • $5.99

____56020-4 **THE LESSON OF HER DEATH** Deaver • • • • • • • $6.50

____56239-8 **REST IN PIECES** Brown • • • • • • • • • • • • • $6.50

____57456-6 **MONSTROUS REGIMENT OF WOMEN** King • • • • • $6.50

____57458-2 **WITH CHILD** King • • • • • • • • • • • • • • • • $6.50

____57251-2 **PLAYING FOR THE ASHES** George • • • • • • • • $6.99

____57173-7 **UNDER THE BEETLE'S CELLAR** Walker • • • • • • $5.99

____56793-4 **THE LAST HOUSEWIFE** Katz • • • • • • • • • • • $5.99

____57205-9 **THE MUSIC OF WHAT HAPPENS** Straley • • • • • • $5.99

____57477-9 **DEATH AT SANDRINGHAM HOUSE** Benison • • • • $5.99

____56969-4 **THE KILLING OF MONDAY BROWN** Prowell • • • • • $5.99

____57533-3 **REVISION OF JUSTICE** Wilson • • • • • • • • • • $5.99

____57579-1 **SIMEON'S BRIDE** Taylor • • • • • • • • • • • • $5.99

____57858-8 **TRIPLE WITCH** Graves • • • • • • • • • • • • • $5.50

Ask for these books at your local bookstore or use this page to order.

Please send me the books I have checked above. I am enclosing $_____ (add $2.50 to cover postage and handling). Send check or money order, no cash or C.O.D.'s, please.

Name _____

Address _____

City/State/Zip _____

Send order to: Bantam Books, Dept. MC, 2451 S. Wolf Rd., Des Plaines, IL 60018
Allow four to six weeks for delivery.
Prices and availability subject to change without notice.   MC 5/00